Her sword whistled through the air.

The man tumbled from his horse. Drue was on her feet beside him before he hit the ground. She removed the fallen knight's helmet. He was not unconscious as she had thought, but stared at her with eyes as blue and guileless as the midsummer sky.

His black hair fell across his forehead, and a droplet of blood trickled from his well-shaped lips.

"Well met!" His voice broke with pain. "I could not have asked for a finer match on which to die."

Drue held her sword against his throat. The skin looked soft and tan, like fine suede.

"Go on." He managed what would serve as a smile. " 'Tis time it was ended."

"Then close your eyes!"

"Nay, lad! When you kill me, you will look me in the eye, just as I will look into yours until I see no more!"

Dear Reader,

As the green of summer fades into the warmer colors of fall, it's time to put away your beach chairs and think about curling up on the couch with a good book. With this month's four titles from Harlequin Historicals, we hope that every reader will find a story to pique her interest.

In *To Touch the Sun,* newcomer Barbara Leigh gives historical romance a new twist with a tale of a man and a woman who meet as enemies and equals on the field of battle. We hope you will enjoy this unique and enchanting love story set in the British Isles during the early 1300s.

Passionate Alliance, Lucy Elliot's sixth book for Harlequin Historicals, takes place in New York City during the closing days of the Revolutionary War.

Maureen Bronson's *Ragtime Dawn,* the lighthearted tale of a minister's daughter with her eyes on Broadway and a handsome music-hall owner, and *Tender Feud,* a fiery romance set in Scotland from Nicole Jordan, round out the month.

Coming up next month, look for Bronwyn Williams, Kate Kingsley, Nina Beaumont and Laurie Paige.

Tracy Farrell
Senior Editor

To Touch the Sun

Barbara Leigh

Harlequin Books

TORONTO • NEW YORK • LONDON
AMSTERDAM • PARIS • SYDNEY • HAMBURG
STOCKHOLM • ATHENS • TOKYO • MILAN

Harlequin Historicals first edition October 1991

ISBN 0-373-28698-8

TO TOUCH THE SUN

BARBARA LEIGH

discovered romance at the tender age of five, when she got chills listening to Snow White sing about Prince Charming. It was then that she realized "there was life after Dick and Jane." Unable to find the kind of stories she sought, Barbara began making up her own and never stopped.

Barbara, who has five children and six grandchildren, lives in Southern California with her husband, a large doll collection, two dogs and a cat. Located high above the family room, the loft where she writes is affectionately known as "fairyland."

Chapter One

England, 1299

A roll of thunder joined the rumble of galloping horses, setting the earth and sky to trembling in unison as the knights rode toward the smoking remains of Duxton Castle.

High above, behind the sightless socket of an arrow slot, a pair of golden eyes beheld the ruin.

Those golden eyes had seen much death and destruction as a panorama of terror had unfolded before them. The child had watched with growing horror as the women clumsily thrust their heavy weapons at the enemy in a fruitless effort to defend their home. As effectively as any foe, the sheer weight of the available arms had overpowered even the most able-bodied of the women.

Druanna and her brother, Garith, had been secreted away in the tiny room behind the fireplace of the solar to keep them safe from the invaders who lay siege to Duxton Castle, as well as from the plague that rent its fury on those who had managed to survive the attack.

"Who comes?" Garith called weakly from the pallet where he lay recovering from his own bout with the plague.

"It is our lord father come to save us!" Pride sounded in Druanna's voice. She pressed her face into the narrow slot, peering into the fading daylight. "Turlock is with him!" Excitement added its emphasis to her words, for Turlock was a special favorite. Champion to Edward I of England and renowned as one of the greatest knights of the Christian world, the gentle warrior always made time for the children of his cousin, the Earl of Duxton.

A scream pierced the gloom. Druanna stepped back, waiting to see if the sound would be followed by a hail of arrows, or worse, fiery rocks from the catapult. When no sound of assault on the castle followed, she resumed her vigil.

"You should come away from there, Druanna," Garith fussed. "It is not good for you to see the pain of battle."

Druanna shook her head. She had seen far too much in the past weeks. Now she would see victory, as Turlock and her father routed the remainder of the invaders.

"It is unseemly for nobility to watch such things. Our lady mother has taken to her bed," Garith persisted.

"I am not a lady," Druanna said stubbornly, "nor shall I be one!" She had seen women fight valiantly before being captured, herded into the courtyard, stripped and set upon by the soldiers. From the distance, Druanna was unsure exactly what had then taken place, but she wanted no part of it. "I will be a knight, like Turlock!"

Garith absorbed her words. It seemed reasonable enough to him. The sickness from which he recovered had made his mind fuzzy. It was sometimes difficult to think clearly. Surely there was no reason Druanna should not become a knight if she chose. Garith intended to do so. And Druanna was larger and stronger than he, though almost a year younger.

Satisfied that there was no argument, Druanna turned back toward the window, unconsciously noting the way her father dispatched his men to seek out and destroy the scavenger that had dared lay waste to his home.

"That's the last of them!" Turlock shouted as he pulled his war-horse to a stop beside his lord.

Duxton glanced over the burned, barren land. Land that had been thick with rich green grass when he left to join the army of Edward I of England only a few short months before.

The Earl of Duxton was a tall man of mighty stature. His blond hair was indicative of the merging of Saxon and Viking blood in his veins, while the velvety depths of his dark eyes bespoke his Norman heritage. At thirty, he had not yet started to gray and he stood in his prime.

"Take no prisoners!" he commanded as his war-horse picked its way over the bodies that littered its path.

Turlock nodded and gave the order as the men followed them through the devastated field. War machines lay like broken toys along the barren way. Burned trees lifted their leafless arms in silent, unanswered supplication reflected in the grim faces of the men.

Ofttimes one of them paused, recognizing a body amid the carnage strewn at their feet.

"Your lady must have given a good battle," Turlock remarked as he overlooked the field.

"Had the King allowed us to leave a week sooner, we might have been in time!" There were tears of anger and frustration in Duxton's eyes as bitter words rose to his lips. He choked them back, letting the cruel, biting wind coursing down from the border blow his anger away.

The thunder rumbled once again as they crossed the drawbridge and made their way into the courtyard. The men scattered, hurrying from one body to the next, searching for signs of life.

"Praise God, the keep still stands!" Turlock said under his breath.

They moved toward it warily, each man aware he must accept whatever it held without flinching. They were soldiers all, and as such, death was part and parcel of their everyday lives. But not the death of their families . . . their way of life.

Though he was a distant cousin to the Earl, Turlock's grizzled appearance belied his noble blood. He was a fighting man and liked it so. His body was iron-tough and belly-swollen from too much food and good English ale. He fought to live and lived to fight, and no man had ever beaten him in hand-to-hand combat. Yet Turlock tugged nervously at his beard as the door to the keep swung open.

The main room was a shambles—tables overturned, chairs chopped to kindling and bodies of the servants scattered about like fallen leaves in the aftermath of a storm.

Edmund of Duxton sighed. "See to their burial," he commanded in a hushed voice. Crossing the room he climbed the worn stone stairs. The men remained below, unmoving, waiting for their liege to open the door to his lady's solar. They clutched their weapons tightly, as though they could fight off the stench of death that awaited inside.

Duxton stopped short as the door swung open. His lady lay on the bed; the old priest praying at her side.

"Do not enter! There is naught but death in this room!" Dropping his prayer book, the old man fell to his knees in terror before realizing his prayers had been answered.

"My lord," he stammered, pressing Duxton's hand to his lips, "I swear you are as glad a sight as would be Saint Michael himself!"

But Duxton could not respond. His eyes and his mind focused only on the figure of his wife. She looked to be at peace, although her face showed the ravages of deprivation and suffering. Her cornflower blue eyes were closed forever and her golden hair hung like a veil across her shoulders. Her skin carried the pallor of death.

Never again would he know the solace of her strong arms. She was young, far too young to die. Unlike other women of her age, Gillian had stood eye to eye with her husband. Though tall, she was as gracefully supple as a reed and had borne two healthy children. Were they also dead? He swallowed, unable to give voice to the question.

"She died of plague, my lord," the priest explained. "It struck the castle during the siege and there was nothing we could do. When the Scots discovered it they would not enter the solar. Those of us who feared plague less than Scots took sanctuary here."

Duxton nodded. His next question was locked tight in his heart. As relieved as he was that his wife had not been ravished by the Scots, he knew many of his men would not have that solace.

"My children . . ." His voice rasped in his throat as fear reached out its skeletal hands to choke him.

"The lad was taken ill, but is recovered. The maid was spared. We thought it best to hide them, lest the Scots return and decide to search the chamber."

The old priest walked slowly toward the fireplace, reaching over the smoldering embers. Duxton realized immediately what the man was doing and helped him loosen the stone. It swung away, revealing a tiny room where the two children waited quietly.

Duxton lifted Garith into the solar, holding him tight against his armored chest, his relief so great he was unable to speak. His son, his heir was indeed alive! Regaining control of his emotions, he turned to Turlock, who lifted Druanna in his great arms.

"We will bury the dead and do our best to provide for the living," Duxton announced wearily.

"It looks as though there is little left here for the living." Turlock indicated the barren landscape visible through the window.

"Those fit to travel will be taken to my estate in Northumbria. The rest will stay here with what provisions we can find. We must be done as quickly as possible. It is mandatory we leave this place."

Like the Scots marauders, Duxton realized he was no match for the plague.

"What of your childer?" the old priest asked. Had the man forgotten them in his grief and anger?

Duxton looked at the solemn-eyed children. Alike as two peas in a pod, his wife had often said. The girl, though younger than her brother, was of a size with him. It was doubtful she would be noticed. And Garith would take his place at his father's side.

Duxton's fear had been too great and his loss too dear. "I will take them with me."

"My lord, you cannot!" Turlock protested.

"I can and I will! I shall not be parted from them again! There can be no more danger on the field of battle than in an indefensible castle."

"But a battlefield is no place for a five-year-old boy, not to mention Lady Druanna."

"I have lost my wife, my home, my servants. There is no one to care for my children save myself. I cannot send them away. I need to know they are alive and well. I need to know they will not die as did the unfortunate souls in this castle." Duxton slammed his fist against the mantle. "Now, find clothing that will cause no remark among my men."

Turlock nodded in understanding, never thinking it would be the last time he would see Druanna wearing a dress.

Realizing the plague had been a blessing in disguise, and that Lady Gillian's death had served to drive the Scots from the land with only a token of the destruction and looting they might else have employed, the men-at-arms took it upon themselves to tolerate the Earl's precocious children. Garith was a relatively quiet lad, who took on the duties of a page with a seriousness that did credit to his upbringing. For several weeks Druanna was kept out of sight. Then she began to make her presence known, and as she was of a size with her brother, the men were hard put to know with which child they dealt.

Turlock became their unofficial guardian. It was he who shortened Druanna's name and unknowingly obliterated her female identity. Just as it was Turlock who insisted both Drue and Garith wear vests of cured leather to ward off the chance of a stray arrow entering their bodies.

The children slept together in their father's tent, until Garith reached his tenth summer and was deemed old enough to serve as a squire. He was then given a cot and corner of his own. At first all went well, for the boy was understandably pleased with his new station in life, but before long Turlock sensed potential trouble.

"Drue, go and fetch your brother from his daydreaming. It's time to practice with the swords."

"Garith does not daydream. He is tired today. He had a nightmare again last night. I heard him cry out in his sleep."

"Has he told you of his dreams?" Turlock questioned. It was bad that the boy continued to have these dreams. If the men heard of it before a battle, their superstitious fears might turn the smallest skirmish to the enemy's favor.

"He says he cannot remember," Drue told him, her golden eyes shining beneath lashes of the same color.

Truly, she was a colorless little thing, Turlock thought as he took her hand and led her toward the practice arena. All honey-colored, like flax in the field. Only her hair was of a somewhat darker hue, as though it were ripening faster than the rest of the crop.

"Listen to me, Drue." He took the child by the shoulders and bent down to place his face on a level with her own. "Surely you are aware by now there are many superstitions among the men in a force such as this one."

Drue nodded solemnly. She knew the soldiers wore amulets and sang chants. She knew there were omens of good and evil that could win or lose a battle even before it began.

"You must realize your brother's nightmares might be considered an evil omen, especially should one occur the night before a confrontation. If his cries are heard, the men might well panic. We must not let that happen! We must see to it he is silent in his dreams, whatever they might be." Turlock looked earnestly into her childish face, wondering if she could possibly understand the urgency of his words. Her next statement allayed his fears.

"He does not cry out when I sleep beside him," she confided. "I stopped doing so when he became a squire, but if you think it best, I will again move my bedroll next to Garith's. In truth, I miss his warmth when the chill of dawn creeps into the tent.''

Turlock smiled and patted the child's head as he got to his feet. It never occurred to him that there might be something indelicate in having the girl sleep with her brother. It never occurred to him that Drue was a girl, nor had it for lo these many years since they had taken her from the plague-swept walls of Duxton Castle. In truth, Turlock was one of the few among the Earl's army who had known Duxton had a daughter. Those who were aware of Drue's sex had forgotten it many years ago and now accepted her as a strong, capable lad.

"Come, I'll let you take your sword to me before your brother arrives," Turlock offered with a burst of unwarranted generosity.

"And will you continue to let me tilt against you as long as I keep Garith from crying out in his sleep?" Drue's eyes sparkled.

"That would be unfair to your brother, child. Your lord father would be angry with both of us."

"As angry as would be should his men bolt in fear and superstition during a skirmish?"

"Drue—" the man stopped and looked down at the determined little face "—you are not being fair."

Her forehead creased with thought. There was a long, pregnant silence before she spoke. "You asked a favor of me and I agreed. Now I ask a favor in return and you say I am not fair."

"You are far too young to demand favors!"

She turned on her heel, taking five strong paces before facing him once again. "If I am too young to be repaid for my favors, I must be too young to grant them. Sleep with Garith yourself! Your snores should drown out even the loudest scream he could muster!"

The man stood still, stunned at the child's sudden onslaught, then he hurried after her, swooping her up under his arm as he marched toward the practice field.

"Very well, Drue, the point is yours. But I will not allow my help to be taken lightly. If you are to have my undivided attention and my private tutelage, I expect you to learn everything I teach you, and the day you shirk in your lessons will be the day they cease."

He set Drue on her feet and handed her a sword. It was small and light compared to the great sword Turlock carried. His was nearly a stone's weight, and it was nothing for Turlock to swing it with deadly accuracy throughout the long hours of battle. From dawn to dusk he could keep the steady rhythm without faltering. It was this Drue must learn. It was to this end she must develop her body, so that it would respond without danger of collapse.

Silently, the man vowed he would somehow see to it that Drue and her brother continued to get only the best of food. No simple army fare for them! They were lordlings, and Turlock had made it his goal that they should eat as such during all the hard years they spent in camp. Instinctively the man realized that only the nobility, having the means to eat good nourishing food, was able to boast of tall, strong sons. So it would be with Drue and Garith. Regardless of their almost Spartan existence, they must be given the best possible tools for survival.

Drue dropped into the crouch position, as she had been taught. Her eyes narrowed as she regarded the man who would be her mentor from that day forth.

True to her word, Drue practiced daily. She was accepted as squire to Turlock himself, and to his delight, the tasks he set for her were done to the best of her ability. Although her strength was not as great as some of the older squires, her skill and cleverness were regarded with awe by her peers.

Drue remembered all too clearly the ravishment of Duxton Castle and the pitiful attempts of the women and house servants to defend it. The young, inexperienced pages had fallen as easily as did the finest lady. Their high-pitched screams still echoed in Drue's memory and manifested themselves in her brother's nightmares. No, she would not let herself be defeated as they had been. She would fight to the death, if need be, but she would fight as a man. Using a man's weapons and developing a man's strength. In truth, Drue never thought of herself as other than a squire. Her sex was unimportant. Only the development of her skills and the muscles of her body were of importance.

It was not as though Drue never visited a castle. Her father held lands in both England and Wales, but Drue never stayed long at any of them. She felt shut in and much preferred the vagabond life of a knight. The swift encounters as the Scots marauders swept down to raid the borderland of cattle, sheep and women sent a thrill of excitement to her soul. By the age of fourteen she acted as her father's standard-bearer.

The signal fires glowed against the night sky in the warning devised over a century before, alerting the border lords that the Scots had again crossed into England to steal and plunder. Drue rode between her father and Turlock as they closed the distance between themselves and the raiders, who travelled more slowly because of the cattle they had stolen.

"Surely we should have sighted them by now," Duxton grumbled. "They were not that much ahead."

"It's that whelp, Connaught, I'll vow!" Turlock exclaimed. "His father recently sent him into service with Robert the Bruce. Connaught's aunt is Elizabeth of Ulster, the Bruce's wife. It seems risking Connaught's life in battle was the lesser of the risks, as he's earned the wrath of either husband or father in nearly every noble house in Ireland. The young cockerel is skilled in the bed as well as on the field."

"Ah," Duxton sighed, a hint of laughter in his voice, "if I but had the time."

Turlock's laugh boomed out. "Had I the endurance I would be willing to give the hotblood a challenge for his reputation."

"In battle?" Drue asked.

"No, lad," Turlock's laughter was joined by that of his cousin, "in bed!"

Drue joined their merriment, but her mind sifted through the information she had picked up through camp gossip. The Bruce was the King of Scotland, newly crowned by his own hand and unacknowledged, as yet, by the Christian world. His cleverness was legend. It was to be hoped young Connaught had not learned his lessons too well.

They rounded a curve in the road and plunged into a copse of trees. As the last of the men entered the dark confines, a branch crashed down behind them and a wild banshee scream split the air.

"Ambush! Ambush!" Drue shouted as men poured from the woods.

The fighting was wild! It was impossible to tell friend from enemy. Drue kept close to her father. She must keep his standard in sight. It was mandatory that the men have a rallying point.

Seasoned soldiers all, the Englishmen formed ranks and began driving the Scots back. The enemy ranks broke, and regardless of the threats and urgings of their leader, disappeared into the trees.

Turlock burst from the pack. "Follow me!" he shouted. "They are routed!"

Seconds later a cry of alarm echoed through the darkness. Duxton spurred his mount in the direction of his cousin's voice. They reached the clearing as a Scot thrust his sword, dropping the point only after Turlock lifted his shield to ward off the blow. Turlock fell to the ground. Duxton shouted his battle cry. The knight's head jerked up. Seeing sure death bearing down on him, he turned his horse and disappeared into the night.

Drue slid from her horse, dropping to her knees at Turlock's side. The sword had skillfully slipped beneath his armor. The wound was painful, and bloody, but Drue knew he would live if given proper care. She vowed to give him that care, just as she vowed to make the Scot pay for wounding her friend.

"The boy's too smart for his own good," Turlock complained as he reclined on a litter outside his tent. "That trick is old, but it's usually reserved for tournaments. And do not think you might want to try the same. A man leaves himself open for a death blow when he drops his point like that. Next time I'll know the wily cub for the fox he is."

"How many other jousting tricks can be used in such a manner?" Drue asked thoughtfully.

"It takes your interest, does it?" Turlock smiled at his protégée's constant quest for knowledge.

"I do not wish to be caught as you were if it can be avoided." She shivered involuntarily. It was the first time she had ever seen Turlock unconscious. Many times she had helped bandage his wounds after a battle, but he'd always managed to return to camp under his own power.

"I'll take you and your brother to the field and show you what I mean. You can practice with blunted swords. That should keep you busy for the better part of the day, and maybe I can rest without having you constantly questioning me about that devil's whelp, Connaught."

"Just teach me his tricks and how to counter them and I promise never to mention his name again."

"Between us we should be able to outsmart Connaught and bring him back to England like a trussed fowl."

Turlock got stiffly to his feet and hobbled toward the practice field. His laughter hung in the air, but Drue did not join in. To her, the thought of capturing the man who had crippled Turlock held no humor, it was an obsession!

Chapter Two

Connaught! The devil's spawn who had wounded her friend and mentor, Turlock. Connaught! The evil force who continually raided the borderlands, making the English army look like fools running in circles to catch the wind. Connaught, who used trickery and wile to obtain his goals and defeat his opponents. How Drue hated him! The very mention of his name was enough to send her into a rage. She longed to meet him on the field of battle.

She especially hated what he had done to Turlock. Since their encounter a year past, Turlock had aged. His walk was the shuffling pace of a man in pain, and while he never complained, Drue was aware that the wound had been slow in healing.

Only when mounted was her mentor the same strong champion she had known from the beginning of memory. Connaught would pay for the suffering his treachery had caused, she vowed once again as she pulled off her gauntlets and stopped beside the barrel of water where her brother stood.

"Another match?" she asked, splashing water on her face.

"Have mercy, Drue! It's too hot to do more today!" Garith watched as she stripped down to her leather vest and, taking a gourd, poured water over her head. The muscles in her arms glistened in the sun. Garith laughed. "I vow, if I don't look to my laurels, you will soon be stronger than I."

"I'm already stronger than you," Drue announced. "Turlock will never let us wrestle one another because he does not feel it proper for the sibling to excel over the next Earl of Duxton."

Garith sputtered. "That's not true!"

Drue smiled quietly. "So you say!" She flexed her arm, watching the finely tuned muscles bulge in her biceps and forearm. "As firm and trusty as my own sword," she challenged. "Can you say as much?"

Garith watched her posturing speculatively. She was as tall as he and matched him in weight.

Drue grinned. "Do you fear I will achieve my knighthood before yourself, my brother?"

He did fear it, but no power on earth would make him admit it. There was something less than honorable about having a younger member of the same house knighted before the heir himself.

"You fight, Garith, but you do it to defend yourself and your lands. You have no heart for it. Your blood does not churn when you hear the sound of the Scots' heathen pipes. You do not thrill to the ancient cries of battle as I do. No, there are many things for which you are more attuned. Leave the fighting to me, and I will leave being a gentle knight to you."

It was later that summer the crisis arose. Like a wraith, Drue's sex came to haunt her, when her father unexpectedly called her to his tent.

"It has been decided that Garith will go into service with the Earl of Arundel," Duxton told her. "It is time you, also, take your proper place in life and learn the gentler graces."

"I do not wish to learn the gentler graces! I would stay in the field with Turlock and yourself."

The Earl shook his head. "It cannot be, Drue! You must learn the ways of a woman. I have kept you with me too long. I am failing in my duty as a father."

Drue dropped to her knee before him. "No man could be a finer example than yourself, and no children more proud of their sire than Garith and I."

Duxton closed his eyes, fighting the acid sting of tears. He would miss this child whose fighting spirit fulfilled his dreams.

"This is no life for you, Drue." He lifted her to her feet. "You should have a home, children, a life of your own. I would settle lands on you when you wed."

"I will win my own lands! Win them with my sword and skill!"

Duxton turned away from her pleading look. "No! You will go to my castle in Northumbria, as you should have done when your mother died."

Drue stood before him; her breath came rapidly. "You allow Garith the freedom of choice, yet you deny me the only life I have ever known. Because he is the heir, Garith has your favor."

Duxton slammed his fist against the table. "Dare you challenge me?" His voice rang with anger, but his heart swelled with pride as his offspring demanded her rights.

Drue's hands began to sweat as she gambled all on her next words. "I do not challenge you, my father, but I would challenge Garith. Let me fight him. If I lose, I will go to Northumbria and bow to your will. But if I win, you must give me your word to let me remain with you and Turlock."

"Garith is older and stronger," Duxton protested. In his heart he did not wish to see either of his children beaten. "You would not have a chance."

"Then your wish for my retirement to Northumbria will become reality, my lord father, with no further protest."

"You will go, protest or no!"

"And I will run away and find a band of fighting men who will appreciate my knowledge of arms."

"No house in England would dare give you shelter against my will!" he shouted.

"Then I will go to the Scots!"

Duxton threw his hands in the air. "So be it! Go! Fight Garith and have done with it! The sooner this thing is over, the sooner your future will be settled."

Drue slipped from the tent, brushing past Turlock as he entered. The twinkle in his eye told her he had been listening.

"See to it that Drue's belongings are ready to be sent to my estates in Northumbria," Duxton ordered his cousin. "As soon as this farcical contest between Drue and Garith is over, you will lead the travel party."

"And are you so certain Drue will be the loser?" Turlock asked as he poured them each a glass of wine.

Duxton took the goblet from Turlock's hand. "How else could it be?"

"It could be, my lord, that you are in for a surprise!" Turlock's great laugh shook the tent and echoed through the hills.

Drue fought Garith that afternoon. Though their weapons were blunted and their bodies well padded beneath their armor, each realized the seriousness of the challenge.

To Garith, it was a matter of pride. If Drue beat him he would be the laughingstock among his peers. The shame of being bested by his sibling would be a blemish on his knighthood.

To Drue, it was a matter of survival. If she did not win, she would be subject to banishment from the life she loved. The only life she knew. Her commitment was made; her mind set. She asked no quarter and gave none.

Their swords met, and the staccato rhythm merged with the shouts of the men as lines formed and bets were called on the two well-matched squires. As the fight continued the blows became measured, but their strength never wavered.

It was the long hours of training that held Drue in good stead. Garith was often slack in his weapon practice, while Drue never seemed to get enough. Now, as time passed, Garith was winded, while Drue still seemed fresh.

Duxton turned to Turlock in astonishment, only to be met by the man's broad grin.

"I tried to warn you, my lord, " Turlock said.

Even as he spoke, Garith stumbled, the pace of the match and Drue's persistence and excellent conditioning taking its toll.

"Stop them," Duxton growled. "Garith will be ruined. Declare the match a draw! Tell Drue I withdraw my demands for the present, but once Garith has attained knighthood, Drue's future will be reassessed."

Delighted that his protégée would not be sent away, Turlock strode forward, loudly proclaiming the time limit had been met and the match was a draw.

By Michaelmas they'd accompanied Garith to Arundel, where he would be trained for knighthood, and Drue was left to her own devices. She practiced daily, not only at skills with the other squires and young knights, but at all aspects of keeping her body in top condition. Her arms and legs were sinewy, and not an ounce of fat dwelled beneath her supple skin. Turlock's pledge of having his charges eat only the best food had obviously paid off. Drue was as strong and handsome as any of the other young men with whom she spent her time. If she had little use for women, she had even less for men, thinking, as did her brother, that the attraction of one knight for another was unseemly.

While some of the knights thought Drue to be a bit strange, they neither questioned nor teased, for Drue was herself a force to be reckoned with. And considering that she was son of a mighty lord, any odd habits could be overlooked.

"After all, a man has a right to his privacy," Henry of Romsley contended. "Drue's upbringing has been harsher than that of the rest of us. I doubt he remembers what it's like to live within the walls of a castle for more than a fortnight. His contact with women has been only with camp followers, so it's no wonder he prefers fighting to the gentler graces."

"The only time he can be alone is when he's in his tent," one of the others volunteered. "I have no doubt he finds himself sick of the company of others and in need of a moment of solace."

It seemed the time for solace had passed, for Drue rode up beside them.

"And have you lost the doldrums of leaving your brother?" Henry asked.

"I was in no doldrums," Drue protested.

"But you kept to yourself."

Drue laughed aloud. "My father was so taken by the wonders of Arundel I was hard put to keep him from making me remain with my brother."

"Do you not wish to be knighted?" Henry asked cautiously.

"I shall be knighted when the time comes," Drue said, repeating the words so often spoken by the mighty Turlock, "and not before."

"It might well be much sooner were you to go into service with one of the noble houses instead of remaining in the field with your father," he reminded her.

"Pshaw!" she snorted derisively. "I have no wish to learn the dances of the court. I am a warrior and so I shall remain!"

"And woe to the enemy should he be luckless enough to meet you in battle!" Their laughter floated through the clear morning air as Henry put spurs to his horse and rode ahead to catch the rest of the entourage.

Although the others doubted the wisdom of vying for knighthood on the battlefield, where the chance of being killed was far greater than that of being knighted, Drue was pleased with her life.

During the first months of Garith's absence there were few battles, and Drue was actually glad when the messenger came summoning them to the court of the young King, Edward II. It was to be a grand occasion, and Turlock grumbled loudly as he was forced to discard his usual wolfskin mantle for one of velvet trimmed with fox.

The king was resplendent in cloth of gold, and Drew was hardly able to repress her laughter at the sight of the long, jesterlike toes on his shoes.

"Drue, remember yourself!" her father admonished as her chin quivered in mirth.

How she longed to share the sight of this effeminate monarch with her brother. To laugh about it with him as she had so many things during their lives together. It was only when the King's friend and advisor, Piers Gaveston, came into the court, the toes on his shoes fully two feet long, that Drue's muffled laughter could no longer be concealed and Turlock whisked her from the hall.

Realizing the impropriety of her behavior, she walked to the tilting yard, silently chastising herself. Her long strides took her across the field in less than no time and she was soon confronted by other squires and newly made knights, who were displaying their skills before the new arrivals.

Drue was angry, both at herself and at the King, the latter for allowing himself to be made a laughingstock. She longed to strike out at something. It was with a deep sense of relief that she took a proffered sword from the man who stood before her.

"Try your skill against the champion of the yard," he offered. "A gold coin says he can beat any man now on the field."

A cursory glance told Drue that beating any of them would be no great feat, including the current champion.

"A coin it is," she said, striking the bargain. "But is your man not a knight in the service of the king?"

"He is!" the young man said with pride.

"Then, as I have not yet been knighted, I feel I should be given a bonus should I win."

The man turned and eyed Drue carefully. He could see his adversary was young and not as thick of body as some. There seemed to be a wiry strength there, but he could not be certain. "What think you, sire," the lackey spoke for all to hear. "Does this lad deserve a special prize should he manage to defeat you?"

"If that pampered son of a soft lord beats me I'll gladly turn over to him my horse and armor, as would be done in a true challenge."

"And if he loses?"

"He will serve me for the rest of his time at court."

Turlock appeared just in time to hear Drue accept the bargain.

"What have you done?" he growled under his breath. "Do you not realize the court is decadent? No young person is safe here. Your father should never have allowed you to come!" He pulled his beard nervously. Drue had never been tested in true battle, with more than a token prize to the winner. He feared for the welfare of his charge, and more than that, he feared the anger of his lord. "What will we do if you lose?" he lamented.

Drue looked at him coldly. "I have had the best training and the best teacher. I have learned all the rules and all the tricks men use to break opponents without dishonoring themselves. I have no intention of losing!"

Without another word she went to fetch her armor.

Turlock fretted as he helped secure the breastplates. "Your father will be upon you for wagering, win or lose!" he warned.

"I shall not lose!" Drue said quietly as she started toward the field.

Word of the challenge had spread, and a crowd had gathered. Many of the men were from the Duxton entourage and cheered loudly as Drue took the field. She stood taller than her opponent, though they weighed within a stone of each other. They saluted as the self-appointed marshal listed the rules, then stepped back.

The knight had no more than assumed a fighting position when Drue dealt him a mighty blow. He reeled, unable to do more than defend himself against the onslaught.

Stumbling backward, he sought to right himself, but Drue
pressed her advantage. Her blows struck with the rhythm
of a galloping horse as she smashed forward, forcing her
opponent to the ground. Slipping her sword under the armor between his helm and breastplate, she held him at bay.

"Dost thou yield?" the thunderstruck marshal managed.

The knight looked into the narrowed eyes of his conqueror. In them he saw certain death should he refuse. It
startled him. This was a game, not a battle to be taken seriously. His eyes wavered as he wondered if he could trip
his opponent, thereby saving face and renewing the challenge.

Drue read his thoughts. She exerted pressure against his
throat. "Even a dulled, wrapped sword can kill, my lord,"
she reminded him.

He let his weapon drop from his hand. "I yield..." he
said as his friends groaned at his embarrassment.

Drue stepped back, offering her hand to help him rise.
The crowd began to cheer. Their cries were soon smoth-
ered as a voice rang out.

"Outstanding, absolutely outstanding!"

Drue turned to see the King and Piers Gaveston coming
toward her, followed by a group of courtiers. She bowed
low, determined not to look at their feet and the outra-
geously funny shoes they wore.

"Never have I seen such a display of aggression!" the
King was saying. "Have you a feud with this man?"

"Nay, Your Grace! I had never laid eyes on him before
this morning."

"He said something to anger you?" Piers speculated.

"Again, no, my lord." This time Drue directed her answer to Piers. "It was but a sporting challenge."

"If that display was sporting I would hate to be your opponent when you are angry!" Drue's conquered opponent declared. Then, realizing his impropriety, he dropped to his knee in apologetic appeal to his King. "Forgive me, my lord!" he swallowed.

The King laughed. "I understand your meaning," he said, turning again to Drue. "Tell me, do you always fight with such intensity?"

"To fight and win is to live, to lose is to die," Drue said quietly. Her mind was not on the words of the King and his favorite, though well they should have been. Piers Gaveston wore lavender shoes with green tassels on the toe, and Drue knew it was only a matter of time before she would again disgrace herself and burst into laughter. The thought of Turlock or her father wearing such things almost undid her. With the greatest of effort she sought to direct her mind to other channels. She lifted her eyes and found herself looking straight into those of the King.

"Well said." He smiled. "And would you defend another with the same intensity you use to defend yourself, should the need arise?"

Drue hesitated. "Should the need arise and the person be worthy," she said finally.

The King chortled with glee and clapped Piers on the shoulder. "Hear him . . . should the person be worthy, he says."

Both men dissolved into laughter, while the growing crowd smiled nervously. Surely there must be some secret between their monarch and his favorite, unknown to the rest of the court.

"If you were in service to a personage, would you then deem him worthy of your best effort?" Piers asked.

"If I chose to swear allegiance to a man and pledged myself to his service, he would be worthy!" Drue said firmly.

The King looked Drue over carefully. "You are not yet knighted," he said as he finished his inspection.

"No, Your Grace."

"And you travel with the Earl of Duxton." It was not a question.

"I am Drue, serving as squire to my lord Turlock. The Earl of Duxton is my father."

The King nodded thoughtfully. "Turlock boasts no household of his own," he commented knowledgeably. "Where will you go to complete your service and be knighted?"

"I intend to earn my spurs on the field. My brother has gone to Arundel to learn the gentle graces the future Earl of Duxton must need know, as is his place. My place is beside my father and my lord Turlock, fighting against Your Majesty's enemies."

Edward smiled again. "And which of my enemies do you see when you attack poor adversaries like Raoul here?" He indicated the newly deposed champion.

"Connaught!" The word burst from Drue's lips without hesitation.

"Ah." The King frowned thoughtfully. "Is he not the young Irish lord, who fights at the side of Robert the Bruce?"

"He is, Your Grace," Drue said.

"A wise choice and a formidable enemy," the King commented. "And would you like the chance to meet him in the field?"

"I would welcome it, Your Grace."

"But only if you served a worthy lord."

"My lord Turlock is worthy," Drue contended.

"And your lord King, is he worthy?" Piers asked softly.

"Is England worthy?" Drue countered. "King or country, it is one in the same." She could see by their faces she had answered correctly, even though a worried frown still creased Turlock's brow. She had no way of knowing what these powerful men wanted, but she realized she must weigh each word, for they were crafty and all-powerful.

Before she could say another word, the King turned away and scanned the crowd until his eyes fell upon Drue's father, who had followed the court to the tilting yard.

"Duxton," he called, motioning the Earl toward him. The crowd parted and the Earl came to a halt before the King.

"I have decided to favor your house!"

Duxton shifted nervously, waiting for his monarch's next words. If the King wished to honor the House of Duxton, it would be far better should the man direct his favors on Garith, the heir, rather than on Drue, whose sex might easily become an embarrassment to all concerned.

"I wish to keep your son, Drue, at my side. I want him to ride with me to battle and bear my standard."

The Earl swallowed. It was an unwarranted honor. It was also an unwanted honor. He could not find the words with which to protest, but Drue had no such compunctions. The thought of having to dress like a jester and wear shoes with tassels on the toes was too terrible to allow discretion to prevail.

"Your Grace—" Drue dropped to her knee "—you do me too great an honor. There is nothing I would rather do than carry your banner into battle and ride at your side. But I have never lived in a castle and fear I would be an embarrassment to you, with my uncouth manners and uncourtly ways. In your wisdom, could you not allow me to stay on the field with my father's men and come to you only when you have need of my service?''

There was a general intake of breath. No one, save possibly Piers himself, ever dared speak to the King in such a manner. Duxton had laid a restraining hand on Drue's shoulder and Turlock had actually taken a step forward, but to their surprise it was Piers Gaveston himself who came to their aid.

Realizing the King's obvious admiration for the young man, Piers decided that, rather than chance his place as favorite, he would champion Drue's idea.

''A true and thoughtful lad!'' he said, lifting Drue to her feet. ''How many times has Your Grace been offended by the vile manners of the warring men of the realm? If young Drue has no wish to learn the gentler graces of the court, we should be willing to allow him to continue to practice his knightly skills and become even more proficient defending Your Majesty, should the need arise.''

Hearing his friend's words, Edward agreed. ''So be it! The Duxton forces will ride with me from this day forth and the Earl will be given a place on my council of war.''

Before anyone could gather their wits enough to do more than bow, the King and Piers were gone.

Drue sat outside her tent on the field near Bannockburn. Sweat trickled down her neck and under the breastplate she wore in anticipation of the call to battle. Of the twenty summers of her life, this was the hottest she could remember. She glanced over her shoulder at the imposing structure crouching like a great beast in the distance. Stirling Castle, their goal. They must take possession before the summer solstice.

Turlock sank down beside her. The ground was bare in this area from the constant pounding of the feet of men and horses, and dust rose, covering him with a fine powder. Rivulets of sweat made shiny paths down his face, disappearing into his beard.

"It is too hot out here," he complained. "The King should attack the bloody Scots and have done with it."

"He awaits the right moment." Drue repeated the words with distaste.

"The 'right moment' has come and gone a hundred times, and still he sits in his tent while thousands of men languish in the heat."

Turlock leaned toward her, peering earnestly into her face. "You could be with him, Drue. Do you regret the decision to stay in the field instead of indulging in court life?"

"There is nothing about the court to interest me!"

"Not even knighthood? You would have had it long ago had you not been so adamant about staying with us."

"I would rather serve as your squire than join the ranks of posturing fools who serve the King," she said.

"Let no one but myself hear you say that, young Drue, or you will no longer bear the standard of your monarch."

Drue smiled at the older man's concern. "I share my thoughts with you alone. Even my father does not know me as you do."

"And well it is, for he thinks you to be the perfect candidate for knighthood and not the hothead I know."

They laughed together for a moment before falling silent. And the whisper of a thought tiptoed through Turlock's mind.

It was against all laws of man and nature to knight Drue. Duxton had taken two children from the ruins of his ancestral home, and one of them had been a female. Yet there was little feminine about the young woman who sat before him. Drue's face was strong, with high cheekbones and a firm, determined chin. Her lips were well shaped, but not overly full. Her eyes were narrow, and they glinted beneath sun-bleached hair clipped shorter than was popular with the court.

Even her body belied her sex. Strong and well muscled from many hours of practice with the ax and sword, her golden skin gleamed with the sheen of perspiration in the afternoon sun. The muscles played in her forearms as she lifted her goblet and drank deeply of its contents. The sinews in her legs bulged against the light hose she wore in anticipation of donning her armor at a moment's notice.

No finer specimen of manhood could be found, Turlock thought proudly. Surely there had been a mistake on the part of the mid-wife those many years ago, or perhaps God had seen his error and, in his mercy, changed Drue from female to male. Turlock did not know the answer nor would he presume to ask. He doubted that Drue herself remembered she had been born a woman.

Turlock was very close to being correct in all his assumptions. In truth, Drue gave no thought to the possibility that a woman's body might function differently from that of a man. As with the other soldiers in her father's force, she grew cold in the winter, suffered from the heat in the summer and was drenched by the rain. She ate when hungry and drank when thirsty, and was subject occasionally to sickness that surged through the army like a devious enemy at unexpected intervals. So it was no great surprise nor cause for undue anxiety when she found herself cramping and purging during her fourteenth year.

Turlock plied her with fresh fruits and vegetables from Spain, and she never gave thought that it might be other than the dysentery that plagued the men of every army from the beginning of time.

Drue fretted at the forced inactivity. Unable to ride, or even walk without disgracing herself, she remained in the tent, cursing her lot. After six days of isolation she went to the stream to wash her clothing. The sun was warm and she felt better than she had for the best part of a week. She spread her clothing over the bushes near the edge of the stream and leaned against a rock, soaking in the sunlight.

The voices of two women disturbed her, but she remained silent, trying to ignore their banter. They spoke freely, unaware of Drue's presence.

"My man will be upset when he realizes I have missed my monthly tides for the second time. I swear it's worse than the flux, and trouble either way."

The other woman chuckled in agreement. "'Tis always a problem when it comes and worry when it does not, leaving you to wonder if you be with child."

The words drilled themselves into Drue's mind. Had this been her problem? Was she to expect this embarrassment every month for the rest of her life? It appeared that these women did, and gladly, too, considering the alternative of having a child while following a man from camp to camp.

Drue's palms began to sweat as she wondered how long she could keep this from Turlock, her brother and the rest of the men. She began to plan ways to protect herself should the women be correct and this undesirable incident repeat itself. Her worry seemed for nothing, however, for several months passed with no recurrence. Eventually she came to believe she had indeed had dysentery, and once again she applied herself to learning the skills of war.

Had she been studying for knighthood in a castle, as was the lot of the sons of most men of her father's rank, Drue would not have been allowed to advance as quickly as she did on the field.

Easily as large as her brother, she was a match for lads several years her senior, and she fought in any competition that could be arranged between herself and the squires of visiting knights.

Although jousting was forbidden without strict supervision, the young men were encouraged to exhibit their prowess in tilting the quintain and lance-throwing. It was during one of these exhibitions that Drue found herself and her brother in an unbreakable tie with the squire of a visiting Irish lord.

As Garith was about to thrust his lance at the target, the Irishman moved suddenly and the lance went askew.

"Foul!" Drue's voice rose above those around her.

"He missed," the young man exclaimed. "It was no foul of mine that caused him to be so clumsy. Had he kept his eyes on the target his lance would have landed true."

While Drue knew the man spoke with candor, she would not admit to her brother's failing. "If it's concentration you want, then let us test yours. Ride against me and see which of us can most nearly touch the center of the other's shield."

"Done!" The young man went off to ready his mount.

"You know Turlock has forbidden this." Garith hurried to keep up with Drue as she went to don her padded armor.

"Turlock forbade a joust. This is a game of skill, and at this game I excel."

He could not deny that. Her eye was good and her aim true. "You have no mount," he reminded her. "Turlock rode out on your horse this morning."

"I'll ride your animal," she told him calmly, "as I did when we tilted the quintain earlier this afternoon."

Garith would have protested further, but knew from the look on Drue's face it would do him no good.

The blunted lances were tipped with tar, which would leave a mark where they touched the shield. The challengers saluted each other and went to opposite ends of the field. At Garith's signal they galloped forward. The first point went to Drue as she tapped the Irishman's shield squarely.

"You'll not match that hit easily," she said as they came together to spot the mark.

"We'll see." His eyes glinted beneath his helmet as he rode away.

The second hit went to the Irishman. The final mark would decide the victor.

As they rode toward each other for the third time, Drue tightened her grip on her lance and aimed carefully. The horses thundered down the beaten path. Accustomed to Garith's gentle urging, the beast Drue rode became agitated by her firm command and shied as she tried to drive him closer to her opponent. Drue's shield arm flew up to maintain her balance and her opponent's lance caught her in the midsection, lifting her from the saddle.

She hit the ground unmoving, the breath knocked from her body.

Garith was the first to reach her side. "He's not breathing," he panted as his hands tried to loosen her armor.

The young Irishman jerked his horse to a halt and ran to the fallen squire. "The horse shied. There was no time to pull back. He took the full brunt of the blow."

Garith shook Drue, trying to shock her into breathing. Then Drue's opponent removed his helmet and knelt beside her. He bent down and breathed into her mouth, then paused before repeating the measure, again and again until the breath of life was restored to her lungs, her eyes opened and she pushed him away.

"You brought Drue back to life," Garith gasped.

"No." He shook his head. "I but forced the breath of life back into his body. It's an old trick used by the Saracens and brought back from the Crusades." He turned his attention to Drue, "Are you all right?"

"I believe so, thanks to you." She ignored the thought that this young man's breath still hovered somewhere deep in her lungs. "In truth, you may have saved my life, and I do not even know your name. We call you only the Irish squire."

He laughed aloud and, taking Drue's arm, helped her to her feet. "And Irish squire I am proud to be. But my father is—" He got no further, for Drue doubled over. She would have fallen to the ground had not Garith hurried to take her other arm.

"Carry me out on my shield," Drue joked, trying to make light of her pain. "I always thought those words rang with honor."

"Your shield is far too small, unless you remain doubled up the way you are now," Garith muttered. He saw nothing funny about Drue's situation. Being the elder, he would be punished should there be anything seriously wrong with his sibling when their father and Turlock returned.

"Doubled over is the only way you can carry me," Drue moaned, "for I swear I cannot straighten my body."

Together they carried Drue to the tent she shared with Turlock.

"By the by," the Irish squire said as he left her on the cot, "I consider the match a draw. But I would give you one piece of advice before I go. Never ride a strange horse into a situation where you must control him solely with your legs. You might have been killed today, for while I missed your shield completely, my hit on your body was dead center."

"Amen to that," Drue muttered. "But I will remember your advice, and hope never to meet you once you've earned your spurs."

"Nor I you. Now fare you well, and I hope no permanent damage has been done."

"I assure you I will be back on the field before the week is done."

But Drue's boast was not fulfilled. It was the better part of a month before Drue was again able to sit a horse. Once the pain that had raged in her belly subsided, she resumed her duties with her usual enthusiasm. It never occurred to her to wonder that she was never again bothered by womanly tides.

As Turlock struggled to his feet, Drue watched him remembering the quick, sprite man he had been before receiving Connaught's blow. Her sympathy turned to anger.

"Now, what are you thinking?" he asked, noting the flush that stained her face.

"I was wondering if Connaught sits on the meadow of Bannockburn, as we do here. I was wondering if he knew how much we hate him and that I intend to seek him out and kill him."

"You will stay by the King's side and hold his banner high for all to see!" Turlock said in a hard voice. "Under no conditions will you leave your post. To do so would be treason!"

Drue bowed her head. "Of course, Turlock, you are right. I will not leave my post. And Connaught will live for yet another day."

"He is a strong and canny man, Drue. Do not be so anxious to fight him. Your time will come, provided I don't happen upon him first."

"My fear, exactly! That you will come upon him first!"

"Do you doubt I can beat him?" Turlock demanded.

"Surely you will beat him!" Drue said staunchly. "Perhaps you will even kill him, and that is the worst of my fears, for more than anything, I long for that opportunity myself!"

Chapter Three

The air snapped with tension as Drue sat astride her mount, her eyes scanning the shadowy figures that moved in a ghostly dance along the horizon.

"Surely there should be some word by now!" she protested.

"Patience, lad," Turlock whispered. "Any minute we should hear the Scots keening the death of their King."

Drue looked over her shoulder. King Edward was mounted, ready to take advantage of the situation. Less than an hour earlier he had been apprised that Henry de Bohun and his scouting party had come upon the Bruce himself, reviewing his troops in anticipation of the day's fighting.

Since the King of Scotland had no notion any Englishman could venture so deep into the Scot Army without being detected, he had ridden out on a small border pony to review his troops, not even taking the time to don his armor.

Realizing his unsurpassed advantage, de Bohun decided to attack, stopping only to send a messenger back to tell Edward of the situation. Now the English army waited for news of the death of Robert the Bruce.

"It seems an unchivalrous thing," Drue muttered under her breath. "Garith would condemn the whole action."

"No doubt you're right, but when a knight has a chance to gain complete victory with nothing more than a skirmish, he would be a fool not to take advantage."

"Are you so certain de Bohun will win?" Drue persisted.

"Certain? Of course I am certain!" Turlock bristled at the thought of his friend being defeated when given such odds. "The messenger said the Bruce wore no armor. He rides a little palfrey and is totally unprepared for battle, as is the rest of his army.

"Granted, the man is an outstanding warrior, but he is still mortal. How can he possibly defeat a knight in full armor astride a seasoned war-horse? No, Drue, there will be no battle today. We wait only to rush to the slaughter. There is little need of fighting men, but rather men to count the Scots' dead."

Drue held up her hand to silence him. "Listen! I hear sounds of battle in the distance."

"Poor devils must have lost all sense of direction, and instead of retreating, they are headed right toward us. It will be complete carnage!" Turlock shook his head.

Drue would have said more, but the King rode up beside her.

"You hear it, too?" he asked, his eyes shining and his cheeks an unnaturally bright pink.

"Aye, Your Grace. The fighting moves this way."

"In a few short hours I will be acclaimed throughout the Christian world as the conqueror of Robert the Bruce. Even my father was unable to accomplish such a feat! I shall be praised by all and my name will live forever!" He stared off into the fog as though he could already hear the sound of adulation.

"The Scots will fight like a swarm of angry bees when they realize their leader has been killed," Drue ventured.

"Truly said!" the King agreed. "But in the end it will come to naught, for Scots without a strong leader are like sheep without a shepherd. They will scatter and we will be upon them. Scotland will be mine, as deemed right and good by God!"

Drue doubted God's plans specifically designated that Scotland should live under Edward's rule, but she knew better than to disagree with her King.

The sounds of fighting became louder and Drue made herself ready for battle.

The fog swirled angrily before them and a figure burst into view. Seeing the standard of his King looming up through the churning mist, he lurched toward it, tumbling to his knees under the feet of Edward's horse.

"Have a care man," Piers reprimanded.

The man looked up as Piers continued his tirade, badgering the unfortunate soldier without allowing him a word. It was Turlock who dismounted and stooped to help the man to his feet.

"What news?" Urgency rang in Turlock's voice as he saw the man's clothing, torn and stained with blood, the dents in his breastplate and his bleeding arm.

The intensity of Turlock's words caught the King's attention. He silenced Gaveston with a wave of his hand.

"Henry de Bohun is dead!" the man managed, ignoring the gasp that rose from his audience. "The Scot cannot be a mere mortal. He fought like a madman! Taken completely off guard, the Bruce still managed to parry de Bohun's blows. Then, de Bohun went in for the kill and . . ." The man paused, closing his eyes as though what he had seen would cease to be reality if he blotted out the world.

"And? Speak, man! Speak!" Turlock urged.

"The Bruce rose in his saddle. He stood in his stirrups, and even then he was hardly equal to the man and horse before him. He raised his arms and, with a mighty blow of his battle-axe, cleaved completely through de Bohun's head, slicing the armor as though it was no more than a loaf of bread."

The King bit his knuckle to stifle the sound that rose in his throat.

"The Scots went mad!" the man continued. "They have beaten our men back and even now fight their way toward our lines."

"We must have time to regroup, Your Grace!" Duxton had appeared during the summation.

"Yes, yes," Edward agreed. "We will regroup and strike when the advantage is more to our liking." He turned his horse. "I will return to the camp to devise a plan!" His horse was already moving away as the sounds of battle grew closer. "Come, Piers, Drue, we must be away!"

Although Drue would much rather have stayed on the field, she knew her place as standard bearer was at the side of the King. In his haste to be away he had not waited for his personal guard, and so it was that only the three of them raced across the open field, the King's banner waving brightly through the morning mist.

There was a copse of trees ahead, and before Drue could do more than shout a warning, a group of men burst from it.

Piers shouted a battle cry and rushed forward, leaving Drue to cope with the King, who gave a little squeak and tried to disappear into the safety of his armor.

Though the enemy was comprised of foot soldiers, it became obvious Piers was getting the worst of it. He swayed in the saddle after a particularly telling blow, and the men bore down in the euphoria of gaining the advantage.

Realizing his favorite was about to be killed before his eyes, the King snatched the banner from Drue's hand.

"Save him! Save him!" he exhorted. "I can defend myself!"

Drue, who had been fighting to keep two of the men away from the person of the King, hardly glanced at him. Drawing her sword, she gave forth with a battle cry that shook the trees and lunged toward her adversaries.

With one mighty sweep of her sword two men fell to the ground, one clutching the place where his arm had been while the other lay still. She ran the next man down with her horse, while she slashed first to the left and then the right until there was only the unfortunate Piers, who was holding his side, and his two adversaries, pressing in for the kill.

She dealt one a mighty blow to the head. His helmet rolled off across the bloody ground, but Drue didn't bother to see whether or not the man's head was still inside it as she plunged her sword into the neck of the other.

Steadying her horse, she lifted the visor on Piers's helmet. His face was gray with pain, but he managed to move his lips into some semblance of a smile. "My thanks, lad. I won't forget your bravery this day!"

"Nor I yours!" Drue replied, realizing for the first time how unaccomplished a knight Piers Gaveston really was. He must have known he had little chance to defeat the men who poured from the trees, yet he had ridden forward undaunted, knowing he faced almost certain death.

Before she had time to say more, Gaveston gestured
weakly toward the King. Drue glanced over to see Edward
smacking a man on the top of the head with the flat of his
sword. It was all she could do to keep from laughing. What
did these men do with their lives? It was obvious they spent
little time practicing with their weapons!

She wheeled her horse around and galloped toward her
monarch.

Edward's frantic gyrations forced his horse to retreat
back toward the trees, and just as Drue neared him, a man
dropped from an overhanging branch onto the back of the
King's horse.

Pulling her mount as near as possible, Drue was able to
grab the man's arm just as he was about to plunge a dagger into the King's back.

Drue pressed her steely fingers into the tendons of his
wrist until the nerves became numb and the weapon
dropped to the ground. With a grunt, she jabbed her knees
into her horse. They leaped away, the man still in her
deadly grip. As he dropped to the ground, Drue twisted his
arm with a quick movement that dislocated it completely.
He lay writhing at Edward's feet as the King's guard rode
up, followed by Turlock and Drue's father.

"We routed them!" Edward cried jubilantly. "They
gave us a battle, but we routed them!"

Piers managed to bring his horse into the group and for
the first time Edward realized the extent of damage he had
sustained.

"My God, Piers, what have they done to you?" All the
excitement drained from the King's voice as he reached out
to take the reins of his friend's horse. There were tears in
his eyes as he turned to Drue and commanded, "Dis-
mount!"

Drue felt her heart turn over. The King was unpredictable. If he thought she had failed to save his favorite, he might well order her killed on the spot. She got from her horse and dropped to her knees.

The words swam above her head. It was as though she was in a dark cave filled with millions of buzzing bees. She tried to concentrate on what the King was saying, but her mind only grasped the fact that his sword hovered above her head as she removed her helmet. She could feel the first rays of the sun burn through the mist and touch her hair. She saw the glint of light as the same rays caught the King's sword, flashing from one shoulder to the other before resting on her bowed head.

Like the summer morn, the clouds in her mind burned away and the King's voice became clear as he said the words immemorial, "I dub thee, Sir Andrew of Duxton! Arise, Sir Knight!"

There was the usual backslapping and embracing as the men-at-arms crowded forward. Drue moved as quickly as she could through their outstretched hands until she reached her father. His eyes were glazed in disbelief, but he managed to embrace her warmly. "No one deserves knighthood more than you, Drue! And no man could be more proud than I."

Turlock's eyes were flooded with tears. They streamed down his weathered face. His throat closed and he was unable to utter so much as a syllable.

It wasn't until Drue and the rest of the entourage had ridden off to escort the King back to camp that Duxton turned to Turlock.

The Earl's weathered face was set as pride warred with the serpent of fear that twisted his guts. "It seems Drue

will have her wish! There is no question now of sending her
to take her rightful place in life.''

"Drue will be a fine knight!" Turlock declared
staunchly.

Duxton placed his hand on his cousin's shoulder. "I do
not doubt the truth of your words, my friend, but the King
would be embarrassed should he come to know he was
rescued by a woman, and that he subsequently knighted
her for her services.''

Turlock nodded his grizzled head. "In truth, I think our
King has little use for women. It might well mean our
heads should he discover the truth.''

"Then it is resolved." Duxton drew his great sword and
held it so the shadow of the hilt cast the image of a cross.
"From this day forth I have two sons, by the grace of God.
The fact that Drue was born a wench must be forgotten.''
He thrust the hilt toward Turlock. The knight repeated the
vow to satisfy his cousin, for Drue's womanhood was
something Turlock had come to grips with long ago. Come
to grips and decided it was of no importance next to the
skill and bravery of this fine young warrior.

"Garith!" Duxton's voice brought Turlock back to the
present. "Should we apprise him of the situation?''

"There is no need to tell him aught but that Drue has
been knighted. I know for a fact that he thinks of Drue as
his brother. Many years ago he came to me and asked if the
sister he dimly remembered had died with his mother. It
seemed simpler at the time to let him believe it to be so.''

Duxton nodded his approval. "We must return to the
camp. There will be much celebration regardless of our
losses on the battlefield.''

Wild with euphoria following the Bruce's miraculous
victory, the Scots attacked before the day was ended. The

fighting was fierce and the English King unavailable for consultation.

Instead of joining his generals to plan the battle, Edward issued inconsistent, inconsequential orders from the bedside of his friend, Piers Gaveston. As Edward was unwilling to leave Piers long enough to so much as oversee the situation, it wasn't long before the English army was in total confusion.

If one of the knights ordered his men to attack, the King might well dispatch a messenger to countermand the order and send the company to the opposite side of the battlefield. It was a soldier's nightmare.

Duxton and the other men of his experience realized the seriousness of the matter and tried to reason with the King, but he would not receive them. As darkness fell the first night the men collapsed in exhaustion, afraid to think what the morning might bring.

Such was not the case with Turlock.

"Be ready to move at first light," he said softly to Drue. "If the King does not leave quickly, we cannot answer for his safety, either from the Scots or from his own army."

"He'll not leave Gaveston," Drue told him.

"Then perhaps you should warn him that preparations must be made to get Gaveston away before a full retreat is called, for surely they will have us in full retreat before another day is out."

"I would not presume..." Drue protested.

"If you do not, who will? Edward will listen to none of us. You saved Gaveston's life. He might feel you had the man's best interest at heart."

"He's right!" Her father's voice echoed Turlock's words. "We've all tried to speak with the King and he will not grant an audience." Duxton removed his helmet and ran his hands through his thick white hair. "Perhaps it

would be best if the Scots took him." The disloyal words
were wrung from his staunch English heart and fell like
drops of blood in the silence. "I understand the Bruce! I
understand his love of his country and his love of war.
What I don't understand is Edward and his love of Piers
Gaveston!"

"If the Scots captured them, they'd surely ransom the
King. But if Piers were captured they might choose to
make an example of him," Turlock said.

"Would they ransom the King?" Duxton looked up in
the flickering light of the camp fire. "With Edward out of
the way, it would be an easy step for an ambitious Scot to
take the throne of England. After the fiasco today there are
many who would not be unwilling to see it happen."

Her father's words rang true! No matter how much the
English hated Robert the Bruce, they could not help but
admire his ability. He had skillfully taken the Scots army
and molded it into a force to be reckoned with.

"Very well," Drue agreed. "I will seek an audience with
the King, but I cannot hope he will listen to me when he
has ignored the advice of the most powerful lords of the
realm."

"It is up to you to make him listen, Sir Drue," Turlock
said, emphasizing her newly acquired title. "Unless you
wish to see the Scots' banners flying from the Tower of
London."

Drue got to her feet. "I will do my best. Pray God, it
will be enough!"

"Pray God it will...." Duxton echoed his daughter's
words as he watched her stride away.

The guard was under instructions to keep everyone from
entering the King's tent, but Drue persisted.

"I was with them when my Lord Gaveston was wounded. All I ask is a short audience to see how he fares."

"He is better!" the guard answered shortly. "Now go your way! The King will see no one."

The curtains parted and Edward's anxious face peered out. "Sir Drue! What brings you?"

Drue dropped to her knee. "I came in hope of discovering the truth of Lord Gaveston's condition. Rumors abound in camp and..."

"And well you have the right to know!" the King said. "Come inside and see for yourself!"

Drue gave the guard a withering glance as she followed her monarch into the tent. The air inside was warm and smelled strongly of medications and blood. To her surprise, the tent was quite luxurious, with cushioned seats of blue velvet and matched hangings to keep out drafts. Piers was awake and smiled weakly when he recognized his visitor.

"I thought you wouldn't mind allowing Sir Drue to assure himself you did indeed live." Edward tucked the blankets closer about his friend as he spoke.

"I am glad of the company and the concern," Piers said. "Few would have cared whether I lived or died."

Drue bowed low before the reclining man. She recognized a sadness in his voice that he would never have shown had he not been weak with fever.

"I believe you to be wrong there, my lord." Drue let the sincerity ring in her voice. "While many are jealous of your friendship with the King, they mean you no ill."

"Ah, Drue, how young and idealistic you are! Remember when we were so?" Piers asked, his fever-glazed eyes searching his friend's face.

Edward nodded. "It is not an easy task, being King," he said sadly. "And even more difficult being the King's friend."

Drue took a deep breath. In a moment they would cease their reminiscing and she would be dismissed without completing her mission. "Your Grace." She spoke so sharply the King jumped. "Your Grace, I fear there is real danger to my lord Gaveston. It would be best if you were to take him from here now and see to it he is housed in safety!"

"What could be safer than in the midst of the English army?" the King demanded.

"A warm house in the heart of Falkirk, from whence we came! The Scots are intoxicated over their victories. Should they break through our lines they will surely make directly for my lord Gaveston. They must be aware he was wounded and they will be on the lookout. It would be a great stroke for them to take Your Majesty's beloved friend and make an example of him before the world."

The King stared at Drue. It was obvious he had not given such circumstance any thought.

"My lord would not even be able to defend himself properly in his weakened condition," Drue pointed out.

"But the Scots bastards won't break through!" Edward slammed his fist on a table, causing a roll of lint to fall.

"Your Grace—" Drue leaned closer "—dare you take the chance?"

"I will not leave you, Piers! Not if it means losing the whole army!"

"Your Grace, may I suggest you go with him? They would never know; neither the enemy nor your own army. You could be back before anyone was aware of your absence. No one would look for a holy man and a wounded warrior traveling with only a few handpicked men.''

The King rubbed his head. "I will think on it," he promised as the guard presented himself at the door. "What is it now?" he asked pettishly. "I'm trying to think."

"Several of the spies have returned, Your Grace," the man said, bowing and scraping his way into the room. "They say they have word of the Scottish plans."

Edward took a deep breath. "I must go! Drue, keep Piers company until I return."

There was a moment's silence before Piers asked, "Is concern for me the only reason you want the King out of camp?"

So the man had seen through their ploy. All the better! If Piers were truly Edward's friend, he would see the wisdom of her advice.

"We fear the Scots may be planning trickery in revenge for de Bohun's sortie yesterday."

"Wasn't de Bohun's death enough?"

"I fear not! The Scots feel they have God on their side since the Bruce overcame an armed English knight. They will stop at nothing to have the King himself. Should they break through, there would be little to stop them."

"What good would it do them to hold Edward?"

"Edward's son is only a babe." Drue looked directly into Piers's eyes as she spoke. "With Edward dead, the Bruce would find it relatively simple to snatch the regency from the Queen."

"The English people would never stand for it!"

"The English people would have little to say of it if the Scots invaded England with no one on the throne save a weanling child!"

"And are you serious on your thoughts about my own person?"

"Regardless as to whether they take the King or no, my lord, they will come after you! With you in their clutches Edward would give them anything they wanted, and they realize it even if you do not!"

Piers nodded his head. "I do realize it!" He reached out his hand and grasped Drue's arm. "I will do my best to get the King away. Will you ride with us?"

Drue's face dropped in disappointment. "I had hoped to see my first action as a knight," she said honestly.

"And you shall!" Piers assured her. "I will see to it! It's the least I can do when you saved me, not once, but twice in as many days."

Drue took her leave, assured that Piers would indeed convince the King it best to steal away rather than wait for the Scots army to surround them.

The crisp night air was like cool nectar in her nostrils after the stuffy warmth of the tent, but it was not the air that made Drue's heart pound so madly. It was the thought that on the morrow she would fight at her father's side as an equal. And perhaps, during that fight, she would find the opportunity to challenge her nemesis, the Earl of Connaught! She smiled in satisfaction. He must accept her challenge now! There would be no question of testing her steel against the knave who had made an old man of Turlock.

Her face creased into a smile as she anticipated her triumph. Yes, they would see . . . they would all see her fight Connaught and beat him at his own game, the way she had imagined every day and night of her life since Turlock's defeat.

Had Turlock known of Drue's obsession, she knew he would have been the first to try to talk her out of it. Connaught was renowned as one of the mightiest, bravest knights in Christendom. But then, Drue had only just been knighted and had not yet built a reputation. She would build her reputation on Connaught's body, a right and fitting revenge for Turlock, and for herself. She could not place why she should have revenge, yet she knew it must be! She would seek out Connaught on the morrow and she would win, or forfeit her life!

The sun burst above the vibrant green of Bannockburn that Midsummer Day morn. The English soldiers, weary to the point of exhaustion, had been allowed no sleep in the fear their Scots adversaries would attack during the short summer night. They staggered to a halt beside the swiftly running burn, aware that the Bruce and his men watched from the distance.

Edward, assured that the Scots would never leave their vantage point to attack, had ridden off beside the litter carrying Piers. Although the men weren't aware their King had gone, their morale was nonetheless at the lowest possible ebb. Even though Edward was within a few miles of Stirling Castle and an end to the siege, his position had not been strengthened.

The English army was engrossed in the preparation for battle, and the even more pressing business of breaking their fast, when they were alerted that the Scots were forming ranks.

The Englishmen stopped and stared across the field as their enemies knelt in prayer.

Aware of the slight commotion behind her, Drue was surprised to see the King had returned.

He smiled, acknowledging her unspoken question. "Piers is safe in Falkirk. We felt it best I return. And it is for the best, I vow! The Scot bastards plan to surrender!"

He laughed and pointed toward the army kneeling in the morning sun. "Ha!" His voice rang out. "Already they kneel for mercy!"

"Yes, sire," Drue replied in a hushed voice. "They kneel for mercy, but not from us! Those men mean to attack!"

Realizing the truth in Drue's words, the King impetuously ordered his army forward. The Earl of Gloucester sounded the charge, and with no thought for his own safety, rode forth into their midst, shouting to his men to follow. A sea of men poured forward, to be met by the solid wall of Scots. Before his King's eyes Gloucester was impaled on the Scots' spears. Leaderless, his own men mulled about in confusion. Combat became a hand-to-hand confrontation. By the time the archers were positioned, their support was impossible. The huge English army was wedged in. Soldiers tripped over one another as the enemy spearmen advanced in relentless ranks, pressing them back against themselves.

"Your Grace, the day is lost!" Duxton dropped to his knee before his liege. "You must be away!"

Edward looked about in confusion. "The archers! Give the order for the archers to fire!" he cried frantically.

But the arrows fell into the English ranks, wreaking havoc on fellow Englishmen. Sir Giles d'Argentine drove his war-horse through the writhing throng of fighting men and gave the order to cease as he drew to a stop before his King.

"Sire, I beg you, be gone from this place. We cannot protect you! All is lost!"

Edward stopped, overlooking the carnage before nodding to the young man who had taken Drue's place as his standard-bearer.

"It is a sad day, Duxton," the King said, "a sad day indeed!"

"It is that, Your Grace," the Earl agreed.

"If it be your wish, I could order your son, Drue, to resume his post as my standard-bearer and so ride with me to safety," he offered graciously.

"I—I..." Duxton stammered. The King was making a generous and unwarranted proposition. One Duxton knew Drue would never accept. "I cannot say how greatly I appreciate the honor you do my house, Your Grace, but at this moment Sir Drue is in the thickest part of the battle. You must think of yourself and of England. I will tell him of your favor, and know you it will strengthen his arm as he fights on for England's glory."

There were tears in Edward's eyes as he reached down and clasped Duxton's hand. No more words were spoken, for the King put spurs to his horse and galloped off.

At the sight of the royal standard retreating across the burn, the Englishmen broke, shattered by the desertion of their King. In truth, his father, Edward I, would have fought to the death, and the soldiers were unprepared for their King's action.

At the first sign of weakening in the English lines, the Scots broke through. Realizing his King was in grave danger, Turlock gave a mighty battle cry, and the knights of England tried to close the gaps in the line as the frantic foot soldiers ran toward safety.

Drue's sword sang as its deadly sweep destroyed all who came within its range. She held her portion of the line until the men, recognizing leadership, began closing with the Scots, forcing them to a standstill. It was then that a huge dark form broke from the melee. Men and horses were covered with blood, whether their own or their enemies one could not tell. His surcoat hung in shreds over his armor. Undaunted, the knight urged his horse on, using his knees to impart his wishes. The gallant animal surged forward, leaving men strewn across the ground like branches broken in the wind.

Turlock shouted a warning, but he was held in on all sides and could not fight his way free. Drue skewered her last adversary and, sword upraised, rode in pursuit. She intercepted the knight as he reached a clearing some distance from the main body of fighting.

Her sword whistled through the air as he pulled his horse to a stop. Before the man could lift his own blade in defense, Drue dealt him a glancing blow against his shoulder. He reeled in the saddle as she struck again, this time across his upper body as he struggled to gain the protection of his shield.

His recovery was swift and his next blow was true. Drue pulled back, realizing she had indeed a worthy opponent. Their horses moved back and forth in a macabre dance of death. The sounds of battle faded into nothingness. There were only the two of them, each maneuvering for the blow that would win the day.

No battle raged as great as that between those two, for the outcome of their match had long since been written in the stars and the winner would ultimately be the loser, just as the loser would eventually win.

They stood in their stirrups, each testing the other for a moment of advantage. Then, as Drue was about to swing back to give herself the added weight of a forceful blow, she caught sight of her enemy's sword dropping to pierce beneath her shield. Sensing the advantage of his dangerous ploy, Drue brought her sword down across his neck.

The man slumped forward and slowly tumbled from his horse. Drue was on her feet beside him before he hit the ground. She removed the fallen knight's helmet. He was not unconscious as she had thought, but stared at her instead, with eyes as blue and guileless as the midsummer sky.

His thick black hair fell across his forehead and a droplet of blood trickled from his well-shaped lips.

"Well met!" His voice broke with pain. "I could not have asked for a finer match in which to die."

Drue held her sword against his throat. The skin looked soft and tan, and like fine suede, easily pierced.

"Go on." He managed what would serve as a smile. "'Tis time it was ended."

"Then close your eyes!" Drue growled.

"Nay, lad! When you kill me, you will look me in the eye, just as I will look into yours, until I see no more!"

This wasn't what Drue had expected. She had killed before, but never so fine a warrior. "And should I spare you," she mused, "would you bring a rich ransom?"

"Take him anyway," Turlock called out, drawing his war-horse to a stop. "It's little enough we'll get from the Scots this day. After the bout he gave you, he'll be worth something to the Bruce. I doubt the man has so many knights of his ilk that he can easily spare one."

Drue withdrew her blade and stepped back, her heart inexplicably lightened with the knowledge that she wouldn't have to kill this man after all.

"Take him!" she ordered the men who hurried toward them. "And be easy! The Scots do not pay for dead men!"

They hoisted him to the back of his horse. His eyes were twin pools of pain. "I doubt you do me a favor, lad, but I give you my thanks anyway."

"Do not call me lad!" Drue lifted her visor and gave him stare for stare. "I am Sir Andrew of Duxton." Without giving him a chance to say more, she ordered, "Take him away!"

Even the sounds of the battle did nothing to excite Drue's blood as she stared after the receding group. It was as though the pain and unspoken admiration in his fire-blue gaze had burned itself into her soul.

"I hope he turns out to be worth ransoming," she remarked to Turlock as they rode back toward the lines.

"Oh, I'm sure he'll bring us a pretty pile of gold," Turlock assured her. "Worth his weight in it, he is, I'll wager!"

"Then you recognize him?"

"Did you not know him?" Turlock asked in disbelief.

"I was unable to identify him. His surcoat was demolished, but he gave me a fight to be remembered! I would never have taken the advantage had he not dropped his sword to pierce beneath my shield, much the same as..." She pulled her horse to a dead stop. "It was him! It was the devil's spawn, Connaught! And I let him live!"

Turlock's laughter rolled out like morning thunder over the sound of battle. "Aye, Drue, it was Connaught, indeed! And now you know how exhilarating it is to fight a man of the highest caliber. In a fight between equally matched knights no man is the loser."

"Is that how you felt after he wounded you with his treachery?" Drue demanded.

"You were not angry that he tried the same trick on yourself. You glory in the fact you saw through his ruse and defeated him at his own game."

"But I would not likely have known, had he not first used the trick on you!"

"He paid you the highest of compliments," Turlock told her. "He knew he could not defeat you by strength or skill. He had to resort to guile, and even in that you were his equal."

"Equal!" Drue's voice rose in righteous outrage. "Equal? I was his master!"

She galloped off, her head high, as Turlock looked on, pride shining in his eyes. "I hope it will always be so, young Drue," he murmured. "I hope it will always be so!"

Chapter Four

"I should have killed him!" Drue muttered under her breath as the weary horses sloshed through the thick English mud.

"An inglorious return," Turlock remarked as his steed plowed along beside her, "but a return, nonetheless. For that we can be grateful!" He chose to ignore her words, and his attitude irritated Drue the more. She repeated her thought more loudly.

"I should have killed him! He will doubtless prove more trouble than he's worth!"

Turlock struggled to hide his mirth. "I doubt not the truth in your words. Still, his worth is great. He is the only true prize we gleaned from the rout at Bannockburn. His capture will niggle at his uncle, Robert Bruce, and we will be offered great rewards for his return. Never fear, Drue! You did well to keep him alive!"

Drue looked back as the wounded man swayed in the saddle of the horse she led. His eyes, twin sparks of blue flame beneath sooty lashes, watched her with an anger that matched her own.

The steady undaunted stare could mean only one thing. He hated being wounded, hated being a captive and hated having been bested by a heretofore unknown knight.

Drue knew his feelings, for had circumstances been reversed, they would have been her own. She did not begrudge him his anger or his hatred, but she wished he had remained unconscious. With him thrown over the saddle of his horse, or borne on a hastily made litter, she would not have been so aware of his eyes boring into her back, of his mouth closed tight against the pain. She would not have had to fight the urge to stop and allow him rest, when she knew the shortest pause might mean the difference between a clean retreat and another skirmish.

"I am surprised they did not try to take him back by force, if he is as great a prize as you believe," she challenged Turlock.

"They still count their dead! Once they realize Connaught is not among them, they will come for him, but by then we will be well away."

"Pray God," Drue breathed as she urged her horse forward. The last thing she wanted was another confrontation with the Scots. They were still euphoric with victory, having claimed Stirling Castle before the English were more than out the gates.

In the panic of full retreat it had taken all Drue's skill to stop the men under her command from scattering and being captured. She had herded them like sheep, using the flat of her sword to keep them moving along the rain-soaked roads as they plunged toward England and safety. Surely there had been no safety in Scotland. Their own marshal had turned the King away from Sterling Castle and sent him riding through the driving rain toward the border, the army following in his wake.

The rain started again and Drue bent into her cloak, cursing the inclement weather that bogged down supply wagons and men alike. She glanced up as Turlock's horse fell into step beside hers.

"If you would keep your 'spoil of war,' I suggest you look to the man's welfare. The dead body of Connaught will bring little in ransom and even less in prisoner trade."

This time it was obvious the man was all but unconscious and only his inherent ability to stay in the saddle kept him upright. Drue handed the reins to Turlock and dismounted. The mud sloshed around her ankles.

Connaught roused himself as she stopped before him. He blinked, trying to clear his eyes, and Drue knew he didn't recognize her. He took the water she offered, spilling more than he drank, before returning the skin.

"We are going on until nightfall," she told him, trying to ignore the slight stiffening of his body at her words. Darkness would not be upon them until almost midnight, and it was not yet time for vespers. "We must put as much distance as possible between ourselves and your uncle's army."

She needn't explain this to him, Drue chastised herself as she returned to her horse. It was as much his fault as anyone's that they must push on! Had it not been for Connaught, there would have been little threat of pursuit. Drue sighed as she stiffly remounted. She had ridden through one full day and night and the best part of another. It would be some hours before she could rest, and her body longed for rest. Still, she must not allow that to become evident. Above all she must set the example for the foot soldiers. Another panic such as the one that had ensued with the King's swift departure from the battlefield must not be repeated!

Drue squared her shoulders, suddenly glad the King had chosen to disguise himself and ride beside the litter of his friend, Piers Gaveston. With the King out of the way, Drue had only her captive to worry about. She looked back once again and was surprised to see the intensity of the feverish, blue gaze that followed her every movement. She must show no weakness to her captive. Her captive—the man who had churlishly made a cripple of Turlock. She hated him as much as she fought her grudging admiration for him.

Only a truly great horseman could retain his seat on the horse despite such a loss of blood. Drue's resolve weakened as she remembered the pain in his eyes when he had returned the water skin. Respect for his courage warred with the well-established animosity she had nursed since Connaught's encounter with Turlock. In truth, it had been easier to hate the man when he was nothing more than a name. Having him at such close proximity gave her pause in her resolution.

She looked back to assure herself her prisoner still sat his horse and was caught in the flash of his eyes as he silently confronted her. Her spine straightened as she met his challenge and forced herself to become more than she had been, while a bit of her hatred chipped away and admiration prevailed.

There was no way she could have known that the sight of her body, straight and strong in the saddle before him, was the only thing keeping Connaught alive. He watched her, vowing with each painful, jolting step of his horse that he would someday find a way to make Drue pay. The fact that a mere lad had beaten him at his own game sent his blood to boiling. He had always been able to defeat his opponent with the maneuver he had used on Drue.

Not that the lad had been any sort of threat. He had only wanted to dispatch his opponent quickly, for his objective was the King of England. But Drue had seen through his ruse, and instead of falling into his trap and opening to his ploy, had struck him down, swiftly and thoroughly. The resulting wound caused him ever more discomfort as the fever coursed through his body with the same deadly intensity as did his anger.

If only the shoulders shimmering before him would slump in weariness. If only the head would bow and nod, but no! His captor rode like a centaur, head high in the face of the elements. Connaught knew he could do no less! He must be as much of a man as the man who had bested him in battle! Desperately he fought the dark shroud of unconsciousness that threatened to enfold him in its deadly embrace. Time and again his eyes focused on Drue, and time and again they blurred with pain as his fever-racked body was drained of its last remnant of strength and his parched lips moved in silent supplication for the will to remain upright in the saddle.

Perhaps what his uncle said was true, he thought as his bound hands clutched desperately at the saddle. Perhaps England truly was a godforsaken land, for God seemed not to hear his prayers.

Surely the night must be upon them, for the world was far more dim than it had been a moment before! Surely they would call a halt at any time. Surely... surely...

It was Turlock who caught Connaught's unconscious body as it tumbled from his horse.

"I told you the man had all he could stand!" Turlock scolded as he laid another compress on Connaught's shoulder. "If he had less than the neck of a bull you would surely have cleaved through, just as the Bruce sliced poor de Bohun."

"And would we not have been better off than we are, had I done so?" Drue asked, casting a glance at the wounded knight. "We have set ourselves up for attack by anything from Scots to wild boars."

"There are over a hundred men camped with us!"

"And ninety of them are wounded!"

"Ten good Englishmen can take on—"

"The wild boar," Drue conceded. "But if the Scots come, we are lost!"

"The Scots will not come. We are too far inside English territory for that. Why, we're hardly two days ride from Duxton!" He looked out the entrance of the tent as though he could see the keep through the dark mist that encircled them.

"They have gone as far as Duxton before," Drue reminded him. "What makes you think they won't do so again?"

"Your father has men posted all across his lands, as you well know! There is no chance of them coming this far without being detected and forced back. Rest easy, Drue! We are safe, and with any luck, your prize will live to be ransomed."

Drue looked at the cot where Connaught tossed restlessly. She looked away. The man irritated her because of what he'd done to Turlock. He was like salt in her wounds. And now she would have to nurse him back to health in order to collect her just reward. He was her captive, and she was honor-bound to keep him alive. To keep the magnificent body alive so this knight would live to fight again. Silently she chided herself for thinking him magnificent, but magnificent was the only word that came to mind.

Even weak from loss of blood and slumped against the neck of his horse he had demanded respect. Grudgingly Drue wondered if she would have been able to carry pain as well as had Connaught.

Perhaps, only perhaps, despite his churlish trickery in wounding Turlock, he was worthy of her efforts to save him.

* * *

Drue had cauterized her share of wounds, but never before had the act affected her.

Any other man would have screamed and writhed, but this one lay stiff beneath Turlock's hands and only once cried out. It had made it all the worse for Drue. She had seen men faint in fear and pain. When she had finished, Turlock took the iron from her hand, and she dropped to her knees beside Connaught's cot and closed her eyes, whether in prayer or simple relief she could not have said. Yet even with her eyes closed she could see his face, his eyes, his lips, the strong lines of his jaw, his dark hair. Fear shook her as she knew instinctively she would never be able to lock him from her memory. His visage was burned into her brain for all eternity and never would she be rid of it.

She pulled herself together, realizing he watched her with eyes so filled with pain she winced that she should have inflicted it.

His lips moved and she waited for the angry curses that would ensue. She had heard them all before; surely he could say nothing new. But he did!

Holding her eyes with his own, his lips moved and his voice, broken with pain, whispered, "Thank you!"

It was so unexpected Drue felt the hatred drain from her. Her hand rested against Connaught's chest. She could feel his heart beat, strong and fast. His skin held the scent of cloves. She should move away. She *must* move away! This was her enemy, and as surely as there was a God, if she gave in to the weakness that threatened her, Drue knew she would be lost.

"You have nothing to thank me for," she told him. "You are worthless if you are dead."

"And so you have saved me, but it was not for that reason I thanked you. You have made it possible for me to fight again."

Drue looked at him askance.

"Had the wound remained the way it was, it would have become infected, and eventually I would have lost the use of my arm. While it's not impossible for a knight to go to battle with only one arm, he is usually less effective."

His hand came to rest on hers. The warmth flowed through her body, settling deep in the core. Her legs suddenly felt too weak to lift her and she remained beside him, aware of his hand clutching hers as she desperately sought words to break the tension.

"After you are ransomed and return to battle I will be more than willing to fight you again!"

The sound of her own voice brought Drue back to her senses. She recognized the surge of excitement. It was the same as she had known when the trumpets sounded the charge and she rode forward, anticipating the first clash of steel against steel or steel against flesh. She recognized the wild euphoria, but it was beyond her to know why it came when she was near this man. Perversely, she was glad he would see battle again, though why she should feel so was beyond her power of understanding. She attributed her lapse to the weariness that permeated her very soul and got to her feet, carrying the bloodied cloths from the tent. Once outside, she slumped to the ground, still holding them in her hands.

As the exhaustion passed she cast the cloths into the pot of water boiling on the fire. But ridding herself of the rags did not rid her of Connaught.

She stared at the blood on her hands. His blood, its color augmented by the firelight. Once again she saw his eyes reflected in the flames. She had carried her hatred of this man for so long, and now that he was in her power, she fought her budding admiration more violently than she had relished the years of hatred.

She knew she must rid herself of this weakness of will. Why did the man have to be so brave? Why couldn't he scream and curse when she tended his wound? Why did his eyes have to be the color of blue fire, his hair black as the darkest corner of hell and soft as down? And above all, why couldn't she find it within herself to hate him today as she had yesterday?

It was as though his blood was soaking through to her soul, softening her heart toward her sworn enemy. She wiped her hands against her cloak, but the offending stain remained. Incensed with herself as well as her prisoner, she ran down the path to the stream and plunged her hands into the cold water, scrubbing furiously with pebbles from the bottom until the stains disappeared. Yet she could not deny the foreboding she felt, that Connaught's blood would remain imprinted on her soul.

Connaught took his time recovering, partially from the extensiveness of the wound, which still caused him great pain, and partially from sheer obstinacy. Drue moved restlessly about the tent. He knew how much she wanted to be away, and ordinarily he would have been in agreement with her, but the longer he could force them to stay in one place the greater his chance of escape.

"I wish they would come!"

Drue's words giving voice to his thoughts startled Connaught so greatly he sat upright, wherein Drue eyed him with speculation, wondering if perhaps she had misjudged his strength.

"We have waited here far too long!" Drue glared at him. "You've been coddled enough! We ride at dawn!"

"What will your friend Turlock say to that?" Connaught asked quietly. "You agreed to remain here until his return."

"It is no concern of yours what he says!" Drue snapped.

The rays of the sun slipped through the door of the tent and shimmered on her hair. Like everything about Drue, her hair, too, was unusual. It seemed to be the only indecisive thing about her; not brown, not blond, not white, it was a combination of each. Bleached from many hours in the hot sun, yet it blended into the honey color of her skin. Her chin was square, a sure mark of an aggressive nature. Her teeth were strong and white, unusual for a warrior. Drue's stride was long and there was a spring to it.

Connaught wondered about his captor's age. It was bad enough to have been taken by the English, but worse still to have been taken by an untried knight. Why, the lad had yet to shave! Connaught had begun trimming his beard before his sixteenth summer! The whole situation was maddening, and even more maddening was the fact that he, Connaught, could not seem to keep from following Drue with his eyes. He was fascinated by this person he believed to be a young man, and even that fascination bothered him. Attributing it to the weakness caused by his wound and subsequent fever, Connaught closed his eyes. He would not look at this English stripling who had all but robbed him of his honor. But his eyes opened of their own accord, and without realizing it, Connaught again watched.

"Get some sleep," Drue commanded gruffly. "You'll need it before you rest again."

"I can sleep in my saddle."

"Of course, but Turlock may not be there to catch you this time!"

Connaught's face burned with anger. Why did this whelp have to remind him of his disgrace? Why must it be rubbed in that he, Connaught, had passed out from fever and loss of blood and had had to be carried into camp? He pulled his cloak about himself and turned toward the wall. "Be damned to you!" he muttered.

"And to you!" Drue said amicably.

Throwing the cloak aside, Connaught got to his feet. "Such never happened to me before!"

Drue shrugged her shoulders. "I imagine there is a first time for everything, even your demise!"

His stare was steely but she didn't seem to notice. Then he laughed and she looked up in surprise. "Perhaps the fever has gone to your head," she suggested.

"I find your words strangely reassuring. If my demise has been preordained, then perhaps I will be here to see yours!"

Drue stopped in front of him. She was almost as tall as he, and although his shoulders were broader and his chest deeper, she knew her own wiry strength would hold her in good stead against him. "Are you planning to attack me?" she asked quietly.

"I have no plans but to be ransomed," he countered.

Her eyes were almond-shaped and they glittered as though lit with sunbeams. Connaught stood mesmerized, forgetting for a moment the angry words he had planned to speak.

"Ransomed!" Drue spat the word as though it was unpalatable. "Turlock left days ago to send our demands to the Bruce and still there is no answer. They want you no more than I!"

"Then why did you take me? I was ready to die on the field."

At his question her mind was wiped clear of any admiration she might have felt for Connaught, with his striking looks and undaunted courage. Her eyes filled with venom. "I took you to make you pay for what you did to Turlock!"

"Turlock!" Connaught tried to make sense of her words. "You mean the old man who helped nurse me?"

Drue bristled. "I mean the man who is one of the greatest living champions in the Christian world! I mean the man you wounded with your foul tactics and filthy tricks!"

"I play no tricks!" Connaught's face turned livid with rage.

"You lie, also!"

He grasped her arm, but she hit him solidly with her fist, catching him across his wounded shoulder. He sank to the bed, his knees buckling in pain. When the waves of sickness receded, he touched the bandage gingerly in an effort to see if the wound had reopened.

The last thing Drue had meant to do was to strike a wounded man, but his words had brought out the worst in her. Even her knightly vows were forgotten when she was near him. Her whole body had been jolted when he had laid his hand on her. Her reflex had been swift and automatic, but, in truth, she had not meant to open his wound.

She bent over him, loosening the bandage. "It did not reopen. I won't have the pleasure of cauterizing it again."

His face was gray with pain and she felt a twinge of guilt at her choice of words. If the memory was distasteful to Connaught, it was as bad for Drue.

She could not forget her inadvertent response to his nearness, and even worse, she could not forgive herself for her weakness. Try as she would to pass it off as hatred, she was honest enough to admit that she admired his bravery in the face of pain or danger. He was a courageous man and a wily one. Drue was aware her reputation had grown since taking him prisoner. No longer was she looked upon as an untried youth. Her sword had been bloodied by the best the enemy had to offer. Only crossing swords with the Bruce himself could have offered her greater respect.

Perhaps she would have done better had she gone to negotiate the ransom and left Turlock with Connaught. The close proximity between herself and her prisoner had caused her to run the gauntlet of emotions from hatred to admiration, from total distrust to grudging interest bordering on a feeling that, under different circumstances, might almost have been considered friendship.

Taking a cloth, she wiped the beads of sweat from his forehead. His eyes captured hers once again, holding them as he delved into her soul, the intensity of his gaze piercing through her habitual defenses, threatening to unmask her innermost secrets. Far more frightening than the intensity of the man himself was Drue's realization that for the first time in her life she wanted to share her thoughts with someone other than Turlock.

It was then she knew the immense threat this man posed to her entire realm of being. Resolutely she shut him from her mind and went about her business, yet he haunted her at odd moments despite her resolve.

Returning from his parley with the Scots, Turlock was more than pleased.

"I tell you, they will give us all we ask to have Connaught returned. It wasn't until we mentioned his name that Jamie Douglas gave consideration to our demands. When your father realized the extent of the prize we possess, he lost no time in tripling the ransom. They will give us no fewer than ten of our knights in return."

"You sound like a canny Scot haggler yourself, Turlock!" Drue laughed. "I do not remember when you have been so excited over anything."

"I am excited!" Turlock agreed. "I have found something I can do besides fight, for whether we chose to admit it or not, young Drue, my fighting days are numbered. It pains me to sit the horse for the long hours of battle, not to mention the forced marches so dear to our King's heart."

"Nonsense!" Drue protested. "You and I have many battles before us. Battles in which we will be victorious!"

Turlock clapped her on the shoulder. "Of course we have, and victorious we shall be! But in the meantime, I will win a victory of my own at the negotiating tables of the Scots, for they sorely want their champion returned." He sank down on a stool near the entry to the tent. "Between us, we will have snatched victory from defeat. The Scots will give more than they get for all their victory at Bannockburn."

"The Scots can afford to give more, since they have taken more in prisoners and land." Connaught's voice caused them to turn quickly.

"You speak true, Connaught," Turlock agreed, "but even I was surprised at their easy agreement. They must value you highly."

"No more highly than you are valued by the English. I remember hearing tales of a castle being given for your ransom."

"That is so," Turlock grinned, "but that was many years ago, when I was the King's champion."

"And are you no longer champion to the crown?"

"Piers Gaveston holds that honor."

To their surprise, Connaught laughed aloud. "Gaveston is the King's champion?"

"Piers is a brave and loyal man," Drue offered in his defense.

Again, Connaught burst into laughter. It galled Drue to hear him laugh. He was a prisoner, he should not be laughing and joking with his gaolers, but here he was, taking a place beside the evening fire as though it was his right. As much as she resented his laughter, Drue found herself wanting to hear it again. It seemed almost melodious to her ears. Deep and rich without being raucous. It made her want to laugh with him.

She watched as the firelight played across the planes of Connaught's face. He was older than she, but younger than Turlock by some years. His teeth gleamed white and even in the fire's glow. There were no gaping holes in Connaught's mouth where battle or rot had rid him of his looks. But then, Drue mused, Connaught would not have spent his life on the field, he would have been trained in a castle, as Garith had been.

Turlock lumbered to his feet. "Damn me for a forgetful old fool," he muttered, reaching inside his tunic. "I bring messages for you both!"

He handed each a packet, watching as they drew closer to the fire in order to read them.

Drue's letter was from Garith. He sent warm congratulations on her luck and foresight in capturing Connaught and said he looked forward to seeing all of them when they returned. Although Garith was now one of the King's men, he assured her he had not forgotten to take special care of her holdings, managing them as though they were his own.

Drue smiled complacently as she read the list of properties, which had increased vastly since she was knighted and would again increase with the ransom of Connaught. She glanced across the fire, to see her prisoner's face alight with happiness.

"It seems you, too, have received good news," she said.

"Aye, I have! My lady wife has given me yet another son!"

Drue felt as though she had been struck. The sensation closely akin to pain, shot through her whole body. She lowered her lids so the man could not see her eyes. "I did not know you were wed."

It was a foolish thing to say. Of course a man of his position was married. He was a valued member of the Bruce's court and army. His holdings would be great and he would want a son to succeed him.

"I was married several years ago," Connaught volunteered. "We were betrothed as children, but I did not meet Enid until shortly before the wedding." He glanced at Drue. "Much the same as your own situation, I'll warrant."

"Not mine!" The words were spoken more vehemently than she would have wished. "It is my brother, Garith, who is betrothed. He will be wed soon, now that he is knighted and has found favor with the King. He is the heir and the one who deserves sons. I desire only my sword."

Connaught's curiosity was piqued. "You must have estates that will return to the crown if you have no heir."

"My brother is my heir, and no, I want no marriage. Women do not interest me."

Connaught was somewhat taken aback, but Drue saw nothing unusual in her words. Women did not interest her. She did not understand them. Their silly posturing and high voices made her head ache. Their clothes were outlandish and obviously difficult to wear. It was said they spent hours on their hair and faces. Their duties as chatelaines of the various castles must be boring and uneventful. Drue would never have given consideration to changing places with one of them, nor did she give a thought to the possibility. In her own mind she was a soldier and a knight. That she had no use for marriage was acceptable as a soldier of the field. Having a family to protect would only prove to be a burden. It never occurred to Drue she could not have married a woman, being one herself, for she thought of herself in every way as a man, as did the knight across the fire from her.

Connaught sat silently, digesting Drue's words. He, too, remembered the moment of weakness she had shown after she had cauterized his wound, when she had slumped forward against his chest. He remembered how, to his everlasting shame, his senses had quickened to a point where he had regained consciousness, when the blackness of oblivion would have best served. Until this moment he had given Drue's action no thought, for his captor was a young man, untried in the rigors of bloodletting. Now he began to wonder, both at Drue and at himself.

Were Drue's words the careless utterings of a hapless lad, or was there a deeper meaning? A meaning inadvertently answered within himself? Connaught watched carefully as the firelight played on Drue's face. It was a strong face. There was no weakness about it. The face of a person used to taking what was needed to survive. The face of a person pleased with life, who desired no changes. But the eyes were guileless. No, it was Connaught's own guilt that chafed him. If it were else, why had he not told Drue of his marriage during the long hours they had spent together playing chess, or chatting of battles they had known? He pushed the thought aside. It was too unworthy to be entertained!

"I now have three sons," he said proudly. "Patrick, who will someday be the Earl of Connaught, is my heir and namesake."

"Your name is Patrick?" The question was out before Drue could silence it.

He nodded as he continued. "Only my wife and Mother Graham call me by it." He saw the twinkle in her almond eyes and quickly continued. "If you would be my friend, call me Connaught."

"I am not your friend, I am your captor. You are my prisoner!"

"A fact I seldom forget," Connaught told her.

"I could be much harder on you," she reminded him. "You go unshackled, unlike any other prisoner in camp. Were I to follow the King's orders regarding those taken at Bannockburn, I would have a chain placed around your neck and you would be made to follow me about like a tame bear."

"I might follow you like a bear, but never a tame one," he told her, his eyes alight at the pleasure of bantering.

"You don't seem so terribly fierce to me," Drue remarked. "I give you credit. You have been a model prisoner. I would I had as little trouble with the others quartered in camp."

"I did not know there were more Scots here," Connaught commented innocently.

"Most have gone, except for the most gravely wounded. Your inability to travel on probably saved their miserable lives. They owe you much."

"I should like to see them," Connaught told her.

"I think not!" Drue saw through his ruse. "It is enough for you to know they are well cared for."

Turlock, who had been watching the exchange from his vantage point in the shadows, disappeared into the tent. Drue and Connaught paid little attention as they continued their conversation. Then Turlock returned with goblets of wine.

"Here." He passed them to Drue and Connaught. "We will drink a toast to Connaught's new son."

"May he live and prosper and be intelligent enough to keep to his own side of the border and not fight the English!" Drue lifted her glass in salute.

"Do you fear my infant child?" Connaught asked in mock surprise.

"I fear no man, but you are more trouble than you're worth regardless of your high ransom. I do not wish to deal with more of your ilk in my old age."

"Hear! Hear!" Turlock reached out, touching their goblets with his own before he quaffed the wine. "One Connaught in a lifetime is more than enough."

"You do me great honor," Connaught laughed. "And I will hope to meet my son before he is forced to come and fight for my release."

"Do not concern yourself for that," Drue assured him. "I vow we want you gone as much as your wife wants you returned."

Turlock poured more wine and began to talk to Connaught. Neither man noticed how quiet Drue became for she realized her words had not rung true. She was not looking forward to seeing Connaught leave. He was a good companion. It was her own perversity that had kept her from accepting his offer of friendship, and she longed to take back her words and accept his hand.

Yet even the thought of touching his hand unnerved her. Strange sensations mingled with the wine and shot through her body, leaving her lightheaded and giddy at the thought of pressing her hand against his. In her mind she savored the strength, the warmth, the vitality that flowed between them when, by chance, they touched. Her eyes focused on Connaught's hands, brown and sinewy in the firelight. He moved them to emphasize his point as he spoke. Every motion was strong and forceful, portraying a man sure of himself and his beliefs.

Drue admired those qualities, for she saw them reflected in Turlock and hoped she, too, encompassed them. But there was a terrible chasm separating herself and Connaught. More than simply the obvious problem based on the fact that they fought for different factions and their loyalty was held by opposing countries, Drue sensed that Connaught contained a force that could destroy her, given the chance.

Again she lifted the goblet to her lips. It could not be! This man held no power over her. Drue was the captor, Connaught the prisoner. Yet somehow she knew she would never again be completely free of him, for at any moment some unknowing knight might gesture in a way that would bring Connaught to her mind, causing the pulse-shattering sensation she found so unnerving. Cursing herself for a maudlin fool and the wine for bringing on the situation, Drue threw the last dregs hissing into the fire and, giving her prisoner and Turlock the slightest of nods, retired to the shadowy confines of the tent.

Chapter Five

It was prudent to keep Connaught inside during the night, both because of his wound and because, as a prisoner, he might try to escape. Tomorrow they would ride on to Duxton, and while hardly more than the keep and bailey remained standing, the castle never having been rebuilt after the siege, Drue looked forward to its safety.

The wind had risen. It whipped through the trees, snapping branches and stripping away leaves. The tent heaved and shuddered. Turlock awoke and walked the camp, a solitary sentry seeing to the welfare and safety of the men. So it was Drue found herself alone with Connaught when she was torn from sleep by his cries. As if in answer to the storm he shouted, fighting unknown battles and unseen enemies.

Groggy with wine and sleep, Drue responded without thought. Dragging her bedroll across the tent, she staggered toward him. "I am beside you," she said, repeating the words she had said to her brother so many times. "There is nothing to fear." But this was not her brother, as she discovered to her ultimate distress when she lay down next to him, to silence his cries before they were heard and considered an ill omen that would postpone their plans to move. Had Drue thought the touch of his hand to be stunning, the feel of his body in such close proximity was tantamount to throwing herself headlong into a signal fire or wearing full armor in the heat of a summer day. Weakness poured over her as though her bones had melted. Was this heat within herself or had Connaught's fever returned?

She placed her hand on his forehead, satisfied that it felt cool to her touch. It was then she realized it was not fever that haunted him but the same demons of the night that had haunted Garith. Connaught thrashed about until she held his shoulders, pinning him to his mat as she hovered above, breathing reassurances against his face. Convincing herself she sought only to quiet him before he aroused the camp, she held him until he relaxed. His eyes opened, glints of blue flame in the shadows, and closed again. He seemed not to see her, and once again sleep came to him, deep and restful, as he unconsciously accepted the warmth of the vibrant body next to his.

Drue was up at the first sign of dawn and began to prepare for the journey to Duxton. Her belongings were bundled in readiness by the time Connaught woke.

Connaught remembered none of the happenings of the night before. He wasn't aware there had been a storm, and there was no sign that Drue had been near him. But his mind was filled with dreams. Dreams of Drue's face above his own. Dreams of Drue's lips so near to his that Connaught could almost taste them.

He rubbed his hands over his face in an effort to wipe away the riotous thoughts bombarding him. Even his bed seemed to be filled with the scent of sunlight, a scent he had come to associate with Drue. He got to his feet, deliberately ignoring Drue as she went back and forth between the tent and her horse. His guilt was so extreme he felt he

must wash it away, and he bolted from the tent toward the
nearby stream the men used for water and washing.

Shedding his clothing, he plunged into the chill water.
He rubbed his body with the gritty pebbles. He wet his
hair, scraping at his scalp as though he would wash away
the cruel images embedded in his brain. Satisfied he was
indeed awake and had control of his mind once again, he
stepped from the stream just as the brush crackled and
parted before him. Drue stood there, her breathing rag-
ged, her face flushed from her efforts to discover his
whereabouts.

There were few men in her father's army that Drue had
not seen unclothed. Thinking of her as a lad, they did
nothing to conceal themselves from her. That Drue preferred privacy was no cause for comment, for her brother
had preferred it also. Many times she had passed soldiers
bathing and never given the situation, or the men's bodies, so much as a thought. But today, faced with Connaught's nakedness, Drue felt her lungs constrict as though
a giant hand had forced the air from them.

She could not tear her eyes from the strength and beauty
of the man before her. The strong shoulders, the deep chest
covered with thick black hair, the flat belly and slim flanks.
The horseman's legs, used to guide his steed with an authoritative touch. Her eyes swept over him, slowly taking
in each line of his body. She had always thought her
brother, Garith, to be the epitome of masculine beauty, but
she now realized she was confronted by a man whose physique was truly spectacular. The thought of having spent
the night in such close proximity to that checked power
made her heart pound erratically.

Connaught turned from her and bent to retrieve his
shirt. Her eyes moved down across his slim hips. Her heart
pounded in her ears. Little ripples ran up and down her

arms as though she had taken a chill, yet she seemed to be burning with fever. A deep, grinding pain wrenched through her body, burying itself deep in her stomach.

Grudgingly, Drue acknowledged her luck in capturing this man. His body was an instrument of war, developed only to dispatch death to his enemies. She envied him his physique. Never before had she envied another person, and it shocked Drue that she should do so now. But the way her heart was pounding, and the way her mouth had dried, it must indeed, she reasoned, be envy.

What seemed to be many minutes as she stood staring at Connaught were, in fact, only a few seconds. But his body was burned into her brain like a white-hot brand she would see each time she closed her eyes for the rest of her life. Drue realized only that new and perplexing sensations were invading her and that the fault was Connaught's!

Her voice returned as anger prevailed. "You are lucky I did not kill you!" She exaggerated in an effort to compose herself. "I thought you were trying to escape!"

"I only came out to cleanse myself. You were busy elsewhere. I gave no thought that you might misread my intentions."

She wished he would dress, and at the same time she gloried in watching the muscles play on his glistening body, still sparkling with water in the morning sun. Walking across the little clearing, Drue sank down against a tree. Her legs were no longer able to support her.

"Dress and be quick," she ordered. "We ride to Duxton!"

Connaught did as he was bid. For the life of him he could not explain his reactions to his captor. His body had quickened when he saw Drue standing before him. It had taken all his will power to fight down the surge that shot through him. Angrily he told himself it was in his mind alone. Obviously Drue gave him no thought except of disgusted impatience because he was not ready to ride. Connaught had a fine body. He knew it might well be the envy of a younger man. It was not unusual to have other men stare at him, but never before in his life had he been so affected by it that he had to turn away to hide his response.

It must have been the close association with the dreams of the night before, Connaught determined. He had been a prisoner a long time, and gone even longer without a woman. Many times the men joked about boys looking attractive after long campaigns. That it had never happened to Connaught before did not mean he was becoming perverted in his desires. But, somehow, he resented Drue's stony stare, a stare that never left him as he put on his clothing.

Seeing Duxton Castle was like a balm to Drue. She rode toward it with a lighter heart than she had been able to claim for many days. Although she disliked most castle living, Duxton was primitive enough to suit her.

Turlock and Connaught rode beside her as they crossed the moat and entered the grounds through the ancient barbican tower. Drue acknowledged the greetings of the villagers, but kept moving toward the battered old building, talking easily with Turlock and Connaught. Dressed and armored, her prisoner posed no threat to her. As long as she had no personal contact with him she was able to shut from her mind the sight that had haunted her throughout the journey.

The main room of the keep was warm. A boar was turning on the spit. Drue looked askance at Turlock, but he shook his head.

"I did not order this, but wish to God I had, for it is a good and welcome sight."

"It is a good and welcoming smell!" Connaught added. The two men laughed in agreement, and Drue held herself in check as a twinge of jealousy niggled at her.

Drue strode toward the stairs as a voice called from above, "Drue! Well come, well come!"

"Garith!" she gasped, hurrying up the worn stairs to meet him. "How came you here?"

"I knew you would come to Duxton rather than go to any of our other holdings," he replied with a laugh. "I came because I wanted to meet the illustrious prisoner who has caused so much gossip in the court."

Drue's eyes traveled to Connaught as he stood in the center of the room below. Even in the dim light she could feel the force of his vibrant blue eyes. "He is there, and you are welcome to his company."

Connaught turned to Turlock. "Drue did not tell me he had a twin," he said.

"Twin!" Turlock repeated in disbelief. "They are not twins! There is a full year between them in age."

"They are so alike it is difficult to credit your words," Connaught said as they came forward.

"I perceive you to be correct, Connaught, though I vow I never saw it before. They are alike as peas in a pod!"

And indeed they were, although the advantage in size and weight went to Drue. She looked the part of the warrior, with sinewy arms and broad muscular shoulders. Though equal in height, Garith could not compare to Drue in physical development.

"They are fine looking lads," Turlock breathed, pride thickening his voice. "Fine looking lads!"

His eyes misted with memories of another entry to this very room. "I never thought they'd grow to this the day we took them away after Lady Duxton died of plague. Garith had been taken with the plague but managed to survive. It was ludicrous to see Drue care for him. Hardly more than babies they were!''

"Garith—'' Drue's voice sliced through Turlock's words ''—this is my prisoner, Patrick, Earl of Connaught.''

Connaught sized up the man before him quickly. While neither of the younger Duxtons had their father's proportions, what Drue lacked in size she made up in agility, which, combined with her wiry strength, gave her a distinct advantage against most opponents. Garith's gaze was that of a gentle lord. The sharp, wary look of a fighter was not in his eyes. It was well, Connaught thought, that Garith had chosen the life of a lord of the realm rather than that of a warrior of the field. The young man would not last long if confronted daily with death and deprivation.

Again Drue's voice was heard. "Perhaps you will help me to convince my brother that he misses much of life with his castle living.''

Connaught's laughter rang out. "You forget I am your prisoner and in poor circumstance to promote the life we have chosen. Besides, I think your brother has chosen wisely. He looks well content with his lot, just as you do with yours.''

These were obviously not the words Drue wanted to hear. While she was pleased that her brother did not challenge her place in their father's army, she made no secret of the fact that she missed Garith sorely and wished many times he was with her in the field. Her life had been sheltered in its own way. She had many companions, but few friends. Of her friends, she considered Garith and Turlock to be the closest. There was an emptiness when one of them was missing. And soon another place would be empty, a place filled by the larger-than-life presence of

Connaught. A place Drue feared might never again be filled to her satisfaction.

Connaught met with Garith's approval. He welcomed Drue's prisoner as though he were an honored guest. An instant camaraderie developed and Drue was hard put to hold her tongue as they laughed and talked together.

It wasn't until after the evening meal that Drue had the opportunity to speak to Garith alone.

"How can you be friendly toward the man who wounded Turlock so treacherously?" she demanded.

"From what I've seen, you turned his own trick against him and struck him soundly. Turlock is far more experienced in battle, and he could have done the same."

"Had it not been for Turlock's tutoring, Connaught might well have killed me!" she protested.

"But he did not, and now he is your prisoner. Your prowess is renowned throughout England. Minstrels sing your praises and Princes point to your deed with pride. There is no doubt in the mind of any man in England that it was skill, not luck, that brought Connaught down. I am proud to be your brother!" Garith's hand closed on her shoulder.

For a moment Drue was too overcome with emotion to speak. Seldom was pride expressed so openly in her circle, even though she was aware both her father and Turlock had been pleased with her achievement. She searched for something to say that would express her own pride in Garith, but her mind was blank. Words were not her forte, but the look in Garith's eyes told her he understood.

Turlock beckoned to Garith from across the room and Drue sat down on a low stool near the fire, resting her elbows on her knees.

Connaught looked up from the piece of wood he was whittling. It was not considered wise for a prisoner to be given a weapon, but it was a small knife, and Connaught was carving an animal for his new son. Drue watched idly as the powerful fingers moved, delicately molding the block into shape.

"You are a man of many talents," Drue remarked.

"Aye," Connaught agreed. "It is to my benefit to be so."

"It would not benefit me to be other than I am." Her voice was defensive, challenging Connaught to contradict her.

"You would be like your brother?"

"Never! I do not want the title or the soft life. I do not long for a roof over my head. If it were not for you I would not be here now."

"So you've said, many times before." A slight smile touched his lips, but Drue deliberately did not return it. Instead, she stared into the flames of the hearth fire. "Does it bother you that you are not like your brother?" Connaught asked.

Drue's head snapped up. It did bother her! She took a deep breath, not wanting to admit what might be construed as inferiority by her enemy. One look at the understanding on his face and she realized it was too late. He already knew....

"I should be more tolerant of the gentler graces," she admitted. "I should take over the management of my estates instead of shifting the responsibility to Garith's shoulders. Soon he will have a wife and sons. It will be burdensome to him to tend to my estates as well as his own."

"I think not," Connaught contradicted gently. "You compliment your brother in every way. What could be more advantageous to both of you than to have each do the thing he does best. The thing in which he excels. With you to do battle for both your own estates and those of your brother, you need not fear that he will end up trapped in a foreign country, waiting to be ransomed when he longs to return to his home."

Drue had never given thought to the fact that Connaught must long to be away as much as she wanted him gone. When she didn't respond, Connaught spoke again.

"The greatest gift you can give your brother is to continue as you are, a respected knight of the realm, able and willing to do battle in his stead while he manages the properties and copes with the idiosyncrasies of the court."

"Am I not cheating him of the excitement of battle by going in his place?" Drue mused aloud.

Connaught's laughter rang out, causing heads to turn throughout the hall. "As much as I love a good fight, there are many times I would give half my worth to stay in my bed and find a 'Drue' to do battle in my place." His eyes twinkled with merriment as he asked teasingly, "Would you not consider returning to Ireland with me after my ransom is completed? We would make a fine team, you and I, and with you in the field, and myself at home with my wife, we would likely see less of each other than we will fighting on opposite sides."

Connaught's jesting offer held some merit, as well as a measure of truth. They would, no doubt, meet again on the field of battle. And his offer to let Drue fight in his stead was a compliment to her ability as a knight. It was the thought of Connaught at home with his wife that sent a chill through Drue's bones as she answered, "Never, my lord. But you have eased my conscience and for that I thank you."

Connaught gave a little bow and returned to his carving, while Drue returned to her thoughts, now eased by

Connaught's words. It wasn't until the men began to bed down for the night that Garith again came to Drue's side.

"Take the solar room," he said. "It will do you good to sleep in a bed for a change. Besides, you need the practice at gentle graces if you are to stand with me at my wedding. I cannot have you lodged in a tent."

Drue glared at him, making no move to respond to his words.

"Drue." It was Turlock's voice that spoke. "It is safer to house Connaught in the solar if any of us hope to sleep this night. I vow, I tire of trying to keep one eye open to see that the man doesn't escape."

Drue bristled. "I have been with him day and night since his capture."

"No one doubts your dedication, but admit, Drue, that it takes both of us to make certain Connaught remains our prisoner. I'm an old man. I long for a good night's rest!"

"Then you sleep with him in the solar and I will remain with Garith."

Had it been anyone other than Drue, Turlock would undoubtedly have agreed. He knew Drue's dislike of domestic comfort. Thinking it a good joke, Turlock and Garith had conspired to put her in a situation where she would be forced to sleep in a bed, if only for the night. They could not have known the trauma they caused. Drue and Connaught had religiously avoided private contact with each other since their departure from the camp. Each had thoughts best left unexplored and each feared their recurrence.

The sight of Connaught's body early that morning had etched itself in Drue's memory and presented itself to her mind at the most unexpected moments. At the first sight of Garith, Drue had hoped her obsession with her prisoner would end. Surely it was only a manifestation of her loneliness, brought forth by Garith's absence, that had produced such soul-shaking effects. But Garith's presence did not bring about the desired results.

Without realizing what she did, Drue had turned to Connaught for a solution of her problem, knowing he would, indeed, understand and give council. The closeness she felt when his words had dispelled her guilt over her relationship with her brother did nothing to diminish her admiration for her enemy. But that admiration was wrong! The whole situation was wrong and she would be better away from him. Still, Connaught was her responsibility and she must take the needed precautions to keep him from escaping.

As was expected, Drue took the heavily curtained bed, while Connaught slept on a mat on the floor. After bathing, Drue had not donned the leather vest she always wore. She was uncomfortable without it and that, plus the unaccustomed bedrobe, kept her sleepless long into the night.

At the first sound of Connaught's low moan, Drue was wide awake. She slid from the bed, and crossed the room to his side. The moonlight gleamed through the shutters and Drue was able to make out Connaught's body, shimmering like a marble statue in its light. Again he moaned, his voice becoming louder and his actions more violent.

Drue didn't want to touch him. She didn't want to feel the warm pliant flesh beneath her hands. She didn't want to feel the smoothness of his muscles as she sought to ease his stress. But, mostly, she didn't want to feel the wild beating of her own heart, which came from only thinking of the things she must not experience.

Many squires looked forward to sleeping at the side of their masters, believing the strength from a champion's body could be absorbed by their own. Drue had never given the premise much thought. She had been in daily

contact with Turlock, whom she considered the greatest of
champions, and if she held any claim to greatness now, it
was because of his advice and tutelage in arms, not because she occasionally drew her bedroll next to his when
the nights were bitter. Still, if there were some merit to the
squires' superstition, there could be no stronger, more
beautiful body than Connaught's. Each pore of her own
longed to blend with the man before her. She fought down
what she knew would be an irreversible mistake.

No, she must not touch him, not with her senses so
aroused by the very sight of him and her emotions raw and
bleeding from the constant chaffing of pride and common sense against feelings she was unable to define.

Turlock! She must call Turlock. His joke had gone far
enough and was a joke no longer.

Taking herself in hand, Drue was about to go to the
door when Connaught bolted upright, a wild cry on his
lips.

She threw herself against him, covering his mouth with
her hands, forcing him back down onto the mat.

"The battle is over," she soothed. "You are safe and
now you must rest."

His arms closed around her and her small, firm breasts
were pressed against his chest. The nipples tightened
painfully, causing her to bite her lip to keep from crying
out at the unexpected reaction of her body to this man's
proximity. A molten flame coursed through her, settling
deep within, before bursting into a rampant blaze. His
muscled legs entwined with hers, strength against strength.

Through the bedrobe she could feel each muscle in his
body play against her. The moon had lied. He was not a
cold, silver statue. His flesh was white-hot with the flame
of life. Her breathing became more rapid as she struggled
to move away.

Caught in the depths of sleep, Connaught held her fast. Still too far from consciousness to understand what was happening, he was aware only of the warmth of a body against his own. He inhaled the scent of soap and sunshine that drenched his senses, rendering him helpless against the onslaught of desire. Burying his face in the taut flesh, he absorbed the warmth, the comfort, the strength that seemed his only salvation.

The need, the overpowering need to become one with this strength, to make this tightly held power a part of himself, was more than he could bear. Here was completion! Here was the end of the quest he had begun so long ago. Here was the fulfillment that would end his nightmares and his longing. His senses quickened and his hands moved across her body.

Like a bolt of lightning, Drue realized Connaught's intent. For a moment she lay stunned, her own desire overpowering both sense and fear as his calloused hands moved with unbelievable gentleness against her soft skin. Drue's mind pictured those same hands in the firelight, carving the wooden figure with delicate precision.

Now they molded her yielding body against his, and her blood began to sing a chant older than the cries of war.

His hands, knowledgeable in the art of love, slipped beneath her bedrobe.

In another moment he would know her as had no other, and in so doing possess the power to have Sir Andrew of Duxton banished from the earth. For one instant of pure madness she longed to give him that power. Then her inherent sense of survival burst through passion-fogged senses and realization washed over her.

With a cry of disappointment mingled with disgust at her own weakness, she struck him sharply.

His eyes opened and his hands fell away as though scalded.

"You had a nightmare, and when I came to wake you, you attacked me! Next time you can wake the whole keep, for all I care. You might have killed me!" Drue extricated herself and crept across the room to the dark recesses of the curtained bed, her heart heavy with the weight of her lie. She lay there, a shivering mass, unable to believe her body had so betrayed her. It was unthinkable that a knight should respond this way to another knight. It was a betrayal of all she believed, of every oath of knighthood she had taken. It would never happen again, she vowed, but the persistent throbbing of her newly awakened emotions mocked her promise. She should have awakened Connaught sooner, or better yet, allowed his shouts to awaken the keep. Anything would have been better than this agony of guilt and desire.

Undoubtedly he had believed her to be his wife, yet the raw urgency of his need had touched the depths of her being, and she would never again be free of the ghost of passion lost.

But it was Connaught who suffered the agonies of the damned, as his sweat-covered frame shook with the aftermath of desire and the realization of shame. He knew in his own mind that there had been no overture of attack on his part. His body still retained the remnants of unrequited passion, pulsing unheedingly as he tried to close out the memory of Drue's flesh against his own. Never, not even with his wife, had he felt such great desire. Never had he ached with such fervor for another's touch. And never had he been so humiliated.

Overcome, he turned his face to the wall, aware he had reached the depths of degradation as tears of pure shame coursed down his face.

Chapter Six

Drue was quiet and morose as they broke their fast the next morning. Turlock looked to Connaught for an explanation and was confronted by a tight-lipped caricature, with red-rimmed eyes and an inexplicably swollen face. If Drue looked bad, Connaught looked worse.

Both Garith and Turlock silently wished they had not insisted Drue and her prisoner spend the night in the solar. Turlock took Garith aside at the earliest opportunity.

"Think you the solar may still be infected by the plague after all these many years?" Turlock asked.

"I think it more likely it is haunted by ghosts of the past known only to Drue. I must admit, I did not care to spend another night there myself, but thought Drue above childish fancies. In truth, I believed Connaught's presence would be enough to drive away the dark memories of childhood."

"Why did you not tell me of your true reason for urging Drue to spend the night in the solar? We are used to sleeping under the stars, Drue and I. It is difficult for either of us to rest beneath a roof, enclosed by thick walls. I was thoughtless and unkind, and apparently Drue has taken out his anger on his prisoner. Never have I seen the man look worse. Even when he was wounded unto death there was more life and...hope...in his eyes. Tonight I shall sleep in the solar with Connaught, and Drue will be free of his responsibility.''

It did Turlock's heart good to see the relief on Drue's face when he gave her the news. Connaught said little, turning away from the older man, unable to meet his eyes. Assuming Connaught was still angry due to Drue's supposed cruelty, Turlock considered the reaction understandable and went about his business, turning Connaught over to a solicitous Garith.

At first, Connaught dreaded contact with Drue's brother, uncertain as to where his licentious desires would lead him. To his relief, he found he had no feeling for Garith other than natural camaraderie. Their relationship fell into place, strained only by Connaught's guilt, which slipped in unexpectedly at odd times.

Relieved by having little contact with Drue except when others were present, Connaught again became the assured charismatic man the Scots and Irish alike loved and sought to free from English clutches.

Turlock went back to join Drue's father in negotiations that would send Connaught from English soil, and Garith took up residence in the solar with the prisoner. To Connaught's everlasting relief, there were no dreams of wild longing, and when either of them was disturbed by nightmares, the other cuffed him soundly.

During this time, Drue kept much to herself, a fact that did not seem unnatural to Garith. He had forced her into a disagreeable situation and she had somehow taken her vengeance on the hapless Connaught, who obviously resented her for it. The farther apart the two were kept until ransom could be made, the better for all involved.

But Drue's problem was not guilt for having punished Connaught in a pique of anger, but rather anger at herself for her own weakness. How she hated herself for that lapse, and, as punishment, she could not forget one single instant of her shame.

Yet her body ached for Connaught's warmth. She longed to touch him . . . only touch him as he passed. It seemed as though she could feel his eyes upon her from across the room. But when she glanced up, he was never looking her way.

Drue vowed she would not again subject herself to such close proximity with a man. It was depraved, somehow. Garith would be ashamed of her, and Turlock would stare in disbelief. She would die before she would have her father know!

Desperately searching for some way to comprehend the overwhelming thing that had happened to her, Drue placed the blame on the bedrobe. The lack of a leather vest, which she habitually wore, had left her vulnerable.

Connaught was like a sickness with her. Physically he was superior to any man she had ever seen. As a knight, his skills surpassed even those of Turlock. In recent years only Drue herself had bested him. It was a heady feeling and one that had broken down her defenses as she allowed her initial hatred to be replaced with admiration and her distrust to become friendship. It was wrong to make a friend of an enemy, and she was paying each day of her life as she tried to blot out the memory of the wildly intoxicating madness that had come over her when his arms closed about her. She felt as though she was being torn in two. Half of her wanting to be near him—only that, she assured herself—and half wanting to destroy him before she herself was destroyed.

So it was they waited, each caught in his own private hell. Garith, who had come to admire the prisoner and dreaded the thought of meeting him in the battle that must someday ensue; Drue, who had all but convinced herself that Connaught had indeed tried to harm her that night in the solar; and Connaught, who had no aspirations regarding himself. He knew it was not murder he had desired to perpetrate on Drue's body, and his shame was as endless as his memories.

Although Drue took great pains to never be alone with Connaught, she found herself seeking him out in the presence of others, using the ploy that she wanted to spend as much time as possible with Garith. At first Connaught felt trapped by his own evil passions, but, as Drue made no move to reprimand him, he began to think his captor believed the attack had been of deadly intent brought on by the throes of nightmare. As the days passed, their distrust lessened and the three of them fell into easy friendship. Together, Drue, Garith and Connaught tried one another in the tilting yard. They dueled and jousted with blunted weapons, and, as the days became shorter, they spent the long evenings playing chess or arm wrestling before the fire. Neither Garith nor Drue could beat Connaught at arm wrestling, but after a particularly rigorous try Garith protested loudly.

"I could best you in a true wrestling match!"

"Hah!" Connaught snorted. "I have yet to be beaten even in my own land. I will take you both on and still you will not best me!"

"Done!" Garith agreed.

The idea of Connaught being so cocksure of himself and his ability made Drue angry. For once she was able to think of him as a braggart! Although Garith and Drue had wrestled often as children, Drue had no way of knowing what tricks her brother might have learned during his time in court. She hoped it had been well spent, for she had systematically beaten Garith whenever they had met. Drue, with her agility, had bested her own father the last time they tried one another, but the Earl of Duxton was an older man, as was Turlock, while the knights and squires they met during the long boring days of enforced encampment were no match for Drue's skill. She smiled to herself. It would be satisfying to see how she fared against a worthy opponent.

Wagering was high when it was known they would meet, for a man had as much chance to win the wager as he had to lose. By the time the three of them took the field, every man and maid at Duxton was there to watch.

It had rained heavily the night before and the tilting yard was an ooze of muddy puddles. Connaught stripped to the waist, flexing his muscles for the crowd's adulation.

"Braggart!" Drue called out after a particularly noisy cheer.

Connaught's eyes twinkled over a flexed biceps and Drue found herself tempted to join the crowd in shouting Connaught's acclaim.

Both Drue and Garith chose to retain their leather vests. Connaught wore leather traces on his legs, but Garith stripped his away and Drue, seeing the wisdom of her brother's action, followed suit. Her legs, even more sinewy than her brother's, gleamed with a golden sheen in the watery sunlight.

Garith stepped forth, but before he could do more than take his stance, Connaught was upon him. Together they rolled in the mud and slime, each trying to attain the better hold. It was not many moments before Drue was aware her brother was no match for Connaught. Having studied the Irishman's tactics for as long as she dared without risking forfeit, Drue broke into the melee and Garith gratefully retreated to the side.

Now it was a dance as Drue forced Connaught to come
to her, only to retreat before his hold could be achieved.
Then, without warning, she leaped out, tripping him and
tangling his legs in hers as they rolled in the mud.

Connaught bellowed in anger as well as pain. His blue
eyes glinted dangerously from his muddied face.

"You don't like this hold, my lord?" Drue mocked.
"Ah, but you used it yourself on my brother only a short
time ago."

Connaught squirmed, fighting to gain leverage, but before he could achieve his goal by means of sheer strength,
Drue kicked free and was on her feet, and her brother took
her place.

"Perhaps you should have challenged us one at a time,
Connaught. The two of us will have the better of you."
Garith laughed.

Drue and Garith changed places often, and although
Connaught was tiring, he gloried in the challenge. They
were covered with mud to the extent that it was impossible to tell Drue from her brother. There was no noticeable
difference, save in their style of wrestling and the fact that
Garith was obviously tiring.

At last Drue realized she must try to put an end to it before Connaught pinned Garith and all was lost. Her eyes
glittered with determination as she closed in for the final
time. Hurling herself on Connaught, she caught his legs
with her own and rocked her body back and forth trying
to force him to yield.

The pain was great, but Connaught's determination was
greater. He would not let this lad have the better of him in
a sport at which he was known to excel! Then Drue twisted
herself about without relinquishing her hold. The pain was
excruciating as Connaught's legs cramped and the muscles tore at the joints.

"Yield!" Drue gasped, throwing her full weight against his chest and shoulders to pin him.

Connaught had long since lost track of which Duxton attacked him. It was impossible to tell them apart as they slipped and rolled through the mud. Connaught's whole motivation was victory, and it had been some time since he had allowed any thought of the midnight encounter with Drue to enter his mind. So it was a double shock when he realized he fought Drue. It wasn't until he saw her face above him and felt her body pressed tightly against his own that he perceived the full scope of the threat to his well-being.

With victory at her fingertips, Drue knew nothing of the man's dilemma. Partially blinded by the mud in which they were immersed, she did not heed the warning in his eyes. "Yield!" she whispered, her voice breaking with the effort it took to hold him down.

But the word *yield* and the husky sound of her voice were more than Connaught had bargained for. His mind reverted to another time when he had seen her face above his and felt the searing heat of her body. Hot blood surged through his veins like boiling oil.

He tried once again to break the hold, but Drue's determination only pushed her more closely against him. Suddenly he hated her above all else on earth. She would shame him before the world. In another moment he would be forced to yield and Drue would pull away, leaving him to the ridicule of the crowd. His head pounded in rhythm with his heart as his hands closed about her throat. They would kill him, Drue's brother and the others, but what did it matter? He would rid himself of this nemesis who taunted him and shamed him with unnatural desire.

"Yield!"

Again, the damnable word resounded in his ears.

"Yield, or I will yank your legs from the sockets and you will never sit a horse again!" Drue's voice was rough and deep, for his fingers were sinking into her throat. She was aware that Garith was trying to pull Connaught's hands away, but she paid him little mind. Her body was singing the song of victory. She had bested Connaught once again. She gloried in it, she gloried in the feel of his body throbbing in rhythm with her own. Her head was spinning, but she gave no thought to the nearness of death. She could concentrate on nothing but the strange euphoria that had overtaken her. Her legs lost their strength, melting as the heat of her body grew more intense. There was a bubble growing within her, a bubble filled with a shattering light that would burst and . . .

She held her breath expectantly, but it was Connaught's voice that shattered her dream as it smashed through, bringing her back to reality.

He knocked Garith's hands away as he released his hold on Drue's throat and grasped her biceps painfully.

Confused, Drue looked into eyes so filled with anguish that she drew back at the sight.

"If you ever touch me again . . . I'll kill you!" With a burst of strength born of desperation, Connaught lifted Drue, throwing her from him as though she were a toy. Sobbing for breath, he managed to roll over, allowing the oozing mud to receive his throbbing body, sucking him into its soothing depths. Even his face was submerged, and he held his breath until he felt a tug on his hair and opened his eyes, to see Garith's anxious face.

Wearily Connaught accepted the fact that even death could not blot out his shame. Once again in control of himself, he pushed his torso from the muck, shaking Garith's hand aside.

"See to your brother." It was an order. "I was harsher than I meant to be with him." It was a lie, but Connaught cared little. The only thing that mattered now was that he get away before this could happen again, for he could not live knowing he lusted after another man! He struggled to his feet. He would write to the Bruce tonight and tell him to give the English all they demanded. He must be away from this land at any price, before it cost him his immortal soul.

Drue was dizzy to the point of being ill as Garith helped her to her feet.

"It was a draw!" he told her happily. "A true draw! For a moment we had the day, then Connaught went insane. I thought he truly meant to choke you, and when I tried to stop him, he brushed me aside like an errant fly! What did you do to anger him so?" Garith babbled on in excitement.

"I bested him, and he knew it! He challenged us and we were about to win. I told him to yield. That was all I said, yet he went wild. He should have been ransomed long ago. We've kept him about like a pet hound. I will send a courier to father tonight and tell him to accept what they offer. I want the man gone from this place. He is dangerous."

Dangerous, yes! Connaught was the epitome of danger. He threatened Drue's way of life and even her sanity.

He challenged her by his mere presence, and she knew it would be but a matter of time before one of them must destroy the other. Yet her heart would ache for Connaught once he had gone. The pride she had known at taking a renowned knight as her prisoner had changed to fascination as his wound healed and his personality began to assert itself. Grudgingly, Drue found herself admiring the man physically and mentally, for he far surpassed any other knight she had known. With the exception of Turlock, no one could touch Connaught on the field. His capture had been more luck than skill, though to save herself Drue would never admit it to another living person. Even thinking such thoughts were dangerous, for Drue dared not believe any knight might best her in battle in case the thought forged her ultimate defeat.

Stoically she stared at her brother, silently defying him to refute her words, at the same time eternally grateful he could not read her thoughts.

Garith liked Connaught, but he saw the truth in Drue's words, just as he saw the ever-reddening marks on her throat. Had Connaught decided to kill her, there would have been little Garith could have done other than try to dispatch Connaught before he achieved his purpose. "We will send a messenger tonight," he agreed.

The messages from Garith reached Turlock at about the same time King Edward received word that the Bruce wanted to come to terms over the ransom of the Earl of Connaught. Since Edward was in residence at Chepstow, he ordered the prisoners brought there. It was a delight to him that the Scots apparently meant to salve his chafed feelings and give in to all the English demands. The defeat of his army and the loss of Scotland to the renegade Bruce, whom Edward's father had managed to hold at bay, still rankled.

The Scots would have their prisoners back, but not before they knew the wrath of a true King. They had chased him from the field like a dog. Now they would see him in his right and true element. Without taking even Piers Gaveston into his confidence, Edward put his plans in motion.

His first act was to demand that Connaught be brought before him. He remembered how great Drue's hatred of the man had been. It stood to reason that Drue, at least, would relish the humiliation he intended for the prisoner.

As Drue made preparations to remove herself and her charge from Duxton, she was aware of new and strange emotions. For the first time in her life she felt unsure of herself in the presence of a man. Remembering the insane anger Connaught had displayed at their last encounter, Drue kept her distance, unable to understand either herself or the man whose presence was a constant gall, reminding her of a weakness deep within herself that grieved to see him go.

Connaught spent much of his time with Garith, and as before, Drue found herself drawn to their company. No more challenges were made, even in the heat of the moment. In her own mind Drue realized that when she again crossed swords with Connaught, it would be to the death.

Many times she would have gone to him to apologize, but found she knew not what she had done.

Could she tell him she was sorry his body was magnificent beyond all others? Could she admit she longed to comfort him when he cried out in the night? Dared she say she envied her own brother his friendship and chided him for befriending an enemy?

There was no answer! She did not know, and had someone wisely seen through the ruse that was being played out in the cold, solemn halls of Duxton Castle, Drue would have called him out as a liar. For the unthinkable had happened. Drue had fallen in love and had no inkling of her malady. She only knew she was miserable away from Connaught's mighty presence. She longed to hear his quick laughter and see his eyes gleaming like sapphires in the dim hall.

She spoke to him only when necessary, and yet she knew, should the need arise, he would be there to offer advice to her as he was for her brother. She cared far too greatly for this man of opposing convictions, this enemy who dwelled so easily among them.

"Why do you not stay in your own land when you are ransomed?" Drue asked as they rode beneath a canopy of trees toward Chepstow. She glanced back, indicating the other prisoners who would be included in the exchange. "I'll warrant they will not be so anxious to retake the field. They will stay with their homes and families."

"Fine chance that!" Connaught laughed. "The Bruce has spent many hours and even more moneys for my release, and he will expect to be paid in kind."

"But surely you will return to your lady wife and your sons?" Drue could not believe her own persistence. It was painful to think of Connaught returning to his home and the loving arms of a woman. Drue brushed it aside as knowledge of a permanent parting. In truth, she never thought of taking Connaught into her arms; that kind of affection was beyond her. But she wanted to be with him. Had she been younger and still a squire or page, she would have willingly offered to serve Connaught, though it meant leaving everything she loved.

The enormity of this realization stopped her cold. It was true! She wanted to be near him. To care for his armor, his horse; to rub his shoulders when he was weary, as she had done for Turlock. Many times she had rubbed Turlock's forehead after battle, and now she dared wonder how it would feel to brace Connaught's head against her heart and feel the raven black hair entwining about her fingers as she sought to stroke away the ache left by the heavy armor.

Her mouth grew dry and her breathing became shallow as her mind formed pictures so real her hands tightened on the reins, causing the horse to toss his head in annoyance.

Connaught spoke, but it was some time before Drue made sense of the words. For the first time in her life, she had indulged in fantasy. She did not know it, and had she known, could not have given it a name.

"With the English out of Scotland, there will be no reason for me to fight on that soil. I will ply my sword in my own country, which has need of strong leaders."

"That sits well with me," Drue said truthfully. "I have no cause to fight Ireland, either for or against you."

Knowing their time together was at an end helped ease the tension. Only a deeply buried memory was allowed to remain as they approached Chepstow, the towering walls floating in the distance like an omen of doom.

Drue saw a great number of men riding toward them. Like brightly colored birds, they swept through the copse of trees on caparisoned horses. Drue ordered her men to halt, giving the prisoners who were walking a chance to rest before being escorted to the castle.

Garith had barely taken his place beside them when Turlock burst through the trees, the scowl on his face as dark and threatening as his unadorned clothing. Drue gasped as she realized her friend had declined the courtly attire and still wore light armor and the huge bearskin cape he valued so highly.

"Turlock," Garith called as the old warrior pulled his horse to a halt. "It is good to see you!"

"So you think now, but you will rue the day you brought your prize here if my ears serve me aright!"

"What do you say?" Drue demanded. "Have the ransom negotiations gone awry?"

"The King is the matter, and he's always been awry to my notion," Turlock returned. "He has ordered a cart-load of chains to be brought to this spot. The prisoners will be shackled neck to neck and, like animals, marched through the streets."

Connaught's face went taut. "You realize this could nullify the ransom agreement!"

"What I realize is of no matter," Turlock growled. "The King is in charge here and his wishes will be met."

"Could we not take Connaught and…" Garith's words were stopped midsentence by Turlock's black look.

"The court is close behind me. I only wanted you to be prepared for what will come and to keep this hothead—" he glanced toward Drue "—from making more trouble than the situation warrants."

But Drue's eyes had narrowed to golden slits. Turlock's warning would go unheeded. She was already planning to take the situation into her own hands. The thought of them dragging Connaught, her Connaught, through the streets in chains was not to be borne.

Had the order been given by any less personage than the King himself, Drue would have challenged the perpetrator to a duel. As it was, before Turlock or her brother could anticipate her intent, she spurred her horse toward the on-coming men.

Her plea was brief, to the point and valid. It was also futile. The King had made up his mind he would make an example of these prisoners and she could not gainsay his order.

The English soldiers dragged Connaught from his horse. His eyes flashed blue fire at being chained. Turning a deaf ear to Drue's arguments, the soldiers chained the men neck, wrists and ankles. The short, heavy chains ran from one man to the next.

Word had spread, and a large crowd gathered to see the spectacle as the prisoners were marched the last weary miles to Chepstow Castle.

Drue was speechless with anger as the shackled men were herded through the streets. When the men did not move fast enough, their chains were secured to horses and they were forced to run or be dragged behind. If one man fell, others tumbled down with him. All were bruised and bloodied by the time they reached their destination.

The prisoners were being ushered into the great hall when Drue brushed past them and bent her knee to the King.

"Your Grace, I protest the treatment given these men who have been under my charge these many months. It is degrading, both for them and ourselves as knights of England, to treat our prisoners in such manner."

"I did not realize you cared so dearly for our enemies. The last I heard you only lived to meet them on the field of battle and destroy them."

"And so I did! I met them and destroyed them, and now I ask your mercy on their behalf. They have endured much and wish only to be returned to their homeland."

"And so they shall be returned, but looking like prisoners, not pampered guests of the realm." Edward sensed more to Drue's plea than met the eye. He watched her closely, noticing how her gaze returned to Connaught. It took no genius to see the superiority of physique of the man in question. Edward observed him closely. He was truly a man among men. If it weren't for his own Piers he might seek to know this Connaught better himself. But at second glance Edward realized it would do no good. Connaught's eyes sought Drue. Their gazes merged, drawing strength from each other.

Edward motioned them forward and spoke softly as they knelt before him. His words, addressed to Drue, were for their ears alone. "I see in your face the same gentle caring I value so greatly in Piers. I know in your heart you must feel the same depth of love for this man I feel for Piers. Do not shake your head. I know whereof I speak. Ah, yes, I know only too well the love that tears at a man's soul and destroys him for all others, save one." His eyes sought Piers Gaveston in silent communion.

Again Drue shook her head, but it was a hollow gesture.

Edward turned to Connaught, who looked more beaten by the words than by the blows he had endured. "If you were as wise as you are brave, you would take this unwelcome gift that has inadvertently come your way. You would cherish it for what it is, a love beyond human understanding."

"You speak of something beneath human tolerance. A low, perverted weakness that damns those who indulge in it," Connaught replied.

The King's eyes darkened with anger. Drue gasped, knowing she could not halt the punishment that must now come.

At the King's command the men pulled tight Connaught's chains, holding him upright to receive the blows that pummeled his body. Unable to defend himself in any way, he took them silently, fighting to retain his balance.

Drue pushed her way through the enraged knights, staying the hand that would have dealt the next blow. "Enough!" she shouted. "He is worthless dead and will bring none of our men back to us. If you kill him you kill those we would receive for his return."

"But he insulted our King!" It was Raoul of Crowley, whom Drue had defeated in the tilting yard so long ago.

She did not release the hold on his arm, but moved even closer, her voice no more than a whisper. "He said nothing I have not heard you say yourself, and if you do not give way to my demands, I will see to it the King is apprised of your true feelings."

She felt Raoul's muscles tense, then release. "Very well," he agreed, motioning to the others to withdraw. "Perchance the King was right in his assumption. Perhaps there is more between you and your pet prisoner than meets the eye."

"And perhaps there is not," Drue returned. "Would you care to challenge us to prove your point?"

Raoul's eyes widened. He had fought Drue once and been easily dispatched. He had no wish to repeat the exercise, nor for anything in the world would he willingly cross swords with the Earl of Connaught, even if the man was somewhat the worse for wear.

"I stand corrected," Raoul stammered. "I can see now there was nothing but concern of a man for his prisoner. Forgive my misconception of the situation."

Drue released his arm. "See that it never happens again! Only the King may think such of me and escape my wrath."

"I understand!"

Raoul would have said more, but Edward called out, "Take Connaught to the dungeons. He can take his scars back to Scotland with him, whatever those scars might be." Putting his arm about Piers's shoulder, the King walked from the room.

Chapter Seven

Drue and Garith went to their father with their plight, but it was beyond his power to overturn the King's command. Drue was drenched in guilt. She could not bear to think of the humiliation and suffering Connaught had been made to endure. In a final act of desperation, she presented herself at the door of the King's chambers.

"His Grace will speak to you after the banquet," Piers slipped out to assure her, "and Drue, do not fret so. He understands more than you realize. Connaught will come to no harm."

The door closed softly behind the King's favorite, leaving Drue enmeshed in dark thoughts.

For the Duxtons, the banquet was a disaster. Each of them was embroiled in his own battle. The Earl faced the possibility of dishonor over the condition of a prized prisoner. Turlock knew not when his former charges would take matters into their own hands and bolt, regardless of the King's wishes. Garith, who valued Connaught's friendship and truly liked the man, was angered by the cruelty his King had so callously displayed, and Drue was torn asunder by the King's accusations and her inability to gain freedom for this man who had come to mean so much to her. If few of the delicacies that were presented were enjoyed, it was no more than could be expected.

The servants still scurried about the hall removing the remnants of the banquet, and the tumblers waited impatiently to take their places before the high table when Drue rose to her feet and made a leg before the King.

"A boon, Your Grace!"

Edward leaned forward, glancing at Piers with a knowing expression on his face. "Speak," he said graciously.

"For the past year we of Duxton have negotiated with the Scots over the release of many English lords, in return for but a handful of theirs. The terms have been reached and the Scots will be here on the morrow to exchange prisoners."

"We are aware of this." The King lifted a pomander of orange and cloves to his nostrils.

"The one stipulation the Scots made was that their men be returned in good condition. Connaught was given adequate accommodations during his incarceration at Duxton Castle. There was no mark on him save the scars of past battles. The Scots had been apprised of this. They are savages, Your Grace, and should they take offense at Connaught's present condition I will not be held responsible! The lives of the English prisoners are on your head."

The King's face flushed, then he threw back his head and laughed. "As always, Sir Drue, your way of winning is unorthodox. We fully expected you to come forth and plead for Connaught's well-being, but to stand there and accuse your King is beyond comprehension!"

"Perhaps, but it is truth, and you hear little enough of that. Only Piers would give you true advice and the others shout him down."

The King looked at Piers, a little smile playing at the corners of his mouth. "They only think they do, dear

Drue." Piers nodded almost imperceptively, and the King continued, "After such a tirade I should have you sent to the dungeons and chained beside your precious Connaught. But I still believe I have discovered the underlying cause of your concern, whether you admit it or not."

Drue would have protested, but the King motioned to a guard.

"Take the Earl of Connaught to Sir Andrew's quarters and see they are given all they need to be ready for the exchange on the morrow." His eyes met Drue's and there was sympathy in their glittering depths. "Say your farewells as you will. After tomorrow you may never see him again. If it were so with myself and Piers, I would want this little time."

His voice faded as though he foresaw the truth of his words.

Drue's head was whirling as she waited for Connaught to be brought to her chamber. She remembered only too clearly how violently he had reacted during their wrestling match and how he had told her he would kill her should she so much as touch him again. She did not doubt the truth in his words, but, somehow, she must have him as well as possible by the time he was presented to the Scots lairds. The dubious truce they had managed to achieve over the past few weeks had more than likely been destroyed with the happenings of the day.

She should call Turlock or Garith; perhaps they would be better able to cope with the situation and less likely to infuriate the already angry man. But she did not want them present. Drue wanted to minister to Connaught herself. As the King had said, this would be their last time together. It seemed to her as final a thing as death.

Men's voices sounded in the passage outside the door. One of the guards pounded on it. "Come!" Drue called as the door opened and Connaught was thrust into the chamber.

He stared at her defiantly, his very stance portending his anger.

Drue ignored him. "The key." She held out her hand to the guard.

The man obeyed and bowed his way from the room. "We would stay outside should you have need of us."

"There will be no need," Drue told them. "This man has been my prisoner these many months. His manner does not intimidate me."

The door closed and they were alone before Drue realized the falseness of her words. His very presence was intimidating. He moved and the chains clanked loudly in the gloomy silence.

Drue motioned him toward her. "Come closer and I will free you."

It was only when he was upon her that she saw the haunted agony in his eyes. She clamped her lips together in a tight thin line. "Was it so bad then?" she asked as she busied herself with the manacles. "You have taken prisoners yourself. Think you it was worse for you than it was for them?"

Still he did not speak. He glanced around the room, taking in the comfortable furnishings. The curtained bed and rich hangings on the walls. It was a room usually given a landed knight in good favor with the King. A room large enough to be shared by the knight and his lady, or his squire, or, if the King's assessment was correct, his lover.

The thought stuck in Connaught's throat, almost choking him with its hateful connotations. He rubbed his wrists as the chains dropped to the floor with a clatter.

"Now for the one about your neck." Drue stood before him, looking him in the eye. "Perhaps I should take Garith's advice. He said I should leave it, then surely the Scots would balk at the exchange and you would be forced to stay."

"You do not want me to stay any more than does your brother."

"Garith likes you. He would be your friend."

"And you, Drue, what would you be?"

There was something in his voice that Drue had never heard before. It held a threat beyond death itself.

Looking into his face, she saw only the lined expression of a tired man. "Tonight I would be your squire, and do not think I intend to make it a habit. Had I any idea of the outcome of our arrival I would have demanded the exchange take place at Duxton, which would have been more convenient and beneficial to all."

"And less painful," Connaught added as the catch released on the heavy iron collar and Drue flung it aside.

She had expected a protest at her proposition, but none was forthcoming, so she went about the tasks of ordering a dinner and bath as she had so many times when she had squired for Turlock.

Remembering Connaught's threat in the tilting yard at Duxton, Drue did not try to help him disrobe. It was only when she perceived him to be having difficulty that she stepped toward him.

He did not stop her, nor could he look away as her strong hands loosened his garments. It seemed as though her face was flushed, but he could not be sure in the uncertain light of the fire. She gasped as she saw the bruises and bloodied gashes on his body. She did not look up. To have looked into the fire-blue eyes she felt searing her flesh would have been her undoing. Somehow, if she did not see his eyes, his face, the expression about his mouth—somehow she would pretend it was Turlock she served, or Garith, who had often bathed in the same room with her.

She was relieved when he sank into the hot tub of water.

"How did you come by this?" Connaught indicated the tub. "I cannot remember it being transported on our journey."

"It is an offering from the King. He feels he was ill advised in his action and looks to make up somewhat for your discomfort."

Connaught's laugh was bitter. "He humiliates me in every way he knows, and then expects me to wash my anger away in his bath?"

"You are humiliated no less than I," Drue reminded him as she took up a cloth and began removing the encrusted blood from the gashes on his body. "My house and my name are dishonored in the eyes of my enemies, and in the eyes of my friends I am cast in the same ilk as the King. You will leave this place on the morrow. I must remain with my shame."

Connaught looked into her eyes for the first time since she'd released his chains. "You could come with me!"

The words were wrung from his soul. His brain had not acknowledged them until after they took form.

"I could not leave my father and brother, as well you know, but I thank you for your concern. It was a kind and gallant offer."

Connaught cursed himself silently. He did not want Drue with him. It would be his downfall, as well he knew. It was all he could do to keep from looking, from touching, from remembering the King's words. No matter how galling, they struck too close to truth to be met in comfort. He would have been better served had he stayed with the others, chained in the dungeons, rather than take the risk of spending another night in Drue's company. He would not think of the last night they'd spent together. He would not!

He stood suddenly, almost toppling Drue before she could hand him a robe.

"Was this, too, the King's?" he asked, trying to erase his mind of all thought.

"No," Drue said solemnly, "it is mine. Now come, there is meat and wine for you, as well as fruits from Spain and white bread."

"How honored I am, while the poor wretches in the dungeon exist on gruel and water."

"My brother has seen that they are well fed," Drue answered. "You need have no anxiety on their behalf."

He ate in silence, digesting her words with his food. It took no wise man to see that the King and his favorite, Piers Gaveston, gave special attention to Drue. Did they, in truth, recognize some inherent weakness of character, some similarity to their own liaison that Connaught could not know? But no! It was himself, not Drue, who was obsessed by his body's responses. God have mercy on him! That he, the Earl of Connaught, had come to this!

The food stuck in his throat and he quaffed down a flagon of wine to wash the taste from his mouth. Having been denied nourishment for the better part of two days, Connaught did not notice the subtle warmth that stealthily seeped through his body as the wine worked its magic. He cast aside the shameful thoughts implanted by the King's surreptitious words and remembered only that this was his last night in England. Tomorrow he would be on his way to his own home and the loving arms of his wife. His wife! She was what he needed! Indeed, it was loneliness that caused these strange sensations and made him imagine the unimaginable.

His mood mellowed as the wine took effect. Teasingly he urged toast after toast on Drue, who for the most part found it difficult to match his good humor.

Lackeys came to clear the food and bathing items from the room. Connaught told them to bring more wine.

"You will have nightmares again," Drue warned. "I do not wish to be kept awake by your caterwauling. Temper your thirst or I will send you back to the dungeon."

Connaught sighed. "It might be best for both of us," he muttered under his breath, but she did not hear.

"Come," Drue urged, "it grows late. You will have a hard ride tomorrow, for your people will be anxious to return to their own soil. Take the bed for yourself. I cannot sleep in the accursed thing." There was a moment's hesitation, then Drue's voice continued. "Your wounds must be salved before you retire."

Connaught's body stiffened. Was this some ploy Drue had invented to torture him? Did the lad not know that a mere touch was enough to send Connaught into a private hell?

Drue's eyes were guileless as Connaught stared into their golden depths. He could find no fault, save within himself. With deep foreboding, he fastened the robe about his hips, his movements jerky, his nerves so tense he could scarce open his hands.

The room was warm and Drue had stripped down to the leather vest. The fire's glow touched her golden skin as she assembled the salves on a low stool. Connaught tried to look away, but instead found himself staring with fascination as the muscle played beneath her skin. He would miss watching this erstwhile friend he had so accidentally acquired. While Drue's physique was no match for his own, Connaught admired its sinewy strength. There was no wasted flesh. Of all the young men with which he had been associated, Connaught felt Drue to be the most nearly perfect. He loved to watch the golden body move about the room. He loved to hear the husky voice that bespoke of youth.

He closed his eyes as her strong hands worked their magic, easing the pain, applying balm to the wounds. He wished the same balm could have been used to sooth his aching heart. Oh God, if it could be so. If only there were an herb, a poultice that would ease the ache, an ache that was surpassed only by the throbbing in his loins.

Drue slowly rubbed the salve into the raw, chafed skin around his neck. Her hands were sure and firm in their touch, knowledgeable as to where to smooth and where to knead to try to relax muscles that could not relax as long as she was near.

A quick glance told Connaught that Drue's mind was far away. He fought his devils alone, and she was oblivious to his battle. Drawing a deep breath, he closed his eyes and gave himself to the gentle ministrations of her hands.

Connaught could not know the tumult in Drue's heart. She was indulging in the forbidden. Playing with white-hot coals of passion that threatened to burst into an all-consuming flame at any second. She could not let him go! This was the last time she would feel his flesh beneath her hands. This was the last time she would absorb the texture of him, and the warmth. He permeated her senses as his scent drugged her mind, leaving her thoughts in a turmoil. She could not concentrate on what she did, and knew only that her hands had left the gentle daubing of salve against abrasions and were now moving across Connaught's magnificent body.

Her fingers tangled in the hair of his wide chest as she kneaded the muscles. He had closed his eyes, but hers were wide open, drinking in every part of him.

There had been truth in the King's words, she thought as her hands worshiped the beauty of Connaught's masculinity. It was love, right or wrong, and though she burned for it, she could not deny its existence. And truly, it did destroy her very soul, for she thought of herself as nothing more or less than a knight . . . totally dedicated, totally sexless. That other knights were not born female never occurred to her. She only knew that, as a knight, the unthinkable had happened. She loved this man, this enemy who had tried to kill her friend Turlock and even herself.

For the first time in her life, Drue felt vulnerable. In this fight she could not win. She closed her eyes, trying to rid herself of the surgings of her body and gain control before she again incurred Connaught's wrath. He no more than she wanted this adulterous interlude.

His hands closed painfully on her arms and her biceps tensed in response. She opened her eyes to find herself looking into the blue-black depths of hell. Golden flares from the fire flicked across them and she shivered as she read his torment.

"I told you once not to touch me again on pain of death." His voice was a husky whisper.

"I remember." Her words were thick with pain . . . and desire.

"The King was right! You have ruined me for all others. And it is only you . . . not your brother, who is so like unto you I thought when I felt nothing but friendship for him I had bearded the dragon in his den. But it was not so. Would that I had shut my eyes and let you kill me at Bannockburn rather than live with dishonor. It may be a love beyond all human understanding, but, God help us, it is love!"

He breathed his admission into the night and it was lost in the answering sigh that escaped Drue's lips. Dizzy with wine and unable to think clearly, Connaught floated weightlessly. Looking down he saw only the face of his beloved, strong and young with smooth skin and solid structure. Connaught's vision blurred and he bent to better see, then his mouth touched hers.

Her lips parted in natural response—a response as primitive as it was devastating, for not since before her mother's death had Drue known the touch of lips against her own.

The heady feeling sent blood raging through her veins. Her senses took control, leading her to responses she had not known existed. As though in a duel to the death, her tongue battled his. The kiss deepened. She clung to him. As strong as she was, his sheer size made her feel less so. It was as though he could easily overpower her, and for one heady moment, that was what she wanted him to do!

The taste of wine was sweet on his lips as she drew his life-breath into her mouth. Their kiss became more desperate as their mouths clashed, then clung, longing for fulfillment when there was no fulfillment, grinding, punishing, torturing until they knew the salty taste of blood, and still they could not break their deadly hold.

Their world spun in a vortex controlled solely by passion. The sound of their sobbing breaths was joined by the wild colors that burst again and again behind their closed eyes. The sensuous feeling of muscular bodies writhing beneath eager hands was mixed with the scent of desire, soap and sunshine, and the taste of flesh and tears.

It was the tears that brought them to reality—that and the mad force of the kiss. A kiss that was forbidden and hence so much more greatly enjoyed.

Connaught jerked away, kicking the bench across the room in an effort to put as much distance as possible between them. His voice caught in his throat as he tried to speak. "I fear we are indeed as damned as the King and Gaveston."

Connaught wrapped the robe more tightly about his body. His eyes were haunted. "Let me return to the others. I would rather spend the night in chains than in sin."

"There will be no sin," Drue said wearily. "My own ignorance caused this. There is little show of affection in an army camp and I did not realize what was happening until it was too late. I will sleep outside the door. You will be undisturbed, by myself or anyone else."

Drue gathered up her bedroll and went into the hall without looking back. Pulling the door shut, she leaned against the solid English oak, drawing from its strength. She had not dared look at him again, for how could she have left him with that haunting sorrow filling his eyes? How could she have left him to the horrors of the night, to the dreams she knew must come? Dreams he must now and forever face alone, alone in the chill darkness. Alone just as she was alone, forever alone....

Chapter Eight

"Drue! Drue! Drue!" the crowd chanted as Drue and her father rode through the streets of Chester. Behind them Turlock's face beamed with pleasure at the recognition given his protégée. Drue's war-horse pranced nervously, unused to the slow pace and milling crowds. She controlled him with her legs, one hand resting lightly on the reins as she raised the other in salute, causing the people to cheer even louder.

It had been thus ever since the prisoners were returned in trade for Connaught. The people of England were grateful. Drue's prize had saved their pride and she was a hero in their eyes, having plucked victory from defeat.

A shower of flower petals fell from a window above them. There could be heard a muffled giggle and several girls' faces appeared, only to once again duck out of sight.

"I believe you have admirers," her father laughed.

"Nay," Drue bantered, "it is you they find attractive. You are covered with petals, while only a few have fallen on me." She brushed them away as she spoke, pleased to see her father's eyes sparkling as he turned and waved toward the window.

As they moved through the walled city, the road widened and Turlock took his place at their side.

"We must watch this fellow, Drue,—" he indicated Duxton with a movement of his head "—or Garith's wedding won't be the only one we attend."

Their good-natured joking rang above the walls as they continued toward the vast Willowford estates where Garith was soon to be wed.

Turlock had given it no thought when he had arrived at the room assigned to Drue and Connaught those many months ago and found Drue asleep outside the door. It was a thing he would have done himself, and to this day he had no notion of the traumatic scene which had taken place earlier.

That Drue was short-tempered and snappy with everyone was to be expected. The King had mauled her prisoner and impugned her honor. Her outrage was justified in the eyes of the court. Few knew of the King's words to Drue and Connaught, and those few were pledged to silence on pain of death. So it was that neither Drue's father nor Turlock had any notion of the turmoil in Drue's soul.

Willow Castle was just what its name implied—a lovely, gentle way of life in a country setting. Surrounded by lush green fields dotted with fat white sheep, it seemed the epitome of boredom to Drue and Turlock. To their surprise, the Earl of Duxton felt otherwise.

"I would that I were marrying the heiress of all of this and could hang up my sword and retire to a life of simple pleasures and peace."

Turlock laughed aloud, but when his cousin did not join him, he turned and looked into the man's eyes. "You jest, my lord, do you not?"

"I always thought someday I would have a place such as this. The Lady Gillian and I spoke of it many a night as we sat before the fire at Duxton. How we would have a country house someday, rather than a fortified castle. Someday…when my days of fighting were over and we could live at peace with one another. My only fear was that I would be killed and not be there to share it with her. Neither of us ever thought it would be Gillian who would die and rob us of our dream." He reached down and smoothed the rich material of the caparison on his horse.

Drue watched him carefully. Here was a side of her father she had not known. He had always been the complete warrior, in her eyes. Never had a word of this new and secret longing been breathed in her presence.

"Surely you would not give up a good fight for a soft life such as this!" Drue could not keep the words silenced.

He smiled at her. "Not when I was your age, Drue, but every man must change as the years weigh more heavily upon him. Even Turlock does not relish a fight as once he did. Is that not right, old friend?"

Turlock did not care to see the accusation in Drue's eyes and addressed his words to his lord. "It is true I am more weary than once I was, but I would not trade a night under the stars and a good battle the next day for all the soft palaces in England!"

Drue's face brightened. "Nor would I!" she declared. "If you like, Father, you may stay with Garith and his wife while Turlock and I go back to the field."

"So now you speak the truth! You could survive well without me!"

"You have taught me well, Father." Drue softened her words with the hint of a smile. "I can survive without anything, save my sword and a strong army at my back." Even as she spoke Drue knew the words were not true. The pain within her had become more acute each day since Connaught's departure. It was as though he had taken a vital part of her, leaving only a gaping, empty void. She was unsure of herself for the first time in her life. Unsure as to who or what she was, unsure of how to deal with the terrible longing she felt for this man who had been her beloved prisoner. Could she survive without him? Could she continue as she was, knowing there was between them a love that could not be extinguished by time and space?

Duxton clapped her on the shoulder. "Well said!" Then, glancing at Turlock, he added, "I wonder if Garith could say as much?"

"Garith is well content with his life," Turlock told him. "Now, enough of this talk. Our conversation should be of wedding feasts and hunts and jousts, not giving up the life we all love."

He spurred his horse forward and the others followed suit.

The estate was alive with people as they rode through the spacious grounds.

"It looks like a Maying festival," Turlock remarked as a bevy of young girls flitted across their path, casting flirtatious glances at the mounted knights.

Drue's armor shone in the sunlight. Her own horse was not emblazoned in rich colors and cloths. Her only condescension for her brother's wedding was to have polished to perfection every inch of equipment worn by either herself or her horse.

The horns sounded joyfully as they neared the castle. Garith himself awaited them as they came to a stop in the courtyard.

He embraced his father wordlessly. With Turlock there was the usual backslapping, but Drue only clasped his arm.

"I wish you happiness, Garith," she said. A happiness I shall never know, she added silently, again feeling the unfamiliar sting of tears behind her eyes. This was another weakness that had manifested itself since her confrontation with Connaught. Never before had she known the urge to weep, but now there were many times when it seemed she might disgrace herself at any moment.

"I want you to come and meet my betrothed," Garith said proudly. "I want you to like her, Drue. To become friends with her. I have told her, should anything happen to me, she could always turn to you for counsel and protection."

"Thank you, Brother." Drue's eyes were soft as she realized the extent of the trust he placed on her. "I vow I will protect your wife and your lands as though they were my own, at all times and with my last breath."

There was a small gasp and Drue looked up to see a young woman standing on the stairs. The wind rippled through her auburn hair and her blue eyes smiled brightly as she moved toward them. Garith hurried toward her, taking her hand and leading her formally down the rest of the steps.

"Allyson, my lovely, you remember my father, the Earl of Duxton?" The Earl bent low to kiss the girl's hand. "And Turlock." While not as graceful as his cousin, Turlock made a leg before the woman who would someday be the lady of Duxton. "And this is Drue!" Garith could not hide the pride in his voice as Drue came forward to bow over Allyson's small beringed hand. Garith could not hide his pride, anymore than Allyson could hide her admiration for the shining knight standing before her.

Allyson allowed her hand to rest in Drue's calloused grip as she looked up through her lashes. Here was the man she had thought her husband would be. Here was quiet strength, determination, a champion among champions. Everyone knew Sir Drue had single-handedly taken the great warrior Connaught as his prisoner and defied the King himself in an effort to keep the captive from undue punishment.

And Drue was taller and broader than Garith, Allyson wailed to herself. How would it feel to be crushed in a wild warrior's embrace instead of gently held by his brother? Allyson could not know, but her heart was racing as she placed a hand on Garith's arm and another on Drue's.

"Please come in and be welcomed by my family," she said, smiling into Drue's eyes. She was somewhat piqued that her future brother-in-law showed no more than polite, impersonal interest.

Drue paid Allyson little mind during the days that followed. The castle readied itself for the festivities of the wedding, and it was up to the knights to go into the forest to hunt for the meat and fowl that would grace the tables and feed the many guests. It was rumored the King himself would be there, and from peasant to peer, all were in a frenzy of preparation.

The day before the majority of the guests were to appear, Allyson hurried down the graceful stairway into the hall to find Drue waiting.

"Sir Drue—" she all but ran across the room "—I thought you had gone with the others this morning."

"They will have enough kill without me," Drue told the girl. "Today I am at your service, should you have need of me."

"But of course I need you," Allyson said, bubbling with happiness. She had come to believe Sir Drue found her unattractive, but these words proved her wrong.

"What do you do all day in the castle while the men are away?" Drue asked.

Allyson was somewhat surprised at this display of curiosity. Then, remembering how Garith had told her of the life they had led with their father and Turlock, she relented. Of course Drue would want to know the ways of women. Having had no memory of a mother, it would be a mystery as to what a lady did with her time.

Taking Drue's hand, Allyson took her with her as she made the daily rounds. From buttery to battlement they went as Allyson issued orders with such verve the housecarls and serfs jumped to obey.

As the horns were heard in the distance, announcing the imminent return of the hunting party, Allyson hurried to see that all was prepared for their comfort. Drue sank down beside a table and stared at the fire.

So this was life in a castle. The woman had run from one end of the building to the other like a headless fowl! Each moment she seated herself she snatched up some ridiculous sewing and stitched as though her life depended on it.

It was ghastly! It was unthinkable that anyone could live so and not die of boredom. How could the girl believe her life was fulfilled when she was hardly more than a servant in her own household. When her every thought was given to the comfort and care of her lord. Of course, it was nice that Garith had found so solicitous a woman to wive. There was no doubt in Drue's mind that Garith would lead a life of gentle comfort if the Lady Allyson had her way.

Yet how could Garith respect this woman who acted like a glorified servant? It was beyond Drue's understanding! Allyson was less than a page, less than a squire, her only function being to gratify her husband's every whim and pleasure. Drue found the thought unsettling.

Although Allyson's eyes followed Drue as she moved about the hall with the returned knights, Drue did everything in her power to avoid her. Only after most of the guests had retired and Garith was busy talking to Lord Willowford, Allyson's father, was the girl able to approach Drue.

"Do you plan to join the hunt on the morrow?" Allyson asked, careful to disguise the hope in her voice. In truth, she had enjoyed having Drue's company during the performance of her duties that day, enjoyed it more than she wanted to admit.

"So I plan." Drue rose to her feet as was meet for a knight when a lady approached. The disappointment on Allyson's face was plain and Drue felt a pang of sympathy for the girl whose life seemed such drudgery.

"Several of the ladies have expressed the desire to go hawking. I had hoped you might accompany us."

Drue looked up in interest. So this was their recreation! Of course! Many times she had seen parties of knights and ladies out with their birds.

"It is Garith you should ask to accompany you, my lady, not myself."

"But...it would be such an honor to have you in our company, Sir Drue. All of England sings your praises in having captured the Earl of Connaught."

Before she could say more they were joined by several other ladies, who lent their voices to persuasion.

"Oh, please, Sir Drue, tell us of the Earl," a small woman with a mouth that looked as though she had recently eaten a quince begged. "It is rumored he is the handsomest knight outside of England."

"For many months he was the handsomest knight *in* England!" Drue laughed. "With the exception of my brother Garith, of course."

The ladies tittered behind their hands. Garith and Drue looked much alike, and if one of them were to be named the handsomest, the ladies silently agreed their vote would go to Drue. There was something challenging about Garith's brother. A determination and, because of his life on the battlefield, an element of mystery.

"But, sir knight, you have not told us of your prisoner. The minstrels sing of Connaught's capture, but surely you must have many stories of the months you held him prisoner." Lady Ann, the wife of one of the Willowford cousins, smiled coyly.

"I would I could have held him prisoner." The quince-mouthed woman batted her eyes in a manner she thought seductive.

"Lady Edith!" Allyson remonstrated.

"Do not use that tone with me," Edith bridled. "I but say what every woman in England has thought in her most secret heart." She turned to Drue, her eyes alight with excitement. "Tell us, is he truly a man among men? Is his body as fine and strong as that of the ancient gods?"

Drue's mouth set into a fine line. She must not think of Connaught's body! She must not! Yet here was this woman, her eyes ablaze, looking as though she would devour Drue's very words!

"He is a fine and honorable knight. Were he not my enemy I would seek him out to be my friend." Drue wanted to close her eyes and look away, but she dared not. Her mind was playing terrible tricks on her, leading her down paths best forgotten. With aching remembrance, she once again saw him standing on the banks of the little stream. Ah, yes, he could indeed have been an ancient god. Surely, no saint would have been such a thorn in her soul!

"But what of his body..." another woman urged.

Drue longed to draw her sword and strike out at this group of harpies. Their clacking tongues should be silenced lest they bring her more pain than she could endure.

"His body was scarred from many battles. He is a strong man. I felt myself lucky to have beaten him on the field of battle and even luckier to have fought him to a draw in wrestling."

Drue turned to leave, but Allyson's voice stopped her. "Are his eyes truly the color of blue fire?"

Drue closed her own eyes, clutching the trestle table as Connaught's face flashed through her mind. "When he is angry I would think you might describe his eyes thusly. They are blue, and it is all the more startling because of the blackness of his hair."

"But surely you could tell us more of him," Lady Edith persisted. "It is said you were with him day and night for lo, those many months he was your prisoner."

Drue knew she must get away! Her hard-earned control threatened to break at any moment. "He is an Irish Lord. His aunt, Elizabeth of Ulster, is wife to Robert the Bruce of Scotland. He is married and has three sons of whom he is very proud. Other than that there is little I can tell you."

Without another word, Drue strode from the room.

For the next hour Drue walked the grounds, unseeing, uncaring for the beauty of her surroundings. The women's words had brought back the demons of memory. Painfully Drue tried to push them aside, but they persisted, just as Connaught's face persisted in appearing in her thoughts. Again she saw the tortured misery in Connaught's eyes as he had looked upon her for the last time before leaving with the Scots lords to return to his own lands.

There had been one moment, suspended in time, when his longing had flashed like lightning across the crowded courtyard. That was the moment Drue wanted most to forget; for it had been more shaming to her than even the surreptitiously shared kiss, which had been a battle in itself. More shaming than the unwelcome response of her body when he was near. In that moment her eyes had flooded with tears, and it had taken all her control to keep from crying aloud. Surely the agony could be no worse when a man was drawn and quartered than when Connaught was taken from her!

The pain of remembrance had lessened as the days passed, but it lay hidden, ready to project itself at the mere mention of Connaught's name. The thoughtless questions of the women had brought it back in unbearable proportions.

It was with great relief that Drue heard her brother's voice behind her.

"I worried for you, Drue. Allyson said the ladies were teasing you for information about Connaught when you suddenly walked out."

"I will apologize if it be your wish," Drue said dully, "but I am a knight and not used to indulging in idle court gossip."

"There is no need to apologize. The women were at fault!"

Drue sighed. "I cannot find it in my heart to blame them, Garith. Have you ever thought how boring their lives must be? They are nothing more than the servant of the lord of the castle. It must be humiliating for them to live so!"

"They would have their lives no other way," Garith assured Drue. "They are trained from babyhood to please their husband and care for his household."

"And for entertainment they force themselves into the business of others to glean information they have no right to possess."

"That they wish to know more about a renowned knight is not unreasonable," Garith said.

"You do not know what they asked!"

Garith could not restrain his laughter. "Ah, but I do! You should have heard the questions they asked about you before your arrival! The knight that captured Connaught is a man to be admired indeed! It was rather galling to have to admit you were both taller and stronger even though I am the older."

"We are nearly of a size," Drue protested loyally. "Even Connaught remarked on our similarity."

"I rattle in your armor like the clapper on a bell. Your clothing hangs on my body as our father's does on yours. And well it should be so! If it were otherwise, I would be on the field fighting and you would be here marrying the Lady Allyson!"

"God forbid!" The words burst from Drue's lips without thought, and Garith choked with laughter while pounding Drue on the back.

"I swear the ladies will not waylay you again," Garith said, when he regained his breath.

Drue nodded. It no longer mattered. The damage had been done. The wound in her heart had been opened and her lifeblood seemed to pour from her veins. Unquenchable thirst filled her mouth. A thirst not for wine or water, but for the touch of Connaught's lips against her own. The pain that shot through her body was so real, she staggered as she reached the door. Garith placed his hand on her shoulder.

"Are you all right?"

"This day has weighed sorely on me. I should have risen earlier and joined the hunt. It will not happen again." Drue turned and looked at her brother. "In all truth, brother, think you our lady mother would have indulged in the activities as do the women here?"

"There is little difference in women, Drue. Their lives are basically the same and have been for centuries. I cannot see how our mother could have lived much differently."

Drue ran her hand through her hair in agitation. "But how can they survive? I would go mad with boredom!"

"They know no better, Drue," he said sagely. "Like my falcon, they are hooded with the protection of their men and not allowed to think or feel beyond their hearth and home. They would not know what to do if given their freedom and are ill prepared for the rigors of the world. I enjoy protecting Allyson. I do not find her prattle boring or irritating. She will make me a good wife and we will be happy together. Someday you will find someone with whom you wish to share your life and will understand what I mean."

"It would be difficult for me to spend my life with a person I could not understand," Drue grumbled. "I fear it will never come to that, dear brother. I shall remain on the field with Turlock. I have given my heart to the demanding arms of battle and can know no other love."

"So be it, then." Garith rested his hand on Drue's shoulder. "But you are wrong about not being able to love someone you do not understand, for you and I are worlds apart in our preferences, still I think we are closer than most."

Drue smiled and clasped his arm before retiring to her own quarters.

Someone with whom to share her life, her thoughts; to speak aloud of the things that troubled her, whether it was the way a man carried his lance into battle or her pity for her soon-to-be brother's wife. What a comfort such a person would be!

A wry smile crept across her face as she strode through the silent halls. She had met the person with whom she longed to share her life. Met him and let him go when she discovered there was nothing to share but misery and shame. Her body burned as she remembered the touch of his hands. Tears filled her eyes as, once again, she seemed to taste his kiss upon her lips. Damn him! Damn him! And yet she, too, was damned, for there had never been, nor would there again be, anyone else for her.

Furious with Connaught, with herself and with life that had cast her such a lot, Drue tore off her clothing. Her body burned as though with fever. It ached and throbbed in a way completely unfamiliar to her. Concerned that she would not be able to take part in the ceremonies, Drue stepped before the highly polished brass that served as a mirror.

Perhaps it was the contour of the metal that threw her body out of proportion, but for the first time she was aware of a small difference between herself and her brother. A small difference between herself and Connaught! What did it matter? She pushed the thought aside. She was a knight! Knighted by the King of England himself on the field of battle. She was a knight and she would have it no other way! Never, never could she live as did Allyson! Never!

The very realization that she had given birth to the thought shocked her into numbness. Had she, in her most secret heart, been thinking of telling Connaught she had been born a woman?

No! Never! It was best forgotten! Buried as it had been these many years! She was a warrior and a knight! She could be no less.

But the memory of his haunted eyes as he left the court-yard with his companions all but undid her. If she were to go to him in Ireland and admit she had been born a woman, if she were to tell him their love was not a sin but a natural progression of life, how would he accept her news? Would he be angry and feel she had deceived him? Would he once again take her in his arms and kiss her, this time without the undercurrent of guilt that crept through their bodies like poison?

She glanced again at her reflection. How could a man accept her word? She did not look like a woman. She was no more like the Lady Allyson than a hare to a stag. While Allyson was soft and white, her arms rounded and plump and her body curved and pliant, Drue was broad-shouldered and sinewy. There was no softness about her. Her muscles rippled beneath skin that had the look of cured leather.

And Connaught had a wife! In all probability a woman much like Allyson. Even if Drue humbled herself and went to him, he would probably laugh her out of Ireland. She was a fool to think of such a thing! It had been only in a moment of weakness that she had allowed it to enter her mind. Even Garith did not remember she had once been a girl, nor had she herself, until…until Connaught had come and made her curse the life she loved and think of giving it up to be with a man she loved even more.

With a silent sob, Drue snatched up her vest and laced it about her body. Once again in her smallclothes, she threw herself on the bed. But sleep would not come, and when it did it was interspersed with vignettes of herself and Connaught. Even in her dreams Drue was unable to project a relationship like that of Garith and Allyson. It was as ludicrous to imagine herself in the part of Allyson, simpering and hanging on every word, as it was to imagine two knights in love with each other.

There was no hope for their love. There would be no one with whom to share her life. She could be nothing more nor less than she was, and should her secret come to light, life as she knew it, would be over. She could not take that chance, not even for Connaught.

The wedding was a celebration of feasting and fighting. Two days of tourneys followed the ceremony, and Drue took the lion's share of victories, fighting as the Lady Allyson's champion. All honor went to the house of Duxton. Garith sat beside his bride and watched Drue fight in his stead.

After a particularly tiring match, Garith went to Drue's tent.

"Turlock tells me you have accepted the challenges of practically every knight here," Garith said.

"If they wish to challenge, I wish to fight! All are pleased and honor is done your lady, who is my patron." Drue said noncommittally.

"I wish to have you enjoy yourself, Drue. I did not invite you here to have you wage battle on every man capable of wielding a sword."

"I enjoy fighting! Would you have me sit in the stands with a flower in my hand?"

Garith's face flushed as he was reminded of the look on Drue's face when she came past in salute and saw Garith holding one of Allyson's flowers while his bride repaired her coif.

"Perhaps I should challenge you!" Garith returned angrily.

"No! For I would as soon beat you as any man here! And I am capable of doing it! I accepted the honor of being Lady Allyson's champion because I knew you could not challenge me. Leave it as it is! We will all be happier that way."

Regardless of her bold words, Drue was not certain they smacked of truth, and from the look on his face as he left the tent, neither was Garith.

Lost in her own maze of problems, her emotions raw from the constant chafing of Connaught's memory, Drue did not notice the way her brother's wife looked at her. What had started as curiosity and admiration for a renowned knight had turned into adoration, and while Garith did not realize the extent of his problem, he was aware a problem existed. It seemed odd to Garith that Drue, who paid little attention to women, now watched Allyson unceasingly. Was there something strange about his new wife that he had overlooked? But no! Drue had said Allyson's way of life was boring, therefore it must be that Drue was jealous of losing his brother to a wife. An understanding smile touched Garith's lips. That must be it, and he would do all he could to let Drue know that no woman could ever come between them.

Drue watched Lady Allyson as she flitted about the castle garden. Her dress flowed as she bounced about like an errant butterfly, her light blue skirts fluttering like wings. There were little shoes on her feet that seemed hardly more than scraps of cloth. It amazed Drue that the girl could walk from one end of the path to the other without wearing through them.

Allyson's hair must have taken hours to prepare in the elaborate style she wore. How she sat still long enough to have it done was beyond Drue's power of imagination. Allyson's hands looked so small and white. It would have been surprising if she could lift a sword, let alone strike a telling blow with it.

Drue glanced at the long shadows. She had been watching Allyson for the better part of the afternoon. Now it was eventide and the girl had done nothing more productive than pick a bouquet of flowers, and a small bouquet at that!

Drue was about to turn away when she heard footsteps behind her and turned to face her brother.

"Ah, Drue, I looked everywhere for you! A messenger has just arrived. He brings a wedding gift from Connaught!"

Drue quickly lowered her eyes in an effort to contain the joy she felt at the mention of his name.

"And what did he send?" she managed to ask.

"Many yards of good Irish lace, so finely woven my lady is beside herself with joy, and some good Irish whiskey for ourselves. He sends you his greetings and thanks for your concern for his welfare while he was our prisoner."

"I would have done the same for any other lord taken for ransom."

"He is grateful, nonetheless! Come, we will tap the supply of whiskey and drink to Connaught."

Drue's face felt stiff, but Garith did not notice as he led the way down the narrow hall toward the cellars. She was remembering the last time she had drunk to Connaught, the night he announced the birth of his son. The night he had cried out in his sleep and she had gone to him. She shook her head to rid her mind of the demons.

"Hurry, Drue! A drink will do you good!" Garith called as she lagged behind.

"Aye, it will," Drue agreed, wishing she could drink enough to numb her mind and blind herself to the never-ending memory of Connaught's face.

The first swallow slid down her throat, turning her insides to fire. Blood pumped hot and strong in her veins. It was like him, this heady drink. It awoke her senses and sent signals blazing though her body, signals best forgotten. It would take more than one drink to blot Connaught from her memory, possibly more than there was to be had. She raised her glass to Garith in salute as they toasted each other again and again.

It was only after the majority of the whiskey had been consumed that Drue felt tears of self-pity streaming down her face. She was glad Garith had already passed out and did not see her loss of control.

With all her remaining strength, she lifted Garith to her shoulder and staggered from the room. The thought of a woman trying such a feat brought forth a burst of laughter. It echoed against the silent walls, causing the guests to burrow deeper into their beds, for there was something bitter and hopeless in the sound. Like the laughter of a damned spirit, made to haunt the earth without hope of redemption for a sin so great there was no forgiveness.... Nor was it asked. For to ask forgiveness, one must first repent, and Drue could not repent of one moment she'd spent with Connaught. She clung to the memory, for it was all she would ever have.

Chapter Nine

"Drue! Drue! Drue!" The word burst from Connaught's throat, shattering the night, echoing through the silent castle.

"What is it?" The Lady Enid burst through the door, her hair falling like midnight shadows about her shoulders. Small and pale, she looked like a wraith coming toward him through the darkness. Her thin lips parted in fear and her eyes almost popped from her head with her anxiety.

Connaught winced at her appearance. Casting the blame upon the light she held, he ordered it away.

"Put it on the other side of the room," he directed. Then, his voice softening, he added, "and then return to me. I will not sleep for a while. Perhaps you would keep me company."

The expectation in her face caused him another pang of guilt. Enid loved him and wanted him and was his wife, yet he could not touch her without longing all the more for Drue.

Since his return, the situation had become worse as the days went by. Enid's clear high voice irritated him. Her long black hair and the whiteness of her skin made him want to turn away. The cloying scent she used turned his stomach and her softness made him feel as though he was sinking into a quagmire.

He wanted a woman! God knew, he needed a woman! And yet, a woman was not what he wanted. Even the woman who was his wife could not fill his aching need.

He closed his eyes, turning his face to the wall, aware Enid had come closer.

"What have they done to you?" she asked, not really expecting an answer. "What have they done to make you so filled with misery and hatred that you cannot enjoy your home, your sons or your wife? I cannot believe they will not be made to pay for torturing you so cruelly!"

"I was not tortured, Enid. I was treated kindly and with respect."

"Oh, yes," Enid returned bitterly, "I saw the kind bruises and respectful gashes on your body. Why, even your mouth was so cut I dared not kiss you. Kindness and respect, indeed!"

Connaught cringed at the mention of his mouth. It had not been a blow that had inflicted that wound, but the abrasion of another's mouth against his own. How he longed to forget that interlude of passion! How he longed to turn back time and erase the cursed memory from the face of the earth, but it was impossible, just as forgetting was impossible. And even more impossible was the truth that he was completely and irrevocably in love with Drue!

"The bruises were the King's doing," Connaught reminded her. "He could not allow us to leave England without some sort of exhibition proclaiming his displeasure over the outcome of Bannockburn. I happened to be there to receive the brunt of his wrath."

"Then, if they were so kind to you and so solicitous of your pleasure, perhaps there was a woman. Perhaps she is the reason you no longer share my bed or allow me to join you in yours." Enid watched him closely, her dark eyes shining in the dim light as she prayed he would deny her words.

"I swear to you, there is no other woman. I scarce saw a woman during the time I was held captive, and then nothing more than a serving wench. Even the English Queen was not in residence when I was taken before the King."

Enid smiled. There was no other woman! Her husband would not lie to her. She was satisfied with his disavowal. Her mind at rest, she launched into telling Connaught what their sons had done earlier that day, never noticing the sigh of relief that barely escaped his lips as he thanked God she had not pursued the subject. But, of course, Enid would never suspect that Connaught's love was for another man. It would never occur to Enid that her husband might long for a love completely foreign to them both. She blamed his oddities and indifference on his imprisonment and roundly cursed the English for imagined wrongs. Had she known the truth she would have cursed them more soundly, but then, had she known the truth, Enid would not have believed it.

She prattled on, hoping to catch Connaught's attention despite the late hour. He watched her through half-closed eyes, thinking that her words, like her appearance, were small and insignificant. She plucked at the coverings on her husband's bed, her movements ineffectual and bird-like. Even the way she cocked her head to one side, then the other, reminded him of an English sparrow—small, drab and utterly uninteresting.

He had tried to talk to her. God knew, he had longed to share some of his experiences, and in so doing, laugh away the shadows surrounding them. But the talk of battle met with abject horror or a blank expression that conveyed her lack of interest more loudly than words.

She did not care to hear of his courage in hand-to-hand combat, satisfied only that he had survived. Her efforts to change the subject irritated him. Thwarted at every effort to converse with his wife, Connaught tried to include her in some of his activities.

"Come hawking with me," he had offered, ignoring her surprise at his suggestion.

"You know I cannot abide the sight of blood," she reminded him. "Then, too, I have not ridden since Kyle's birth, except in dire necessity."

He dismissed her excuses with some relief. Having a woman with him would slow his progress and limit his enjoyment. It was difficult for her palfrey to keep pace with his destrier, and it was impossible for those tiny, soft hands to control a larger horse. Riding the palfrey, she looked like a child joining her elders for an outing.

It never occurred to Connaught to question Enid's reluctance to ride since the birth of their last child. Bearing children was part of a married woman's duty.

Their marriage had been arranged when they were children. Enid had brought him lands and wealth and given him sons. In return he had provided for her with his name and titles, and, out of respect for her proficiency as mother and chatelaine, had remained true to her for the most part, and had not taken a mistress. Nor had he desired anything more than an occasional brief encounter with the women who followed the army from camp to camp.

It was only recently that he had come to believe there might be something more to a relationship between two people than that which he and Enid shared.

Even now he longed to talk of the strike his falcon had made and of the boar they had taken in the woods. He ached for a companion who did not flinch at the mention of death and who did not in return bore him with a recital of the shortcomings of the chambermaids.

Enid had been raised to take her place as the chatelaine of her husband's castle. From childhood she had given orders and expected the castle steward to see they were obeyed. Her soft hands never lifted anything heavier than her needlework. Her mind never grasped anything outside of her domain. She neither talked nor thought of any activities other than those in which she was directly involved. And while she longed for Connaught's company, she was dimly aware that he seemed less than enthused at her recitation on the antics of the traveling acrobats who had entertained the household some months earlier, or on the productivity of the herb garden.

It mattered little to him that she had set every available serf and maid servant to cleaning the castle in honor of his return. He seemed not to notice the polished brassware, the fresh rushes mixed with herbs that covered the floor, the linens, which had been soaked in a mixture of wood ashes and soda and pounded to cleanliness before they were dried in the sun. So indifferent was Connaught to his surroundings, he had insisted his great wolfhound be allowed to sleep on the freshly laid rushes.

His sole remark regarding their sons was that Patrick had grown almost as tall as his mother, which was an exaggeration. Enid sniffed diffidently as she remembered. She was still an inch or two taller than their child, and happy that the boy showed signs of gaining Connaught's stature as an adult.

Enid's father had not been a tall man. In truth, Connaught towered above her whole family. She could walk beneath his outstretched arm without it touching the top of her head. To diminish the difference in their heights,

Enid wore her hair piled high on her head when her husband was in residence, though the weight of her tresses caused her neck to ache and her head to pain her. She wondered if, indeed, it mattered to Connaught how she wore her hair. He seemed not to mind that she was so much smaller than he. During their betrothal and the first months of their marriage, Connaught had found her diminutive stature quite enchanting. Regardless of her lack of size, she had borne him strong sons, and it was about them she spoke until his eyelids drooped heavily and his breathing became measured, though he fought the sleep that would come.

She rose from her chair and moved across the room, stopping at a low table to pour her husband a cup of wine. Her movements were graceful and seductive. She took a sip from the cup before handing it to him. "Here, my lord, it will make you feel drowsy and soon you will find peace."

The black look on Connaught's face startled her. For a moment she thought he would knock the goblet from her hand, then, recovering himself, he took it from her and quaffed the contents in one motion.

Somewhat taken aback, Enid recovered the vessel and withdrew. "Try to sleep, my lord," she urged. "I will sit here with you, unless . . . unless you wish me to lie beside you." Her voice ended on a hopeful note but Connaught took no notice. He still pondered her words, *you will find peace!*

God! How he longed for peace! But there was no peace for him. His soul writhed with the knowledge that he was forever damned by his all-consuming love for Drue. Peace! Could he but find it in the bottom of a barrel of rich heady wine, or in a cask of foamy ale. Even the solace of the good Irish whiskey that he loved was denied him. The spirits that usually left him ready to sing and joke with any

IT'S A WILD, WILD, WONDERFUL
FREE OFFER!
HERE'S WHAT YOU GET:

1. *Four New Harlequin Historical™ novels—FREE!* Everything comes up hearts and diamonds with four exciting romances—yours FREE from Harlequin Reader Service®. Each of these brand-new novels brings you the passion and tenderness of today's greatest love stories.

2. *A Lovely Victorian Picture Frame—FREE!* This lovely victorian pewter-finish miniature is perfect for displaying a treasured photograph—and it's yours absolutely free as an added gift for giving our Reader Service a try!

3. *An Exciting Mystery Bonus—FREE!* You'll go wild over this surprise gift. It is attractive as well as practical.

4. *Free Home Delivery!* Join Harlequin Reader Service® and enjoy the convenience of previewing 4 new books every month, delivered to your home. Each book is yours for $3.19*—80¢ less per book than the cover price. And there is no extra charge for postage and handling! If you're not fully satisfied, you can cancel at any time just by sending us a note or a shipping statement marked "cancel" or by returning any shipment to us at our cost. Great savings and total convenience are the name of the game at Harlequin!

5. *Free Newsletter!* It makes you feel like a partner to the world's most popular authors...tells about their upcoming books...even gives you their recipes!

6. *More Mystery Gifts Throughout the Year!* No joke! Because home subscribers are our most valued readers, we'll be sending you additional free gifts from time to time with your monthly shipments—as a token of our appreciation!

GO WILD
WITH HARLEQUIN TODAY—
JUST COMPLETE, DETACH AND
MAIL YOUR FREE-OFFER CARD!

*Terms and prices subject to change without notice. Sales tax applicable in N.Y.
© 1990 HARLEQUIN ENTERPRISES LIMITED.

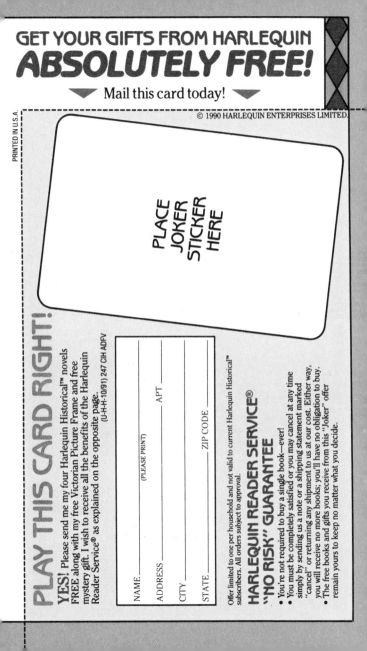

IT'S NO JOKE!

MAIL THE POSTPAID CARD AND GET AS MANY AS SIX FREE GIFTS!

and all who would listen now only made him maudlin. He had sent some of that same whiskey to England to honor Garith's wedding. Connaught wondered if Garith had received it, and if the strong, wild liquid had been used to toast the bride by the groom and his kinsmen.

Had Drue lifted the cup and felt the surge of power that shot through the blood like a call to battle? Had Drue tasted the liquid fire, allowing it to penetrate the body, boiling like passion through the veins?

Connaught wiped his eyes. Sweat stood out on his forehead as he relived the effects the drink had on himself and imagined Drue reacting in kind.

"What day is this?" he asked, so suddenly that Enid jumped.

"It is the feast of Saint Gregory," she answered quickly enough, but there was a look of puzzlement on her face.

Connaught closed his eyes. Yes, the gift would have arrived and the wedding be over. Would the brothers hold a celebration of their own? Connaught wondered. Would Drue be tasting his offering even now? And would the memories flood Drue's mind as they did Connaught's?

"Bring me spirits. This wine holds no relief for my problems. I need something stronger!"

Enid did not bother to question, but ran from the room, only to return shortly with a gourd brimming with spirits.

"Do not drink it as you did the wine, my lord, or you will surely undo yourself," she warned, a crease of worry furrowing her brow.

Connaught paused before taking the first sip. "I drink to my captors, who are most likely celebrating this night. I join them in their merrymaking. I toast them and wish them happiness!" With each sentence he again lifted the gourd to his lips.

"Please, my lord, you will make yourself drunk." Enid had never seen Connaught in such a state. He seemed bent on self-destruction.

The spirits reached him quickly. He blinked owlishly, willing his eyes to focus.

"I but celebrate with my friends," he said, brushing her words aside. "They drink my whiskey, toasting Garith's future happiness, and I drink with them. Somehow, I believe they will feel the communion between us and know I join them in their merrymaking."

He raised the gourd again, waving it now as though he touched another's goblet in a toast.

"I drink to the bride. May she be as fruitful and obedient as is my own dear Enid." He lifted the liquid to his lips, watching Enid's pretty face light with pleasure, though it was still shadowed with concern. "I drink to Garith! May he live long and have many strong sons." Again the gourd found Connaught's lips. His hand trembled slightly and Enid reached out, covering his hand with her own.

"Enough, my lord, you will be drunk, and Jaime Douglas himself comes on the morrow."

"Nay, turn loose my hand." There was a note of danger in his voice. "I drink to Drue, who captured me and will not let me go!" He ignored the confusion in his wife's eyes as he raised the gourd once again. "For you, Drue," he held the gourd out as though offering it to an unseen entity. "We both must taste the dregs of this sweet drink. Far sweeter than wine and far more deadly than hemlock. It tastes of tears and despair; of memory and remorse; of love and hatred. There is no cure, there is no forgetfulness! Even in death, I will remember... I will always remember!"

His words were slurred and Enid could make out but a few. Latching on to what she could understand, she knelt beside him, taking the now-empty vessel from his hand.

"What will you remember, my lord?" she inquired. Although she did not understand the ghosts that drove her husband to drunkenness, she recognized the look of love that shone on his face, and, believing it to be for herself, moved closer, resting her head on his mighty chest. "Do you remember the nights we spent together before you went to fight with your uncle? Do you remember how happy we were?" her voice went on, but Connaught could not remember. His memory seemed to have ended the day he looked into Drue's golden eyes. Had he died at that moment he would have been content going to his reward, his eyes locked on Drue's. For Drue possessed everything Connaught admired in a man. Courage, determination, strength, loyalty—they all were there, and more...so much more....

Without realizing he moved, Connaught's arms tightened about his wife as she snuggled against him. With his blood beating like the thunder of highland drums through his veins, he could not stop his errant memories. Once again Drue's face floated before him. Once again he was invaded by Drue's presence. Unseeing, uncaring, he turned to the love so readily offered, desperate to purge himself of the phantom that threatened to possess him. It was only later, as he lay in the darkness, that he realized he had not destroyed the phantom of Drue, but only a portion of himself. His breath caught in his lungs as he pulled himself free of Enid's soft body and lurched to his feet.

Throwing on a robe, he sought the solace of the battlements, realizing again that he would never be free of Drue. His body grew cold as the icy fingers of fear clutched his heart. He had damned himself with his admission. He alternately cursed and prayed, searching for an answer to his dilemma, but his prayers were to no avail and his curses fell on sleeping ears. The only answer he received was the memory of Drue's face when last he'd seen it, just before he rode away. Only then did he realize the magnitude of his sin, for he knew now that his unbridled love had also damned Drue.

With his fingers he clutched the rough stones of the battlements, as though their age and strength would give him surcease, but it was not to be. The first glimmer of dawning fought to overpower the endless night as he looked out over the shadow-strewn land. What if he were to leave it? What if he were to return to England and declare his love to Drue? Surely they would accept them there. King Edward himself openly loved Piers Gaveston. Connaught and Drue would be loathed but tolerated.

Connaught's mind worked at a dizzying pace. He would go to Drue and present his case. They could be together, always.... Connaught would leave his holdings to his son, Patrick. Then he would be free to live as an errant knight, free to fight for hire to the highest bidder. Free to love Drue, Drue, Drue....

The guard awakened him sometime after dawn. The sun beat down on Connaught's aching head as he moved slowly toward the cool darkness of the tower stairs. The thoughts and acts of the past night seemed no more than a dream to the tired man as he returned to his rooms.

The bed had not been made, and while Enid was no longer present, the outline of her body remained, a reminder of the night before.

Connaught tried to clear his mind, but memories persisted, exceeded only by his guilt. He had used Enid cruelly, and she was his wife! He dressed slowly, chastising himself for his weakness. He would apologize at the first opportunity, he vowed, but just as he was about to go search her out, the door opened and a glowing Enid burst into the room.

"My lord husband, Jaime Douglas has arrived and is awaiting your pleasure in the hall."

"Enid, I—" But his words were lost as she threw her arms about his neck and pressed her lips against his.

"We will talk of it again tonight." She lowered her lashes seductively.

Connaught caught his breath. He could not remember what he had done or said before going to the battlements last night. He could only remember letting himself be saturated with the memory of Drue, letting it permeate his very soul until there was nothing in the world but Drue and their love for one another. Even in making his wife so obviously happy, Connaught found only guilt and misery. Placing Enid's hand on his arm, he escorted her down the great stairs to meet their guest.

"All is quiet now," Jaime Douglas was saying as they sat at the high table watching the jugglers perform after the evening meal. "Mind you, I do not expect it to be so for any great time. No, it is only a matter of days, weeks at the most, before that fool Edward of England will do something to once again insult the Bruce."

Connaught nodded. "Do you not feel it would be wise to have a force trained and ready to counter the swift border raids that will occur?"

"Nay," Douglas shook his head. "I do not believe there will be raids. I look for another war. Edward is still smarting from Bannockburn, but he will not be allowed to lick his wounds for long. Already his council advises full-scale battle rather than raids. Only a few English lords do not join in the cry. The Duxtons, Pembroke, and, from what I hear, Gaveston himself.''

''The Duxtons will not join the fight?'' Connaught's voice mirrored his disbelief.

''So far they have remained on their own lands and tended to their own business. Only the youngest, Drue, and old Turlock have seen so much as a skirmish since you were ransomed. But there, it matters not to you. Your lands are on Irish soil.''

''No longer!'' Connaught laughed. ''The Bruce has deeded me a castle in Scotland, with lands and a small township. I stopped briefly on my way here. It was bleak and barren. Too remote for my taste.''

Its very remoteness reminded him of Drue. It was strong and had withstood many battles. With such a power behind him, how could a man help but win, Connaught thought, not listening to the drone of Jaime's burred voice.

It was many minutes before Connaught realized Douglas was not talking to him, but to his small son instead. Patrick stood solemnly taking in the man's words, young Devin at his side.

''And what will you be when you are grown?'' Jaime was asking the boys.

''I will hold these estates, as has my father and his father before him,'' Patrick told him.

''And you?'' Jaime turned his attention to Devin.

It was a difficult question for a six-year-old child, especially one who would not inherit, but Devin was undaunted.

''I want to be exactly like my lord father.'' Devin's eyes shone with pride as he looked at his sire. ''That's all I want.''

Connaught cringed. He wanted to shout, ''You cannot know what you say,'' but the words choked in his throat.

"Our father is the greatest knight in Christendom," Patrick added. "He always wins! He has never been beaten!"

"Is that so?" Jaime winked at his friend, and was a little taken aback at the abashed look on Connaught's face.

"I was beaten at Bannockburn when I was taken prisoner." The words were wrung from Connaught's lips.

"But that didn't count," Devin said staunchly, "you were surrounded by the enemy and had to fight them off a hundred to one."

"Who told you that?" Connaught asked sharply.

"Why, our lady mother said—"

"Your lady mother was wrong. I was not surrounded and I was not overpowered. I was taken prisoner by Sir Andrew of Duxton. It was a fair fight."

The boys faces dropped, then Patrick touched Connaught's hand. "Is that when you surrendered?"

"That was when I was taken prisoner," Connaught said spiritlessly, "I did not surrender until some time later."

The boys looked at each other in confusion, but even Jaime Douglas did not have an answer to this riddle. Realizing there was more to the matter than met the eye, Jaime turned the subject to something dear to the heart of man and boy. "Why don't we get the horses and go hawking?"

When the boys had clattered off to ready themselves, Jaime turned to Connaught. "I thought to find you aglow with happiness at being reunited with your wife and children. Instead, I see before me a troubled man. If the country life is not to your liking, be assured the Bruce can use your skills and will welcome your presence at his side."

Connaught shook his head. "No, not yet a bit. I should stay and give Enid a chance . . . give myself a chance. We must learn to know each other again. It is not easy."

But Jaime discounted his friend's problems. "All of us have been held prisoner at one time or another. Even the Bruce spent time behind bars. It is nothing shameful, man! You act as though it was something to be kept hidden. You did nothing wrong!"

"Say it is a blow to my pride, my manhood. I feel less than I was before I was captured. Do not fret yourself, Jaime. I will work it out in my own way."

"Assuredly you will," Jaime agreed. "All you need is rest and the love of a good woman, and you have both of these, from what I have seen."

Connaught nodded in agreement. "That I have, Jaime, that I have." But these things could not ease the ache that came each time the thought of Drue entered his mind. He turned away from his friend and looked out over the green expanse of land, his land, spreading before his eyes.

Jaime Douglas watched him for a long moment, then, stepping beside him, laid a hand on his shoulder. "Connaught, I know not what demons besiege you, but should you need a friend, I am here."

"Thank you, my friend," Connaught said, "but I fear there is little any man can do."

"Then perhaps you should seek council of a priest. I have my own confessor traveling with me. I doubt you could shock him after the many sins I have confessed." Jaime laughed at his own joke, but his heart ached for this fine young man who was so grievously troubled.

But the thought of telling anyone, even a priest, of his sins was something Connaught did not care to imagine.

"I will give it thought," he promised evasively.

His decision was made rather abruptly. Returning from the hunt, Patrick and Devin were chortling happily over the bagging of a wild boar.

"And he felled him with only one blow!" Patrick's voice reflected his awe.

"Our father is a great warrior and a great hunter," Devin said proudly. "When I grow up to be a man I wish to be like him in all ways."

The child's eyes shone with such pride, Connaught was forced to look away. "Do not say you would be like any man, Devin, my son. Only look to be yourself, the best and the bravest person possible."

"If I were the best and bravest person, I would surely be you, my father," Devin said in open adoration.

"No! You will not be like me! You must not be like me!" The words burst from Connaught's lips with such vehemence even the birds of the wood stopped singing.

There was a moment of unbroken silence before Devin found his voice. "As you wish, Father," he managed, as he fought the tears that threatened to undo him.

But Connaught was instantly aghast at his outburst. He knew his son had paid him the highest of compliments, and in return, Connaught had shouted at the child. Drawing close to Devin, he took the little boy's hand.

"Forgive me, my son. I would be honored if you grow to be the man you believe me to be. Surely no father could be blessed with such fine and loyal sons." His embrace took in both boys, holding them close to his heart. He owed it to them to exorcise the devil that held him prisoner. He owed it to the babe, Kyle, still in the nursery—a child Connaught could not bear to face, so strong was the memory of Drue and the night they had toasted the child's birth. He owed it to Enid, who had remained faithful to him though she had seldom seen him through the years of their marriage. He owed it to himself, for he had not asked for this curse to be visited upon his heart. He would go to the priest and ask for deliverance and salvation.

* * *

Father David had traveled many miles with Jaime Douglas. During that time he had heard many confessions—words wrung from the souls of dying men, petitioning God for forgiveness; meaningless words confessing little and meaning even less. But never had he seen a man more tormented than the Earl of Connaught.

Time and again the man had approached him, only to turn away at the last minute, until finally Father David took it upon himself to seek the Earl out alone.

"My lord, Jaime Douglas has said we will leave on the morrow. I wanted to thank you for your hospitality." The priest raised his watery blue eyes to those of the troubled man.

"It is my lady wife who deserves your thanks, Father. I will see that she is apprised of it."

"I have much enjoyed my stay here. It is good that you have been ransomed and returned to see to your estates and your family." The priest watched Connaught closely, hoping the man would find the courage to speak his mind and purge himself of the troubles that so obviously rent his soul. "I have most enjoyed the company of your sons, Patrick and Devin. They are fine lads."

Connaught started noticeably, as though waking from a deep sleep. "Aye, they are fine lads," he agreed. Then, gripping the little priest's shoulder, he hurried on. "I have a confession I would make to you."

"Not to me, Connaught, but to God. I am but the vessel through which His forgiveness flows."

"And if there is no forgiveness?"

The priest saw the anguish in the man's eyes. If it were possible he would have saved Connaught the agony of confessing and would have given absolution at that moment, for the man's pain was so intense no loving God could possibly withhold forgiveness.

"In God's love there is forgiveness for everything. We have only to ask and resolve to sin no more."

"If it were but that simple," Connaught whispered. "I sin each time I allow myself to remember. I sin as I sleep, and dream. There is no peace for me, waking or sleeping. My own sons torture me with their prattle, and I torture myself, for I can no longer find it in my heart to be husband to my wife." He might have continued, but Father David touched his arm.

"Come, we will go to the chapel, and all this will be dispelled through God's everlasting love."

Connaught did as he was told, and when, broken by shame and remorse, he had finished his confession, Father David granted him the absolution he sought.

"Listen to me, my son," the priest soothed. "Yours is a sin of the mind only. You have been under terrible stress. If you were to see this young man today it would be in a different light. The English court is decadent! Sin abounds! It is no wonder you were infected by it. It was like a sickness, and now that you are back in your own land the sickness will heal itself. Wait! Give it time. Time will heal this poisonous memory and purge it from your heart. It is in the hands of God. His will shall be done. The time of reckoning is near, not only for this young knight who tempts you so slyly, but for the whole English court as well. Mark my words well, the time of reckoning is at hand!"

"But how will I know..." Connaught was confused by the priest's words.

"You will know when you come face-to-face with temptation and overcome it," he said forcefully. "Now, go in peace with the Lord's blessing."

"And you, Father," Connaught murmured.

It was many minutes before he roused himself from the prie-dieu on which he knelt. Many minutes before he dared believe there was any truth to the priest's words. But as he left the chapel, Connaught was aware of a lightening of his heart. Truly the time of reckoning *was* at hand, and he would face it as he faced death, without fear. The furrows had ceased to crease his brow as he entered the great hall. His sons ran toward him and he lifted them in his arms, his laughter mingling with theirs as it echoed through the vast expanse of the ancient structure.

Enid's eyes were bright with hope. She cast a grateful glance at the little priest, who stood silently in a shadowy corner. His smile of encouragement warmed her, and she hurried across the room to share in their happiness.

Connaught looked up as Enid came toward him. God help him, he still did not want her, did not love her with the deep unquenchable desire he had felt for Drue, but he must never let her know. He must make her believe that everything was as it had always been between them and that the shadows of the past had been driven away.

He had questioned the fact that Father David had given him no penance, but now he saw the man's wisdom. Enid would be his penance, and perhaps his ultimate salvation.

As his family gathered round, Connaught swore he would prevail! He would free himself of this unwanted love. He would, with the help of God and the love of his little family, forget there had ever been a person named Drue.

Chapter Ten

"We have come too far into Scots territory," Turlock complained as he glanced back over his shoulder once again. "It is only a matter of time before they stand and fight. We will be lucky to escape with our lives."

"Perhaps we should withdraw and return to the border," Drue suggested halfheartedly. She longed for a good fight regardless of the cost.

"You would not withdraw even if I agreed, and I would not go back without you."

"I have fought alone before. I need no nursemaid to hold my hand," Drue returned hotly.

"You need your head examined to see if your brain has been jarred loose by some unremembered blow. You take risks of which no man should live to tell." He shook his head, remembering the heart-stopping chances Drue had been taking. "You fight as though life's only meaning is to mete out death."

"I do as I have always done," Drue protested. "I fight for my King and country. You taught me all I know. How then can you reprimand me for doing it well?"

Turlock shook his head again. "I do not mean to reprimand, Drue. I only feel a desperation of unrest within you. It is not healthy. It smacks of destruction."

Before he could say more, a messenger came galloping toward them, forcing their tired horses to dance aside to avoid collision.

"What news?" Turlock demanded.

"The Scots! A huge force! They wait on the other side."

Drue looked at the craggy peak, dotted with patches of early snow. The gray sky threatened more of the same. She wondered if it would be wise to force the battle before the snow came. Her silent question was answered by Turlock.

"We will ride forward and see for ourselves, then decide what to do."

The messenger took them to a point where they were able to see the full valley. Bleak and shadowed, it swarmed with the enemy, portending no good.

"The King is to join our forces with his own. He will come through the southern pass," Turlock commented.

"We should look for a place of our liking and force the Scots to come to us."

"Not likely!" Turlock leaned forward in the saddle. "See there! The Bruce himself is with them! They will not be tricked so easily. Theirs will be the advantage and theirs the victory."

But Drue's eyes had riveted on another banner—the banner declaring the presence of the Earl of Connaught. Her heart turned so painfully she clutched at it to ease the ache. It was Turlock who put voice to the words.

"Young Connaught has again joined his uncle, it seems. Stay clear of him, Drue. We allowed him to become too close when he was our prisoner. It was not a good thing. A man must either be friend or enemy. He cannot be both. Not on a battlefield."

Drue nodded at the wisdom of Turlock's words. Yet she strained her eyes for some glimpse of Connaught's towering figure. She studied each dark head, trying from that almost impossible distance to ascertain if he were indeed among them.

"Come," Turlock turned his horse. "We must go."

The next few hours were like fire and ice to Drue. While she longed to see Connaught, to feast her eyes on him once again if only for a moment, she knew that, should she be close enough to see him, she would undoubtedly have to fight him, and she did not want to pit herself against him in battle. For the first time in her life, she thought longingly of Garith's warm, comfortable castle and the safety he knew there. She would not have traded lives with him, she vowed staunchly, yet she wished that some miracle would transport her to a place where she would not face the possibility of fighting Connaught.

Thoughts of him raced through her mind. Memories she had managed to suppress except during unbidden dreams. His face, the smiling sparkle of his eyes, the sound of his laughter. His body, glistening with water... God help her, she must regain control of her thoughts or the vision of Connaught would rise up before her on the field and ultimately be the cause of her downfall.

With sudden decision she swung around and went in search of Turlock. She would stay in camp and dispatch the armies from there. It was a job she hated, but anything was better than coming face-to-face with Connaught. Before she was able to tell Turlock of her plan, an alarm sounded through the camp.

"What news?" She burst into the command tent.

"That fool Edward blundered onto the Scots' encampment and attacked!" Turlock was livid with rage. "There's nothing for it but to hit them from behind. It will be no surprise, I vow. They know we are here and will be expecting it. Take the right flank. I will take the left. Between us we may be able to buy the King enough time to get away.''

Drue hurried from the tent to where one of the squires was holding her horse. She slipped quickly into the heavy armor and mounted in record time. Shouting encouragement, she urged her men forward. From the corner of her eye she could see Turlock doing the same. It was imperative that they attack at the same moment, so she waited until she was certain all was in readiness, then gave the signal.

The situation was worse than she had thought. The main contingent of the Scots army was engaging the King's forces, but due to the sheer numbers, there were more than enough men to give Drue a good fight. Her battle cry shivered above the sounds of war as she led her men in full charge, while Turlock's voice thundered from across the way like a mighty echo of doom.

As they had done many times before, Drue and Turlock swept through the enemy, forcing them back upon their own men. The English soldiers joined together to form a wedge that narrowed as the Scots battled to hold their ground.

By the time the wedge had become a straight line, the Scots were tumbling over one another, crushed back on their own men. Realizing they were nearing the King's forces, Drue allowed her men to break their formation and fight hand to hand. The Scots knights began fighting their way toward them. Within minutes they were dealing destruction on one another.

There was little time to distinguish anything other than who was friend and who was foe. Drue and Turlock were separated as the battle heightened. Suddenly, with the wary foreboding of one who has survived many battles, Drue was aware of eminent danger. Dispatching her last opponent quickly, she glanced about the field. Turlock, swinging his battle-ax with deadly precision, was in no obvious danger, but Drue's eyes fell on a group of knights bearing down on one lone enemy. Even as she would have turned away, they closed in for the kill.

Drue could feel the perspiration drench her body despite the chill in the air. Her legs tightened, urging her horse forward. Without thought she cried out in a mighty shout, "He is mine!"

But the knights did not slacken the intensity of their blows. None paid her heed, for the fight was deadly and the prize great.

"He is mine!"

She shouted again as her horse burst into the melee. For a moment she thought she saw the spark of recognition behind the slitted face guard, followed by a split second of hesitation. That hesitation was all the English knights needed as they swung their swords downward for the kill.

Connaught skillfully blocked one of the blows, but the other came quickly behind. It staggered him and he reeled in the saddle, leaving himself open to the death blow.

Wild with desperation, Drue realized the man she loved above all else was about to be killed before her eyes. Throwing herself forward, Drue blocked the blow with her own body.

"He is mine!" Her voice echoed through the dark pit of unconsciousness as she fell from her horse onto the bloody field.

Connaught continued the fight. His arms moved automatically, dispatching death with unknown strength while his mind refused to accept the happenings of the past few minutes.

He had been assured that the Duxton contingent had refused any part of this unwarranted invasion. Never would he have consented to lead his forces had he believed any of them would be there, but there they were. Turlock still fought strongly, while Drue...Drue lay somewhere on the field.

It had not been a one-sided love existing only in Connaught's imagination. The sacrifice had been demanded, and Drue had unhesitatingly taken the fatal blow. Connaught's throat closed with rage while unshed tears stung his eyes. He swung his great sword with renewed vigor as blood pumped through his veins in utter desperation.

Was this the will of God that Father David had promised? Was this the moment of reckoning he had been told to expect? If so, he would have rather lived a thousand lives in hell than to see Drue struck down in an effort to save him.

Without conscious thought, Connaught continued striking out at his enemies, knowing in the black corners of his mind that his own worst enemy was himself. His arm ached from the constant swinging of the heavy sword, but he no longer noticed. His legs cramped from controlling his horse, but he no longer felt the gripping pain. His head throbbed from the constant crash of steel against steel, yet he could not hear it, for the sound of Drue's words screamed in his ears.

With sudden resolve, Connaught turned his steed and cut his way across the field. Only a few skirmishes now remained, along with the moans of the dying. He ignored the pleas of friend and enemy as his eyes searched each prone, twisted body. He wanted to remove his helm and cover his ears with his hands in an effort to shut out the sound of Drue's voice, yet he knew it existed only in his mind...as Drue existed only in his memory.

As he neared the area where the confrontation had taken place, he was aware a number of scavengers had crept surreptitiously onto the field, stripping the soldiers of their armor and valuables.

The wintry light was fading as he carefully searched each face, finally dismounting to be more thorough.

As each fallen warrior was inspected, Connaught's heart twisted inside his great chest. He had to know if Drue was dead. He had to know that there was no hope of ever seeing the golden eyes light in recognition.

A slight, bent figure tugged awkwardly, trying to remove the armor from an inert body. The man's movements caught Connaught's attention. He went toward him, dreading yet needing to know at the same time.

With each step, he heard Drue's voice. With each step, the terrible dread grew like a poisonous bubble, threatening to explode and destroy him. With each step, the words rang in his brain until the world was filled with only the pain of those three fatal, irrevocable words.

"He is mine!"

The little man scurried away, glad to escape from this massive knight who lifted his fallen brother as though it were no feat at all. It had been all the scavenger had been able to do to lift an arm in the effort to remove a gauntlet, yet this huge fellow had lifted the unconscious knight as though he were light as a child, and in truth, as tenderly as if he had been.

It seemed strange, though, the little man mused, for he would have sworn the two fought on opposite sides during the battle. Perhaps there was a chance for reward after all. Perhaps the English would pay to know what had happened to their fallen hero.

He glanced back over his shoulder and was astonished to see the knight striding away, his face almost touching that of his comrade, as though he sought to force the breath of life back into his friend's body.

The man's crooked back straightened somewhat with sudden resolve. He would wait until the dead and missing were counted in the morning and then present himself in the English camp. He would send a message to the King himself, for surely there would be a reward when he related what he had seen.

"They have Drue!" Turlock's face was white with shock as he spoke the words. The timbre of his voice stopped even the King's chatter and brought the men to sudden silence.

"How can you be certain?" Piers asked. "We still have men searching for him. Drue has never been captured. He's too clever to be taken!"

"I tell you Drue is their prisoner, and this scurvy little rodent will bear me out!"

With that Turlock flung the little man into their midst. "Tell them!" Turlock bellowed. "Tell them what you told me!"

The ferret-faced little man took in the group before him. The English King, his arm about the shoulder of another man, patting him affectionately from time to time. The men in brightly colored clothing; like a flock of prize peacocks preening themselves. Only the gruff old bird who had handled him so roughly seemed not to adhere to the fashion. Yet the fashion wasn't his chief concern; it was the atmosphere of the court that turned the little man's stomach.

These were supposedly warriors, come to Scotland to fight a war against the Scots. And though the fellow had little love for Robert the Bruce, at least the Bruce was a man, just as the grizzled old warrior beside him was a man, just as he, Tam MacBurgh, was a man. But even a man must survive, and unless Tam missed his guess, the one they called Turlock would be tighter with a reward than the canniest Scot. No, it must be to the King he made his appeal.

Scrambling to his knees, he prostrated himself.

"Your Grace, I came from the battlefield to relay what I saw with my own eyes. I felt you would want to know to what end came one of your bravest and most hallowed knights."

"And who is this knight, little man?" The King's voice was smooth, but his eyes had narrowed.

"I do not know his name, and his surcoat was torn asunder and covered with blood. But before I could gather aid to carry him to your camp, a mighty Scots knight tossed me aside and lifted the man in his arms, carrying him away as though he were a babe."

The King and the little man eyed each other. Both were aware there was more to the story than had been said.

"Why would such a thing be of interest to me? Men are carried from the field after every battle."

"Your Grace, I am not a fighter. I gain my reward by helping the fallen warriors."

"You gain your reward by helping yourself to the riches of the fallen warriors, I'll warrant!" Piers laughed.

Tam shifted his weight. "I saw the battle, and I saw the knights meet. They were fighting on opposite sides, and the one who fell did so in trying to save his enemy."

Turlock shook the little man like a a dog worrying a rat. "You lie! It is not so!"

"I swear, my lord. That is why I dared come to you. If your friend is alive, he is well cared for. It was the man he saved who returned for him. Had I not known they were enemies I would have sworn them to be brothers.''

''Know you the name of this mighty knight who came and carried our man away?'' the King asked quietly.

''Aye, Your Grace, that I do! It was the Earl of Connaught!''

The King gave a whoop of pure joy. ''It was Drue!'' he chortled. ''Never fear, lads. He will be cared for with all consideration, unless I miss my guess.'' He plucked a purse from his sleeve and tossed a few gold coins to the man. ''If Sir Drue is truly alive there will be more,'' he promised.

Tam bowed low and scurried toward the door. The men were obviously pleased that their companion was in all probability alive, all but one of them. The old war-horse, Turlock, had sunk down onto a stool and buried his face in his hands. It seemed strange that he would be the least excited, when Tam had believed the big man cared the most for the welfare of the young knight named Drue.

Ah, well, it was not for him to understand these men, only to do their bidding and receive the reward. He rubbed the gold pieces between his fingers as he melted into the shadows.

The constant jolting caused Drue's mind to return to reality, if only to find a way to lessen the pain in her head. She deserved pain. More than that, she deserved death! She had acted the fool during a battle. Her sudden recall of events leading to her demise were far more painful than the blow itself.

What had possessed her to place herself in a position where she would endanger her own life in order to save an enemy? She hated herself for it. She would undoubtedly hear harsh words from Turlock over this impulsive act. She delayed opening her eyes to face his wrath, for surely it was

Turlock who strode so mightily from the field. He had carried her many times as a child, and she instinctively felt the tender protectiveness in the arms that held her. Secure in their aura of safety, she knew she was shielded from harm as long as those arms were there. Shielded from harm, but not from his righteous anger! Yet, as her senses became more alert, it seemed strange that there was no hesitation in the stride that moved them across the field.

Drue weighed many stone and she wore full armor. It had been years since there had been occasion for Turlock to lift her. It would take a man of great strength to do more than stagger under her weight. She remembered carrying Garith, but he had not been armored at the time.

She became aware of other voices. These were not the clipped tones of the English, but rather the melodious burr of the Scots. Cautiously she opened her eyes.

It was painful trying to focus on the profile so near her face. But even through hazy, blood-blinded eyes Drue could make out the well-remembered features of Connaught. He looked straight ahead, intent only on reaching the safety of camp, unaware of Drue's scrutiny. Her eyes caressed the high forehead and long black lashes that shaded the sapphire-blue eyes, the well-shaped nose and firm, yet sensuous lips, and the strong determined chin set proudly on the powerful neck. Below that, Drue dared not look, though the remainder of Connaught's body flashed through her mind as though she had seen it in all its naked glory only yesterday.

Like the sudden piercing blow of an arrow, pain shot from the core of Drue's being and exploded in her anguished head. She set her teeth to keep from crying out as anger filled the void of unrequited love. She had foolishly tried to save this man, and for her efforts he had taken her prisoner and was carrying her into the enemy camp in full view and full disgrace! Misery and hatred, both for herself and for Connaught, welled up within her until she could hold her silence no longer.

"Damn you, Connaught, put me down! I would rather you dragged me bound into your camp than be carried like a helpless child!"

The sudden impact of her voice so surprised Connaught he almost dropped her.

Recovering himself, he eased her to a standing position. "In truth I am glad to see you recovered. I could as easily have carried my war-horse as you. There cannot be much difference in weight."

"You could have left me behind. You could have allowed me to be retrieved by my own people. You did not take me fairly in battle and it was not your blow that felled me." The words were strong, but Drue still clung to Connaught's powerful body for support as the world spun around her.

"You were left for dead and the scavengers were already upon you when I arrived. I did not know that you lived and wanted only to see that you were returned to Garith for proper burial."

Connaught shocked himself by the coolness of his words. He had known in his heart that this beloved enemy was not dead. He knew it when he held her weight in his arms and would not relinquish her, even to throw her over his saddle, as was usual when one knight captured another. More than that, he knew he would have brought Drue back to camp with him alive or dead, for his soul cried for this confrontation that would purge him forever of the unwanted love threatening even now to overwhelm him. The grief he had known when he thought Drue to be dead had been so overpowering he did not know if he could bear it. To live without Drue was one thing; to live in a world without Drue was something so agonizing he dared not touch it, even in his imagination.

But he told her none of these things. Instead he asked, "Can you walk?"

"Certainly!" Drue was not sure she could stand alone, much less walk, but she must not let him know. If she was to be his prisoner by her own folly, she would do it on her own terms.

Through sheer determination she managed to take several halting steps.

"We will make better time if we walk together," he told her.

Realizing he could easily have thrown her over his shoulder and introduced her to camp in that degrading manner, Drue held her tongue and accepted his help. His body seemed to burn through the armor that separated them. She could feel the heat permeate through the metal that had successfully shielded her from the enemy's weapons but could not shield her from the desires of her own body. She looked up again at Connaught's face, glorying in his nearness, though she must never allow him to know. Just as she must never allow him to know any of her secrets; to tell Connaught would be to court certain destruction.

He cared nothing for her, she assured herself, only for the ransom she would bring and the friendship they had shared. He would have forgotten the encounters that had embedded themselves in her memory. He would have forgotten the unquenchable desire and the scantily disguised passion that had threatened to undo them. He would have forgotten their never-to-be-forgotten kiss, which was as real to Drue as it had been the moment it had become not a thing of dreams but a reality. Of course, he would have forced all these things from his mind.

Her assumption was at least partially correct. Connaught was, in all honesty, trying to force those exact things from his mind. Had he not been assured by Father David that the time of reckoning would come and that he would be relieved of his obsession for Drue? Had he not been assured that Almighty God would be his source of strength and would aid him in his struggle? Surely if God's will were to be done, it could not be so devised that Connaught could continue to carry this festering wound within himself. The fact that Drue had been delivered into his hands indicated Father David's prediction would come to pass.

Yet why did Connaught's heart continue to pound with joy as his arm held Drue closely against his body? Why did his hands linger as though even the armor Drue wore was a caressable extension of the strong, sinewy body beneath? Why was he haunted by memories and the scent of sunlight? The deep, husky tones of Drue's voice were blown out of proportion, leaving him weak with desire—desire heightened by the one moment he had stolen as he lifted Drue in his arms to be carried from the field. The moment when he had broken his vows to God and to himself and allowed his lips to once again touch those of his beloved. It was the slight intake of breath in response as they warmed and molded themselves to his that allowed him to know Drue lived.

Perhaps that moment of weakness had undone all the good his prayers had achieved. Once again he silently asked for forgiveness and strength to overpower the dragon that would surely destroy them both. Here, in Scotland, there was no place for such a love. If it were so much as suspected, Connaught would be dishonored and sent back to his own lands, regardless of his affiliation or his record as a warrior.

It must not happen! He would fight this thing, and as Father David had promised, he would find a way to be free of the unbidden love that threatened him with hellfire, both in this life and the next.

Hardening his heart against his base emotions, he pushed on toward the camp with his prisoner.

Chapter Eleven

The relationship between Drue and Connaught was strained. There was none of the easy camaraderie that had typified their friendship during Connaught's incarceration. Not only were the Scots openly hostile to a prisoner who had freedom of the camp, but Drue was aware there were other English prisoners who did not fare as well. Connaught saw that Drue was kept away from them at all times, though so close a watch demanded his constant attendance.

"I swear sometimes I cannot tell which of us is the prisoner and which the captor," he declared one day as he and Drue sat in Connaught's rooms at Stirling Castle.

"Perhaps you will have some sympathy for my dilemma during the time we waited for you to be ransomed." Drue's voice was haughty, but her eyes gleamed mischievously.

"You had Turlock to spell you when you wanted to get away."

"That's not true! Turlock was the one who 'got away.' I remained with you, as well you know!"

Connaught groaned and agreed, "As well I know, indeed!"

"If you want to leave you have only to chain me in your quarters. I would still be there when you returned."

"I doubt it. You would find some way to disappear."

"And would that be so terrible?" Her eyes searched his and Connaught lost himself in their golden depths. It was like looking into the sun. All else faded and he knew only the blinding heat that burned through his brain and seeped through his body. How could he tell Drue it would be terrible? That to him the very thought of having her ransomed and losing the solace of her presence was like a sickness to him? Had it been so with Drue when Connaught was waiting to be ransomed? But no! Drue had wanted him gone. Even in those last passion-filled moments in England Drue had been able to pull herself together and leave the room with some semblance of dignity. The remembrance of that dignity was precious to Connaught, and he cursed himself for his own weakness.

Once again he swore he would see this test to the end and earn the peace he so earnestly sought. Once again he prayed that God would grant him the strength to overcome this unbidden love that thwarted him at every turn. He must keep Drue with him until his penance had been paid and his sins of the flesh forgiven.

The only redeeming grace, as far as Connaught was concerned, was that Drue seemed so completely unaffected. Several times he caught her looking at him, but Connaught thought little of it. In his mind, she was watching for the opportunity to escape, and he did not intend to give her that opportunity, at least not until he could again call his heart and soul his own. He would keep Drue with him until the sound of her voice did not cause his mouth to become dry. He would keep her with him until her scent did not permeate his very pores and burst like a thousand tiny stars in his brain. He would keep her until the warmth of her body even as she walked beside him did not cause his heart to pound like the drumbeat of a thousand war-horses charging to battle. He would keep her with him until he could bear to remember the sweet, salty taste of her lips without his blood turning to boiling oil and burning like poison through his veins.

He watched her in the glimmering firelight, loving and hating her at the same time. He wondered what she thought, sitting there so serenely as the lights and shadows played on her face. The very picture of the perfect gentle knight.

There was nothing in Drue's expression to tell of the turmoil that raged within. She was aware that Connaught was watching her. She could feel the heat of his gaze as it caressed her as surely as though it were his strong, gentle fingers touching her hair, her face, her body. She ached for his touch...just that, nothing more. A hundred times she had invented reasons that she might be near him. That their hands would touch across the chessboard or as they plotted a course on a map. With the excuse of clumsiness she would move her horse close to his, to feel the brush of his thigh in passing. And yet she was sure the love she felt was one-sided.

Connaught had not so much as mentioned the fact that she had saved his life on the field. Apparently he felt it his due. His only thought was to obtain as large a ransom as possible. If only she dared talk to him the way she had talked when they were together those first few days at Duxton, but that had been rendered impossible by their own foolish emotions. She closed her eyes and breathed deeply, trying to expel the thoughts that once again threatened to creep through the barrier of consciousness. She would not, she must not think of him. She must force down the desire to once again taste those lips that were to her like a forbidden drug and a thousand times more deadly.

What if she were to tell him that she had been born a woman? What if, sitting there, without so much as moving, she was to put an end to this farce? Would he take her in his arms and kiss her? Or would he be righteously angry at the pain he had been made to endure by her inadvertent deception? It mattered little, for Drue knew she could never bring herself to speak. By doing so she would be condemning herself to a life of drudgery. She would be a prisoner forever. A warrior's soul in a woman's body, tied to the life of a chatelaine, a life she abhorred. Separated from all she knew for one moment of pleasure. It could not be! It could never be, though her heart ached with longing to know the mystery of fulfillment so close at hand.

The sounds of a party arriving in the courtyard brought Connaught to his feet and put an end to Drue's musing. Within minutes a man hurried across the room and dropped to his knee. "A message for you, my lord." He held out the missive.

Drue watched as Connaught read it, his face tightening with an emotion she could not understand.

"I will speak with you later." He dismissed the man before turning to Drue. "It is Enid, my wife."

The words struck Drue like a great blow. The very mention of the woman was a form of torture.

"She was with child." Connaught's voice was flat, void of all emotion. "The babe was born dead and now it seems Enid cannot recover. She asks that I come to her."

"With child!" Drue felt betrayed. Her heart was filled with agony at the realization that he had gone from her to the arms of his wife. With anguish, as she was forced to accept the fact that he had given his love to another woman. It mattered not that he was unaware of Drue's womanhood. The thick, green poison of jealousy oozed through her veins as the words were torn from her throat. "You left me and went back to her without so much as a thought. I agonized that you had to go with the feeling between us unresolved, but it was all one-sided. I see that now! It was as you said, a moment of weakness that would never happen again."

The words were wrung from her heart—words that took form without conscious thought. Words so deeply buried she had never expected to give them voice. In her own mind, Connaught belonged to Drue, just as she belonged to him, but apparently he did not feel the same. She shut her eyes against the amazement on his face.

"It was not that way," he protested, forcing down the fierce surge of happiness that thundered through his body. Drue cared! During all those dreary months of separation, Drue had also suffered. He must make her understand, but the words would not come. His mind was spinning with shock, and all that came from his lips was a weak explanation, "Enid was my wife long before I met you. Where else would I go?"

But Drue was so distraught she neither heeded his words nor gained control over her own. "I was filled with guilt and misery both for myself and for you. I almost followed you. I thought of coming to you and..." Only Drue's inherent sense of self-preservation kept her from speaking the words that would condemn her forever to a life she could not bear. She stopped short, suddenly realizing how close she had come to revealing all to a man who did not care. "And offering my service to your King to be near you."

Connaught uttered a silent prayer for the inner strength that would free him from the unbearable joy he knew as

Drue revealed her love for him. His hands burned to touch her, his arms ached to crush her to him. In those few seconds his joy was so great he was unable to think of anything save that Drue loved him. Even his guilt, his sin was not as great as his euphoria.

"It was so with me. I tried to forget, to put you from my mind, but I could not. Your face was before me awake or sleeping. I longed for you above all others and despised myself for it. I could not be husband to my wife or father to my sons. All I could think of was you. It was only after I confessed my sins that I found some surcease, for Father David assured me it was in God's hands and all would be put right in his eyes."

"Father David was wrong! God was wrong! What was between us will never be right! Let me go, Connaught! I swear I will raise the ransom myself and send it to you, only let me go!"

Connaught looked into the golden eyes staring desperately into his. Drue was too close. The demon was not yet purged. He must fight until it was. He could not let Drue go until he was free of the love that undid him each time he lowered his guard. His lips hovered above hers. He could feel the warmth. He could taste Drue's breath against his mouth. He wanted to merge with her into one single being. "God help me!" The words burst from his throat as he fought to keep from taking Drue in his arms. There was no way his dream could be fulfilled, no way that would not leave him doubly damned, and yet, and yet . . . "I cannot . . ." he murmured. "I cannot let you go."

Drue returned to her place by the fire, her face and mind mercifully blank. Had he kissed her in that brief moment of passion she would have betrayed herself. Yet if her secret were known he would expect her to play the part of a woman, and that she could not do! That she could never do, no matter the cost.

It was some time later when she heard the door close and was aware that Connaught had gone from the room. He would leave her again. Leave her here at Stirling Castle among her enemies. She must escape before he returned, for there was no future save misery for either of them. Drue was a knight, and a knight she would remain until she died.

"Turlock sends you greetings." The words were so hushed they seemed almost an extension of Drue's imagination.

She did not look around, but her shoulders tensed in response.

"How do you come to know Turlock?"

"I met him when I took news of your capture."

Drue turned now, regarding the ferret-faced little man with disdain. "If this is true, you probably know more about the progress of my ransom than I do myself."

"There is no progress in your ransom. Connaught will not come to terms." Tam MacBurgh watched closely. His uncanny instinct told him there was something here he did not understand. The gaze that met his was like a golden ray of sunlight, clear and unblemished. This knight was not of the same ilk as was the King of England.

"Can you get a message to Turlock for me?" Drue was asking.

"There is a possibility, though it would be most dangerous."

"Turlock will see that you are rewarded for your efforts, but I must send word to him before Connaught returns."

"Very well then, tell me what you want him to know and I will relay it to him."

"I would rather write—"

Tam held up his hand, cutting off her words. "I will not carry a written message. If I were caught and searched I would forfeit my life, not to mention my usefulness to you."

Drue hesitated. "How do I know you will not run to the Bruce with your information?"

"With a verbal message all you would have to do is deny you gave it to me. It would be your word, the word of a respected knight, over that of a . . . messenger."

There was no other choice. Drue knew she must escape and this man seemed her only chance.

As a prisoner held for ransom, Drue had presumably given her word of honor and would not try to escape. She was therefore allowed the run of the castle in Connaught's absence. She stayed well within the confines and did not attempt to go near the gates or the outer bailey. Instead, she slipped into the dungeons, where the other English prisoners were held.

The guards, secure in their position, paid little attention, for knights came and went without question. In truth, most did not realize Drue was English, for she had been seen with Connaught before he left. The guards did not even attempt to overhear the conversations Drue held, for there was much laughter from the prisoners and it was obvious the young knight tried only to cheer them. Had the guards been told the prisoners were told to laugh on cue as Drue related plans for escape, they most likely would not have believed it.

"What word?" Drue stood watching the Scots dismantling some of the buildings in Stirling. The Bruce had ordered that it be rendered indefensible so the English could not hold it through a siege as they had done prior to the battle of Bannockburn. The constant confusion of men milling about had made it easier for Tam to gain entry to the castle and approach Drue.

"Turlock will be waiting outside the north gate as you requested. The first night of the dark of the moon, he will be there." Tam could not help but feel it was a mistake for this young knight to return to the licentious court of England. Surely he would be better off an honored prisoner of the Scots than risking corruption. Besides, Turlock had been tight with his purse strings. It might be for Drue's own good if Tam were to whisper some hint of the escape to Jaime Douglas. Perhaps the Scots would be more generous.

There had been no word from Connaught, nor did Drue expect it. She went on with her plans, readying the men for the quick escape that would set them free. Although she did not completely trust Tam MacBurgh, she could not fault his information and realized he was her only link with Turlock.

Her heart beat wildly as the party approached the castle. Pipes and drums announced the importance of the personage. Drue hurried to the wall to overlook the road. Surely Connaught would not come at so inappropriate a moment! Tonight was the dark of the moon and Turlock would be waiting. She held her breath, staunchly denying the part of her that longed to see Connaught again though it destroyed her plan.

But it was the Bruce himself who came riding through the gates. Drue smiled. There would be much celebrating and confusion this night. The men would not notice her whereabouts.

* * *

As though extensions of the shadows themselves, the silent figures slipped through the murky darkness. Piles of rubble helped to disguise the movements of Drue and the band of prisoners that followed her.

"When we reach the north gate we will be met by Turlock and his men. They will have horses for us secured in the wood some distance away. The only real threat is between the gate and the trees. Stay close to the rocks. Move as silently as possible," Drue admonished the men once again. She could not shake off the feeling of unrest that beset her each time she thought of Tam MacBurgh. The little man had given her word that Turlock had arrived. She had not seen him since. It was unlike one of his ilk not to be there to receive the reward she had guaranteed when escape was completed.

Shrugging off her qualms, Drue began sending the men across the open space between the ruined wall they crouched behind and the north gate, their passage to freedom.

As had been promised, the gate was unsecured. One by one they disappeared. Sounds from the castle became more raucous, the laughter louder, indicative of heavy drinking. Another blessing, Drue thought. They would be well away before the guards roused themselves enough to find their fallen comrades in the dungeons.

There was a strange tightness about her heart as she realized she might never see Connaught again. She knew she would not willingly put herself in a position where she might again confront him. He was her nemesis! He was the destructive power that could persuade her to give up her very identity just to know the magic of his kiss, and that must not happen!

"The men have reached the gate, save for you and me," a voice called, interrupting her thoughts. "Go next, Sir Drue, and I will follow."

Tam MacBurgh had somehow materialized at her side.

She nodded silently and crept across the open area, slipping easily through the gate and into the night. She could see the last of the men disappear into the trees as she sped among the rocks.

A shaft of light shone though the gate above her and she paused for a moment before accelerating her steps. Her heart began to pound. As she reached the foot of the hill she dared look back. She had been right; there were men swarming through the gate. Damn Tam MacBurgh! He had betrayed them as she had feared.

"Drue!" Turlock's voice rumbled from the depths of the forest. In another moment they clasped each others arms. "I thought never to see you again. Connaught would not set a price for your ransom. If it had not been for Tam—"

"Tam has betrayed us. The Scots already come. We must away!"

Turlock looked up and saw the proof of her words. Muttering something under his breath, he thrust sword and shield into her hand. "We will cover the escape." Then, turning to the others, he let the authority in his voice sound through the night. "Go! We will follow!"

His answer was the thunder of many hoofs against the soft earth. Together Turlock and Drue mounted their horses and rode in the wake of the escaping men.

Horses screamed suddenly as the men fell back upon themselves.

"It is a trap!" a voice cried. But it was too late. The trap was sprung.

The men fought desperately, for each knew they were dead should they be again taken. Swords whined through the night like angry hornets. Drue and Turlock joined the melee.

"Scatter!" Drue shouted. "Regroup across the border!"

The men disengaged themselves from the Scots and obeyed her order, while Drue and Turlock fought on, allowing the others retreat.

Drue had no armor and defended herself only with sword and shield. Any telling blow could be the end for her, she well knew. Turlock also understood the seriousness of her dilemma and continually attacked the majority of the knights to keep them from her. Again and again they parried and thrust as the Scots fell back, only to return once again, realizing the enormity of the odds against the two English knights.

Drue and Turlock took the offensive, all the while retreating toward their goal, the border between England and Scotland. Darkness was their friend, but the dawn came undaunted through the thick foliage. Without the cover of night it would be easy for the Scots to hunt them down.

The Scots, seeing their advantage with the growing light, accelerated their attack. Sparks shot through the lifting night like wildfire as steel struck steel. Drue dared not miss. She must parry every blow. It was her life and Turlock's at stake, but even as she gave credence to the thought, she heard a shout of victory. Turlock was down.

Like a wild thing Drue fought her way to his side, leaving a path of wounded, disbelieving men in her wake. Heedless of the circumstances, she dismounted and fell to her knees beside the prostrate figure. "Turlock!" Her voice broke as she saw the seriousness of his wounds.

"Turlock." This time it was no more than a whisper. His eyelids fluttered and his chest heaved painfully with each intake of breath. "It is good this way, Drue. It is what I would have chosen. To die fighting...at your side. You are my pride, my greatest accomplishment. Above all else, you are most dear to me."

"Turlock, you will not die! They will get help! Your ransom is far greater than mine could ever be," Drue argued desperately. "You cannot leave me!"

"Each time you fight you will feel me at your side..." His voice faded and the Scots grasped Drue's arms, pulling her from him.

"Turlock!" Her voice split the dawn. "Turlock!"

There was no thought of tears. How could a soul shed tears?

"Take Sir Drue alive," an authoritative voice called out.

"What of the other?" a knight asked as Drue was subdued.

"Leave him! Turlock was a good and courageous man. Let his people come for him. I would the outcome of this night had been different."

Drue was led away, only vaguely aware that the Bruce himself had spared her life, for her soul was shattered by the magnitude of her loss.

Chapter Twelve

"**Y**ou were given the freedom of the castle! Even after Connaught was gone, we allowed you to roam as you would. And for this kindness you betrayed us. You broke your word and tried to escape!"

Drue let the words fall around her. She did not look up, but continued staring at the floor in front of the Bruce's feet. Leather thongs cut into her wrists, but she hardly felt their discomfort, just as she hardly heard the lashing of the Scottish King's words.

"You have betrayed your honor as a knight," he said, pacing back and forth across the audience chamber as he spoke.

"And what of your word?" Drue's voice was flat and toneless as though she truly did not care what his answer might be. "The Scots said they held me for ransom, yet no negotiations were made. The English were offered no terms of ransom on my behalf."

The Bruce forced her head up, peering into her face. "Who has filled your mind with such lies? Or do you seek to shift the blame of your own misdeeds? Connaught is a man of honor! He would do all in his power to see that your ransom was arranged with all expedience."

"If that were so, Your Grace, Turlock would not have deemed it necessary to give his life to secure my release!" Drue's voice was emotionless, as though some integral part of her had died with her friend. The pain of loss had not yet begun. She still suffered the blessed numbing of body and spirit that comes just before the realization of agony.

The Bruce looked sharply at her. He had seen the signs before and knew Drue was in a state of shock. He cursed under his breath. First Connaught had answered the summons of a whining woman and then his prisoner had seen fit to organize a mass escape. Now a brave and renowned knight was dead. A knight who, although an enemy, was a man the Bruce knew and admired for his bravery and prowess. The Bruce was well aware that the young knight standing before him was Turlock's protégée. For that reason alone, it was in his heart to let Drue off with a light punishment. Perhaps he should wait until Connaught returned and let him cope with the problem.

Jaime Douglas entered the room, undermining the King's plans for mercy.

"All but ten of the prisoners escaped, Your Grace," Jaime reported. "We followed them across the border, but Duxton met us there with his army and we were forced back. They followed us and retrieved Turlock's body." He said the last words more softly, his eyes on Drue as he spoke.

The King, too, turned his eyes to Drue. "By rights I should have you executed—" he stroked his beard thoughtfully "—but there has been enough killing this day. I will take a page from the English book of punishment."

Without giving anyone a chance to question further, the Bruce strode from the room.

* * *

"You will not!" Connaught's voice echoed through the narrow halls as Jaime Douglas hurried to keep up with the man's pace. "Drue is my prisoner! I will not allow such a thing!"

"My God, man, be reasonable! Sir Drue led an escape, one which was made good to the tune of over thirty men and knights returning to English soil without a crown in our purses."

"Turlock is dead! It is punishment enough! I will see that Drue is ransomed immediately!"

Jaime grasped Connaught's sleeve, pulling him to a halt. "Think, man! Sir Drue is your prisoner no longer unless the Bruce says it is so! The man tried to escape while you were gone. The Bruce recaptured Sir Drue himself. He may do with him as he sees fit."

"No!" The word was wrung from Connaught's heart, and Jaime sensed an emotion deeper than any within the old warrior's understanding.

"I know this man is your friend, Connaught," Jaime was saying, "but the Bruce has not ordered anything so terrible. He could easily have had Drue drawn and quartered for what he has done. The King has decided to mete out the same punishment as was given the Scots nobles captured by the English some time ago. They will be caged and hung from the castle walls until they can be ransomed. Drue will no doubt survive nicely."

Connaught closed his eyes, trying to shut away the visions that threatened to drive him out of his mind.

He had entered the gates of Stirling Castle as the announcement was being made. The prisoners were to be stripped, caged and hung from the walls like animals. They were to be left on display day and night for the edification of the people of Stirling and as a reminder of the dishonor of the English.

Jaime was right! It was not so great a punishment, but it was a punishment Connaught dared not imagine. Drue, suspended in golden glory before the eyes of the populace. Drue's muscles glistening in the sunlight as the flesh burned in the heat of the sun. Drue shivering in the cold of night and Connaught unable to do more then agonize. It must not happen! For if he did not go mad with desire at the sight of Drue's nakedness, he would drive himself wild at the thought of his captive's misery.

So it was that Connaught made his way toward the Bruce's private chambers, with every intention of demanding Drue's return to his custody. He would not allow this to happen! Beads of sweat stood on his forehead, belying the coolness of the day. Somehow he must convince the Bruce that Drue should be returned to his care. He would beat Drue himself if the Bruce so ordered. Allow himself to be chained to his prisoner. Anything! But Connaught knew he could not stand to have Drue's strong young body displayed before the jeering soldiers. Drue was his! So much a part of Connaught he had hardly been able to give Enid a decent burial before riding back to Stirling.

Now, Connaught's guilt would never be assuaged. His terrible admission before going to his wife's side had caused Drue to attempt this escape. His neglect in making arrangements for the ransom had caused Turlock's death. He could not add to his sins by allowing the Bruce to place Drue on display. Yet, in his heart, Connaught knew it was not only Drue he sought to protect, but his own sanity.

Connaught remembered all too well the wiry strength of Drue's golden arms about his body as they wrestled at Duxton. He remembered the long limbs gleaming in the firelight as they played chess, passing the long winter's nights. He remembered the strong hands kneading his weary body that last night in England. The magic in Drue's touch. The strength and life that flowed through those hands, setting his blood on fire until his brain exploded in the unescapable clutches of that one unbidden moment of madness...that one kiss that would haunt his soul through the darkest dungeons of hell.

No! Regardless of Father David's promises, Connaught would forsake his very hope of heaven to keep Drue from this punishment.

He watched as Jaime Douglas disappeared through the heavy doors to the Bruce's chamber, to ask for an audience. As he stood waiting, Connaught knew it was not for Drue he made this request, but for himself.

He squared his shoulders as Jaime came to the door and motioned him inside.

"You *demand* that Sir Drue be returned to you?" The disbelief in the Bruce's voice was obvious.

"Drue is my prisoner!"

"No longer! You left him here with the run of the camp. He attempted to escape. Sir Drue is my prisoner now!"

"Your Grace—" Connaught dropped to his knee in supplication "—Drue saved my life on the battlefield. We quarreled shortly before I left. He would never have attempted such a thing had it not been for that."

The Bruce stroked his head thoughtfully. "Quarreled?'

Connaught had not meant to say as much and was now trapped by his own words. "I had not made any overtures regarding his ransom. It came out shortly before I went to my wife's bedside. Drue was understandably angry, hence the attempted escape."

"Then there was truth to Sir Drue's words," the King mused.

"If Drue said no ransom had been negotiated, it was true."

"And had you demanded Sir Drue swear to remain prisoner on code of honor?" the King asked.

Connaught shook his head. "Drue was unconscious when I brought him to our camp. I believed him to be dead. When I discovered he lived I did not think to ask him to swear an oath. We had become friends during my stay in England. I did not think he would try to escape. Nor would he, had it not been for our . . . misunderstanding."

Connaught's mouth went dry when he thought of the words spoken during that conversation. Drue had all but admitted loving him, just as he loved Drue. Just as he had always, would always love Drue.

"If you will let me see Drue I will make him swear on his honor as a knight that he will not attempt escape again. In the same vein, I will swear to facilitate obtaining ransom quickly and be done with it."

The Bruce's eyes met Jaime's across the room. Connaught was a good and trusted ally. They would do all they could to comply with his wishes, even though neither could understand the vehemence with which the man pleaded for his captive. With sudden resolve the Bruce motioned to Jaime Douglas. "We will go forth and see what Sir Drue thinks of your offer."

A spark of life touched Drue's face as she looked up and saw Connaught enter the cell she shared with the other captured men. She had not thought to see her captor again, any more than she believed she would live through the punishment the Bruce would devise. The prisoners had been kept in the dark about their fate, but there was much laughter among the guards and it portended no good.

"I would speak to Sir Drue privately," Connaught said, glancing around the squalid surroundings.

The King nodded. "Very well. Take our prisoner to the guardroom. The others will be 'made ready' for their punishment." He snapped his fingers, and the guards came forward and led the prisoners away. "When you have finished, bring Sir Drue to the battlements."

So that was to be their fate, Drue thought numbly. They would be cast from the battlements of the castle to their deaths on the rocks below. A rotten death for a warrior! Somehow she must devise another means of securing her fate.

"I would go with my men!" she demanded.

"Later!" Connaught caught up the thong that hung from her secured wrists and led her from the chamber. "Now you will explain your actions to me."

The guardroom was empty as the soldiers busied themselves with the other prisoners. Connaught shoved Drue onto a low stool and stood above her. Unwilling to give him the advantage of height, Drue struggled to her feet. The heavy shackles clanked ominously.

Connaught ran his fingers through his thick hair. "If I am able to secure your release into my custody, will you swear to remain my prisoner until ransom is secured?"

Drue did not answer. She stared at the sapphire blue of his eyes, so unusual in contrast to the dark tan of his face. She stared at the strong blunt fingers and calloused hands that could be deadly or gentle at will. She stared at his lips. Lips that would never again know the touch of her own, though she longed for it through eternity. It would be better to die than to live forever in an agony of unfulfilled love.

"I would share the fate of my men," she repeated.

"You are a fool!"

"Better death than a life of loneliness," she said softly.

"I am sorry about Turlock." The words were inadequate, but they were all Connaught could manage as the depth of her despair penetrated his soul. He longed to put his arms around Drue and give comfort, as he had comforted his sons in their time of sorrow. His arms ached to know the solid pressure of Drue's body against his. Connaught's hand reached out inadvertently.

Drue could not know his intent, but sensed the kindred sorrow. Her body reacted where her mind dared not. She took his hand and pressed it to her lips. It was as though all the fury of a summer storm sent shock waves, like bolts of lightning, crashing through their bodies.

He could feel Drue's breath against his flesh as she again spoke.

"Please, my lord, let us end this farce. I do not fear death as greatly as I fear the future. There is no life for me either with you or without you. Let this cup pass. Let me go and end the otherwise endless misery between us."

He fell to his knees before her and pressed her hands to his face, dropping kisses on the strong war-calloused fingers. These were not the work-worn hands of the gentle sex, but hands like his own. Their touch was like the touch of his own. He knew the pain of each blister and callus, for he had developed the same. Drue was an extension of himself. It was narcissistic of him to glory in his captive's strength, and yet he was unable to stop himself.

Her hands closed over his, knuckles white with tension. "It is no good, my lord," she whispered. "There is no future in this for either of us."

Something burst in Connaught's brain. He could no longer think clearly. There was only one goal in the world. Only one thing that mattered...and that one thing was Drue.

"My wife is dead. If you would swear fealty to the Bruce, he would allow you to remain in Scotland. We could be together." Even as the words formed, Connaught felt degraded. His love for this knight had brought him to the very depths of damnation. Now, as Drue's eyes widened in surprise, anger rose in Connaught's heart. He stood, jerking Drue up with him.

But it was not the shock of Connaught's words that reflected in Drue's face, but her own wild hope. If she told him now that she was not a man, if she revealed herself to him and cast herself on his mercy, would he indeed allow her to swear fealty to the Bruce and remain with him as his equal? Would he keep her secret and let her fight at his side?

Her lips parted to say the words that would condemn her and free her at the same time, but his mouth crushed the forming words, drawing them into his being, devouring her lips, her thoughts, her soul. She cried out as his mouth plundered hers, delving through the barriers known only to herself. In her heart she had already forfeited the battle. The hot pounding blood melted even the solid muscles in her legs and she clung to Connaught as they trembled beneath her. Forgetting all else in the wake of newly discovered desire, Drue returned kiss for kiss, answering his passion with her own.

The powerful love, so long repressed, filled Drue's being. She would give Connaught the greatest gift she possessed, the secret of her womanhood, relying on his love to protect her with his silence and understanding. She opened her eyes as their lips parted.

"Connaught," she murmured, her voice deep and husky with desire, "I would be your woman."

To her horror she found herself looking into the black depths of hatred. It never occurred to Drue that Connaught had not understood the meaning of her words, anymore than it occurred to Connaught that Drue was telling him she was other than a man. In a panic of self-hatred and desperation, Connaught flung Drue from him. Hampered by her shackles, she stumbled and fell to the floor, while he stood above her, shaking with anger and self-contempt.

"You will not do this to me again! I will not allow you to destroy my immortal soul!" He opened the door. "You wish to share the punishment of your men? Then, so be it! Share it and be damned!"

He called to the guards as his footsteps echoed through the empty hall.

The guards did not immediately appear and Drue was able to pull herself to her feet. She staggered forward to the table, leaning on it for support. The events of the morning had happened too swiftly. The gauntlet of emotion had been too devastating. She could not absorb it, and all she could remember was Connaught's mouth on hers, followed by the wild look of hatred in his eyes as he cast her away.

How could she have been so wrong, so stupid, so foolish in her desire to love and be loved? She had thought Connaught would rejoice when she entrusted him with her secret. Instead, his rejection had been swift and complete. True, he might have desired her during a moment of weakness, but when she had offered to commit herself to him and had asked commitment in return, he had not been able to hide his aversion. She tried to blot out the hurt of Connaught's rejection. She could not have known that he did not feel the mad rhythm that pumped through her bloodstream when they kissed.

She had assumed her love had been returned in kind and she had been wrong!

She looked down at her hands, clenched against the rough wood of the table. Hands as roughly hewn as the table itself. Scarred and tough, with the strong wrists of a swordsman filling the shackles until they chafed the flesh.

Those same shackles would have slipped over the dainty hands of a lady, and the lady would have walked away unscathed.

Drue had been foolish to think Connaught would accept her as his woman. Even the camp followers were more attractive than she, as well she knew.

Connaught was a rich and powerful lord. He could have any woman he wanted. Drue knew as much and had known from the beginning, but before God, she had believed the unwanted love she had borne him had been answered. His rejection was more cruel a blow than any she had taken in battle. The pain did not ease, nor would it. Without Connaught's love there was nothing left save darkness and death.

The time she had spent with Connaught had been rich with camaraderie. Their friendship had grown and blossomed into a love of unsurpassed dimensions, or so she had believed. Now, however, she could see the love was hers alone, as was the mistake.

She had been a fool! A fool! And as such she was being punished for her blunder. Not only had Connaught rejected her offer, but the very fact that she'd suggested she would be his woman had earned his everlasting hatred. His rejection had been complete and unbending. Never again would she know the touch of his hand. The taste of his mouth. The warmth of his body against her own. Never again would she hear the whisper of his sighs or the sound of his laughter as they shared a private joke; the exhilaration as they hunted the stag or wild boar.

Oh, God! it was so unfair! Never had she loved anyone as she loved Connaught, nor would she. In him she saw the reflection of all that she would be. To love, she must respect, and no other person had lived up to her expectations. Had she but left the situation alone and held her silence, their friendship, at least, might have been preserved.

The memory of the hatred in his face sent chills through her body. She felt as though she would never be warm again, as indeed she would not, for it had been the knowledge of Connaught's love that had warmed her through the long, lonely months they spent apart.

And though they had fought, the love that grew between them could not be denied. She had thought Connaught loved her as surely as she loved him—until she offered to be his woman. Yet, in that moment, she had believed it was what they both wanted. She had thought he would rejoice that she offered herself freely. She had even hoped he would understand how difficult had been the choice to share a secret that could destroy her and bring her father's house crashing down around them.

Perhaps it might have gone better had she explained her situation before offering herself, yet in that breathless moment of passion and longing she had scarcely managed to form the sentence, let alone think of a way to tell him of her most secret fears.

Her words had been as spontaneous as the kiss they'd shared. She had looked into his eyes expecting to see a love that matched her own, not the anger that was more painful than his words or the roughness as he thrust her from him.

Perhaps her bid for his love had come too soon after the death of his wife. She understood little of a man's grief for a spouse, but could not believe Connaught's sorrow could be more than what she felt over Turlock's death.

They had both suffered the loss of a person who shared their lives, and their love had reached out and drawn them together in heartache as it had in happiness. Only Connaught's repudiation kept them apart, and it was beyond Drue to understand his sudden repulsion of her love.

Her mind reached back over the years, remembering the laughter, the challenge, the camaraderie, before daring to touch gently on those moments when their passion had burst forth with such force that nothing short of divine intervention could have stopped them from seeking some release from their unbearable need. A need that now would never know fulfillment, as their love would never know culmination.

She wanted to go after him. To beg, yes, beg him to forget her foolish words, her unwanted offer, and allow their lives to return to the heaven-hell it had been since the day their eyes had met on that field of battle. But his voice still echoed through the room and the stones vibrated with his hatred.

For the first time in her life, Drue drank the dregs of total defeat, her soul was seared with the total absence of hope. She reeled as the depths of despair engulfed her, sending waves of agony coursing through her body, leaving her as weak and shaken as if she had taken a killing blow.

Her trembling hands clutched at the little table, toppling the basket of fruit that stood in the center. As the contents spilled to the floor, Drue spied the knife. Apparently one of the guards had left it, in his haste to escort the prisoners to the battlements. She tucked it into her sleeve as the guards entered the room.

The other prisoners stood chained together along the battlements as Drue was led from the darkness of the tower into the brilliant sunlight.

"And have you and Connaught come to an equitable agreement?" the Bruce demanded as Drue was forced to her knees before him.

"There is no agreement between Connaught and myself," Drue said staunchly.

The Bruce looked closely at the prisoner. Something was amiss here. Drue's face was swollen and looked to be bruised. "Send for Connaught and we will resolve this matter," he commanded.

As the guard disappeared into the tower, the Bruce turned his attention to the other prisoners.

"Get on with this!" he ordered, and the guards sprang forward. "Strip them and secure them in the cages, then lower them from the castle walls until their ransom arrives. We will see how the English fare with the type of punishment they devised for the Scots."

Drue's breath escaped slowly as she realized the potential danger of the situation. If she were stripped naked, her womanhood would be discovered. At best, Connaught would kill her. At worst, she would be raped by the guards. She heard Connaught's voice as he approached, but it held no hope for her. He would do nothing to save her. She had offered herself to him and she had been repulsed.

She looked at him with barely concealed longing as he bowed before his king.

"Has Sir Drue agreed to give his word of honor to remain our prisoner?" the Bruce demanded.

"Sir Drue has no honor!" The reply was wrung from Connaught's heart, and the intensity of seething hatred emanating from his powerful body shocked even the Bruce.

"Is Sir Drue then to be punished with the others?"

Connaught's hands closed over the hilt of his sword. Perhaps this was the purging of which Father David had spoken. Perhaps seeing Drue's body, naked before the world, would free him of his desire. Connaught had seen many naked men in his lifetime. How could this one be so different? A body was a body, and Drue's would be no different from any other. Yet Connaught could not speak the words that would strip his captive before the world.

"Is it your wish that your prisoner be stripped and caged with the rest?" The Bruce's voice rang with impatience.

Drue watched Connaught. She knew he hated her. She could see it in his eyes, in the way his hands, white-knuckled and tense, clutched his sword. His face seemed almost gray in the sunlight. She longed to take back her offer, but it was too late. Within her world, a woman was less than nothing. Revealing herself to Connaught had only made him hate her the more, crushing the last remnant of respect he might have held for her in the bargain. She let the handle of the knife slip from her sleeve into her hand as she watched Connaught nod his head. His movements were stiff, almost puppetlike, and all eyes were upon him as the Bruce spoke again.

"Very well, strip the prisoner and cage him with the rest."

As the guard stepped forward, Drue plunged the knife deep into her chest. Though the binding about her wrists hindered her movements, the quick shock of pain told her she had struck true.

"Stop him!" a voice shouted. "He has a knife!"

But it was too late. Drue collapsed as the guard eased her to the ground.

"Drue!" The word was ripped from Connaught's soul. He knocked the guards aside and turned her over. "Drue..." This time his voice was hushed as he saw the blood welling up around the blade buried to the hilt in her body. "Drue." There was no sound, but Drue's heart heard his cry and she opened her eyes, trying to focus on the face above her own. To memorize it for time immemorial, to hold it throughout eternity.

She concentrated only on the man above her, lost in the brilliance of his eyes, drowning in the vortex of fire-blue desperation. Echoes of the past crept through her consciousness as the numbness of shock gave way to the blood red cocoon of molten pain, and she repeated the words that had sealed their fates so long ago.

"I will look into your eyes until I see no more."

Chapter Thirteen

Connaught's footsteps rang through the halls as he carried Drue toward his apartments. Servants scurried from his path, aware that somehow tragedy had struck on the battlements.

The Bruce followed his kinsman, his sharp eyes watchful, his mind filled with unsettling thoughts.

"I cannot understand Drue's motives," Jaime Douglas was saying for the third time. "The punishment was neither harsh nor painful. Sir Drue is a knight. Surely he was aware stronger methods could have been taken."

"If he lives, we will question him. In the meantime I have sent for my own physician." The Bruce spoke loudly enough for Connaught to hear, but the man paid no heed.

The dead weight of Drue's unconscious body was burdensome, but Connaught would not share it. His thoughts, his prayers, his very life was centered on each shallow breath he willed into Drue's lungs. The doors to his apartments swung open as he carried Drue through them. Swung open and shut in the faces of the Bruce and Jaime Douglas.

"Your Grace, I . . ." Jaime began apologetically.

"Leave them," the Bruce ordered. "If Sir Drue lives we will question him later. If he dies, it is best Connaught be alone with his grief. I have watched many men die." The Bruce sighed as he remembered his brother Edward, once High King of Ireland, and Scotland's own William Wallace. "It is not an easy thing to lose a fellow-at-arms, whether he be friend or enemy. When I face death for the last time, Jaime, I would you were at my side, for I know no man more loyal than yourself."

The two turned away, diverted by their own melancholy thoughts, unaware of the drama of revelation building on the other side of the closed door.

The surgeon impatiently removed the knife.

"We will bind him tightly," he said, placing the weapon on a low table. "There is little else to do. The man is all but dead."

Connaught reached out, lightly touching the leather vest Drue always wore. He remembered how identical Drue and Garith had been when, slick with English mud, they had wrestled against him.

"Here." The surgeon's voice interrupted impatiently. "Cut this leather thing from his body and get on with it. I have other things to do besides wait on a suicidal prisoner."

Connaught's hand closed over that of the doctor. "Then go and do them. I do not want you here. Drue can die without your ministrations."

"But the King said—"

"And I say begone, before I plunge the knife into you!"

There was madness in Connaught's eyes and the doctor thought better of arguing. Without another word, he left the room.

"Get out, all of you!" Connaught shouted, unable to disguise the grief that filled his throat and choked his voice. "Get out and leave us alone."

He did not look up until he heard the final closing of the heavy door.

With great effort he lifted his eyes and looked at Drue's face. It was drawn with pain, but the strength Connaught had come to admire was still there, as was the self-sacrifice that Drue disguised under the cloak of bravado.

It was only this last insane act he could not comprehend. Had it been the immensity of their sin that had caused Drue to destroy so precious a life? Or had it been Connaught's final rejection when Drue had damned them both with those fateful words? They still rang in Connaught's ears: "I would be your woman!"

And still the sin was Connaught's! He had led Drue on. Unable to stop himself, Connaught had played on the emotions of the younger knight until Drue was no longer in control.

He, Connaught, had broken every knightly vow. His illicit love had made his marriage a sham and his wife's death a blessed relief.

Oh, God, that he should come to this! That he should so use another human being in the name of love and then cast that person aside when the love was avowed and returned. And as punishment he would live out the rest of his life in a world filled with darkness and death, for Drue was his light... Drue was his sun, his warmth, his love....

Yet before darkness fell once again, Drue would be no more. He reached out, intending to dress the wound that still oozed blood. In his haste the doctor had wrapped the bandages over Drue's garments. If the bleeding were to be stopped, Drue's clothing must be removed.

Connaught's hands halted in midair. He could feel the heat of Drue's body radiating into his pores. Could he touch Drue, even now, without yielding to desire? Would he propagate his sins by drinking in the muscular beauty even at the portals of death?

No! Even he had not fallen so low. He would call the servants and let them care for Drue! After all, this was a willful captive who sought to escape not once, but twice, the second time through the cowardly act of death.

Connaught got to his feet, intent on summoning his lackeys, but before he could take two steps he knew he could not bear to allow any hands other than his own to touch Drue, nor other eyes to see. Drue was his, only his, and Connaught alone would know the vision of that naked flesh.

His hands shook as he loosened the lacing. Turning Drue to her side, he slipped the leather garment from her body. Inadvertently his hand brushed the newly bared flesh. The vest was coarse compared to the smooth skin, which sent tiny currents of shock through Connaught's body. Desperately, he centered his attention on her back, but the well-muscled contours became a thing of beauty to his eyes and offered no surcease.

Her skin glimmered with the sheen of a polished marble statue. Drue must live! Connaught could not let this finely hewn body, a carefully crafted machine of war, be wasted in a moment of madness. Nor could he look at it, lest it fill him with guilty desire. He would center his gaze and his complete concentration on the deadly little wound that threatened to end the usefulness of this knight among knights.

Not until it was cleansed and the bandages wrapped tightly did Connaught allow himself a moment's respite. Drue was breathing more evenly now. Unless the fever was greater than usual with this sort of wound, there was a chance life would not be snuffed out. A chance Connaught intended to see through to accomplishment.

It was as he directed his concentration on the steady rise and fall of Drue's breathing that the first niggling realization penetrated his consciousness. Though the knight's chest was full and heavily muscled, it was not the chest of a man. Above the tight, white wrapping the difference between the structure of his own powerful torso and the one before him became more prominent. He rubbed his eyes, unable to believe what they beheld.

No! It could not be true His tired mind betrayed him.

Desperately he searched for a logical explanation. The day had faded as he battled for Drue's survival and now shadows crept across the room. That was it, surely; it was a trick of the light. Drue was a man! Had he not captured Connaught in battle and later wrestled him to a draw? These were feats not to be taken lightly! Many knights had tried to take Connaught and been sorely beaten. He was renowned in his own country and in Scotland for his prowess at wrestling, yet Drue was his match, as well he knew. Still, there must be some reasonable explanation for this phenomenon. Never had he seen a body such as the one before him.

His hand reached out, curious fingers tentatively touching the firm breast. It was not as he remembered Enid's lush bosom, yet it did not have the resiliency of his own powerful chest. Slipping his hand beneath his doublet, he tested the flesh and tone of his own body and then touched Drue once again.

It was true! There was a difference. While this was not a woman's breast such as he had ever known, it was definitely not that of a man's! It would be impossible to develop a body to the extent Drue's was and leave even the slight softness he had discovered.

Again Drue's words came to him, echoing through his brain with such force it left him dizzy. Perspiration beaded his brow. It could not be! He had lived with Drue for many months. He would have noticed had there been anything unusual about the knight. The only thing out of the ordinary was their attraction for each other.

"I would be your woman!"

Connaught covered his ears with his hands in an effort to shut out the memory. Had Drue indeed been trying to tell him this most sacred secret?

Once again, Connaught reached out. Now his hands shook as though palsied with age. The remainder of Drue's clothing fell to the floor. Disbelief laced with outrage raced through Connaught's body. The hips were narrow, the stomach well muscled and flat, the legs burgeoning with the powerful muscles of a horseman. But between those masculine legs lay not the sword of manhood but the sheath of a woman instead.

"Merciful God!" Connaught's cry echoed through the silent room. The ramifications of his discovery were almost too great to bear.

He had been beaten, not once but many times, by a woman! The fact that their love was not a sin, but a normal flow of nature, was no comfort in that moment.

He, Connaught, had been taken prisoner and held for ransom by a woman! He had learned to admire and respect the strength and stamina, the power and the skill of this warrior, this fellow knight who was, indeed, nothing but a woman!

He looked long and hard at the still features. It was beyond him to see any feminine beauty in the high brow framed by close-cropped hair. The wide-set eyes framed by pale golden lashes held no charm. The cheekbones were high and the nose too pronounced to be admired as beautiful. The lips . . . oh God, how he remembered the ecstasy and promise of those lips, yet they were not sensuous and full, nor did they pout and pucker. They laughed above strong white teeth, and spoke of war and sang out battle cries. And once they'd spoken of love.

He allowed his gaze to move on. The taut, golden skin, the rippling, well-muscled body, the strong, bulging legs, the calloused, skillful hands, all belied the proof of womanhood that lay before him.

Father David had spoken true. The time of reckoning was at hand. It all fell into place now. His attraction to his fellow knight. The kisses they'd shared, which would not be denied. Drue's words when she had surrendered her secret to him. And her reaction when she heard what the punishment was to be.

Had the guards stripped Drue with the rest of the prisoners, it took no imagination on Connaught's part to realize what her fate would have been. He had seen women raped all too often. It was a spoil of war and the right of the soldiers to take their turn with any female who dared try pass herself off as a man.

Fear, pure and simple, washed through Connaught's body. Fear mingled with relief so great that he gathered her to him, then drew back as though he had been burned. Even in the face of his newly attained knowledge, Connaught would not yet accept this highly developed body as that of a woman, and therefore could not treat it as such.

Even in the throes of fever, Drue was not docile. Her whole being was taut, with each sinew waiting for the command to spring into action. Yet he loved her, as he had always loved her, as he *would* always love her.

Drue moaned and Connaught moved to her side, pressing her war-roughed hand against his cheek. "It will be all right, Drue," he whispered. "No one need share your secret. You are safe with me. I will protect you. I will pro-

tect you with my very life, now and forever. I will protect
you with a clear conscience and a pure heart. There is no
licentiousness in our love. It is a good and true progression of nature. And you will live! I will not let you die! I
will not let you leave me.''

His voice echoed through the silence as, for the first
time, Connaught dared verbalize his love. In his heart he
repeated his vow. He would not let her die! He would not
let all the bright promises be snuffed out due to ignorance
and pride. He would forgive her for overcoming him in
battle. He would forgive her for not telling him she was a
woman. He would forgive her for causing him the agony
of sleepless nights as he writhed in guilt for his supposed
sins. But he could not allow this farce to continue. He
would take her at her word, the poignant promise that still
haunted his mind and heart. He would let her be his
woman.

Through the murky depths of pain Drue heard his words
of love. Over and over he told her he would protect her.
His voice droned in her ears and she fought for consciousness.

She must tell him. She must let him know! She was Sir
Drue, knight of England! She needed no protection, not
from Connaught or from any man! Yet the touch of his
strong hands was reassuring, and she listened from the
threshold of death for the sound of his voice.

In the end it was anger, not love that brought her back
to the world of the living. Anger at being trapped by her
own words.

Drue lifted heavy lids and tried to focus fever-glazed
eyes.

"You know..." she managed.

He leaned close. "I know and I love you, as I have always loved you without daring to admit it. You will be my

woman, Drue. I will take you to my castle where you will live as my lady and my love.''

Drue stared at him in disbelief. Could it be that he visualized her in the role of his wife? Memories of Garith's bride, the simpering Allyson, flashed through her mind and she cringed, remembering the miserable, uneventful existence on which she seemed to thrive. It was impossible to imagine herself picking roses in a garden, or eagerly awaiting Connaught's return from battle while supervising the servants to insure his comfort.

It was equally as impossible to imagine herself tripping about a castle in a billowing gown. The thought was so grotesque it bordered on ridiculous, but from the look on Connaught's face he did not find it so. It was as she had feared so long ago. He honestly believed she would spend the rest of her life as his chattel . . . his slave! . . . and enjoy doing so in the name of love. Her eyes closed, shutting out his face and the unwelcome vision of the life he promised so blatantly.

Drue felt herself sinking into the black cocoon of unconsciousness. The truth rose to her lips, and she whispered the words that damned her to loneliness in this world and the next: ''I would rather be dead!''

Chapter Fourteen

Connaught could feel Drue's eyes following him as he moved about the room, instructing the servants.

"We leave on the morrow," he said aloud, as much to the servants as to the silent Drue. "I am moving the household to my castle on Loch Morrill. I have sent a messenger to collect my sons. They will meet us there."

He watched Drue closely. Her eyes flickered at the mention of his children, but it could not be construed as interest. Rather, it was an acknowledgment of his words. He thought introducing Drue to his sons pure inspiration. Women liked children; surely his handsome brood would soften any heart. But Drue showed no sign of caring one way or the other.

When the packing had been completed, Connaught dismissed the servants and sat down on the chair at Drue's side.

She did not wait for him to speak, but asked. "How many days journey is it to Loch Morrill?"

"Five days, maybe six...."

"I will ride my horse. We can make it in two."

"You will ride in the cart and we will take the full five! I do not wish to have you dying from exhaustion after all the time and effort I've spent to keep you alive." He smiled, softening his words, but Drue did not respond in kind.

"I do not wish to be hauled in a cart like a side of beef!"

"And I do not wish to bury you along the way. I want you to see this craggy, barren land the Bruce has bestowed upon me. I think you will find it the perfect place to complete your recovery."

"I am recovered enough to be ransomed. Why have you not seen to it?"

"Do you really not know?" His blue eyes searched her golden ones and she looked away.

She knew! Oh God, but she knew! Connaught had discovered her secret and now he expected her to submit to him as a woman. Drue had gambled and lost, not once but twice!

In that one split second of weakness in the guard room she had submitted to her overpowering love for this man and betrayed herself. Now her words had come to haunt her, over and over again. To her disgust, Connaught expected her to conform to the mold of the women of their era, and this was a thing she could not do! Drue knew it, even if Connaught did not!

The vest that had stood her so well for so many years had itself betrayed her and deterred the thrust that would have ended her troubles forever. In her misery, Drue even felt betrayed by Turlock. Turlock! Her friend, her mentor! The only man who had accepted her for what she was and gloried in it! Turlock, who had died and left her alone to face the unfaceable.

Connaught's voice brought her back to the present.

"As far as ransom goes, I will send a messenger to Garith and tell him I have his sister as my guest."

Drue grimaced at his words. "He will not know of whom you speak. Garith has long since forgotten he ever had a sister. Indeed, when I was ten or so, we actually searched for the grave of our sister, whom the villagers assured us had been born to our parents at Duxton. We found our mother's grave, but no other, and assumed the little girl had been buried with her, as indeed she had.''

Connaught looked sharply at Drue. ''What do you mean?''

''All who were with my father after the siege have forgotten a girl child was taken from the castle. In the minds of the soldiers, two lads joined the army.''

''What about your father?'' Disbelief reflected in Connaught's face.

''My father has long since resigned himself to my vocation. I am a knight! I have been honored for my prowess by King and country! If anyone ever had second thoughts about the propriety of my position it was Turlock, and he is dead.'' As she said the words a shudder passed through her body. ''I would I were with him.''

Connaught laid his hand on her arm. The muscles tensed beneath his fingers. ''Do not say such things, Drue. Turlock did not ask that you die with him. He would have wanted you to live, just as I do! This isn't the end. It is only the beginning. The beginning of a new life... for both of us!''

Drue sighed. How could she make this mule-headed man understand?

''I do not want a new life! I liked the old one!''

''Did you?'' he asked softly.

''Of course I did!''

''Did you like the sleepless nights when your body longed for mine? Did you enjoy hearing me thrash about in waking torment? Did you never long to break your vow of silence and admit you were a woman and you loved me, as I loved you and lay tortured because I thought I was committing a sin against God and nature?''

"I am a knight! It is a sin against God and nature to love another knight!" she said self-righteously. "I did not think of myself as a woman, nor do I now! If you love me, you must accept that, Connaught, else there can be no true love between us."

"There is already true love between us," he said staunchly. "A love greater than other men imagine even in their wildest dreams. I am, even now, willing to betray my own King and kinsmen to protect you. I love you beyond life itself... beyond man's knowledge of love... beyond honor."

Drue's breath caught in her throat. "Then let me go!" She did not plead. Her voice was strong and firm, for she realized one of them must surely be destroyed by this love.

Somewhere in the dark recesses of his mind Connaught understood the urgency of her request. It was in his heart to tell her his love was so great he could not be without her regardless of the eventual cost, regardless of the ultimate pain, but the words would not rise to his lips.

"You have made this request before," he said lifelessly.

"That is true," Drue agreed, "but it is nonetheless valid. There is no life for me here with you."

"You are wrong! All has changed now that I know what and who you are!" His strong hands closed on her shoulders. "Now more than ever I cannot let you go!"

"Now more than ever I should leave you," Drue whispered. "For your sake as well as my own."

"No!" The word was soundless on his lips, yet it echoed through the room with the force of a battle cry. "You are mine! You are my challenge, my love, my woman!"

Drue's eyes swept across his face. Across the wide brow and past the eyes that snapped with fire-blue intensity, before centering on his lips. He was speaking, yet she could not concentrate on his words. Not while those lips moved so near her own. As though pulled by some unseen force Drue leaned toward him, longing to blend her mouth with his, fusing lip to lip. The thought itself made her tingle. Her body tensed with quiet anticipation as she hungrily watched him. Her own lips parted, readying themselves for the onslaught that must surely come.

He uttered words of love. Words that meant nothing to Drue as her whole attention centered on the kiss for which she longed. Her hands closed on his biceps, kneading them instinctively. Her body filled with a heat surpassing any fever she had known. The warmth flowed through her blood and seeped into her taut muscles, melting them as his hands, as though possessing magical powers, caressed each one.

His mouth moved over the strong contours of her face and down the powerful column of her neck. She clung to him, unknowing of all else, save this man who had so awakened her. Never had she felt so alive. Never had she known the enchantment of floating on a crest of fire.

Her breath came in great gasps, catching in her lungs and threatening to render her unconscious by its sheer magnitude. Muscle molded to muscle as two magnificent creatures sought the ultimate fulfillment, the ultimate release, the ultimate love.

A cry escaped Drue's lips as Connaught crushed her against his body. Immediately he released her, holding her cradled in his arms as he smoothed her hair from her forehead. Her skin felt cool and slightly damp, and he chided himself for taking her too far, for being unable to control his passion even in the face of Drue's precarious health.

"Forgive me, love, I had not meant to hurt you."

"It was not in pain, but in love that I cried out," Drue protested.

He kissed her lightly. "The pallor of your skin tells me differently, but I love you the more for saying so."

"Connaught," she began, but he stopped her with a kiss so achingly tender it took her breath away. "Connaught..." She breathed the word as one would a prayer.

"Rest now, my love." He drew her arms from about his neck and placed them on the soft fur that served as a blanket. "We leave for the loch before dawn. It is a rough and wild place, much like your beloved Duxton. You will meet my sons and grow to love them. They need the love of a mother just as I need the love of a woman."

The word *woman* brought back all the memories of Allyson. Drue reached up to press her fingers over Connaught's lips before he said something even more damning, but he kissed her fingertips and ran his tongue over the calluses on the palms of her hands.

"Someday the calluses will be gone and your hands will be soft against my face," he whispered, "someday when you are my lady."

Drue turned away from the open love she saw in his eyes. She could not bear to see the hurt she must inflict. Like the knight she was, her thrust was quick and true and she was unaware that in his euphoria Connaught did not hear her utter the single word "Never!"

Drue's eyes narrowed dangerously as she overlooked the courtyard. It had taken nearly all her strength to walk from the bed to the window, but the sight before her made her more determined to overcome the weakness.

She turned to Connaught. "I will not be carried out in my bedrobes."

He regarded her for a long moment before agreeing. "Very well, but you will ride in the cart. I do not care to spend my mount because you are too weak to sit a horse alone."

"It is not I who had trouble staying on my mount." Her words brought back visions of the forced march to England when Connaught had been her prisoner.

"I intend to see that it remains so," Connaught told her. "Now come and I will help you dress."

Though the wound was healing Drue found it painful to move her arms. She was grateful for Connaught's offer and even more grateful when he brought forth her vest. She hesitated a fraction of a heartbeat before removing her nightshirt.

She could feel the heat of his eyes as they swept across her body. Her breasts felt tight, clutched in a torturing grasp that only Connaught could sooth. She wanted to rub the sensation away, or better yet, to take his hands and place them on her body. She imagined Connaught's hard calloused palms caressing the softness that had been so long hidden.

Drue reached for the vest. It slipped to the floor between them as her movement brought her beyond the point of resistance and his hand fulfilled her fantasy, cupping her breasts in adoration.

She lay back, grateful for the support of his arms, while his fingers worked unthought-of magic through her body. The pain was coaxed from her breasts by the skill of his ministrations. Tightness turned to heat and pain to ecstasy. She thrust against the roughness of Connaught's hand, a roughness that only stimulated the more.

She could feel his breath moving against her skin. Her hands kneaded his arms and shoulders, working toward his neck as she realized his intent. Her heart pounded wildly as she awaited the moment when his mouth would sooth away the last remnant of pain.

The gentle moistness of his tongue contrasted delightfully with the roughness of his hands. Her hands pressed against his neck, wordlessly urging him to take away the wild sensations that filled her, but the relief she sought did not come. Instead, pain shot down through her body, centering itself in the very core of her being, leaving her once more unsatisfied, unfulfilled and burning with desire. Her body pressed against his, and she knew that he, too, longed for the ultimate release.

He lifted his head, looking long and hard into her golden eyes. A sigh escaped his lips as he released his hold and bent down to retrieve her vest. That he fought a battle within himself was obvious. It was the crux of the battle that was not clear to Drue.

She did not bother to take the vest from his hands, but instead stood straight and proud before him, the unspoken question hovering like a wraith between them.

"Had I continued, it would have been to culmination." The words tumbled from his lips. "What we have is too hard won! I will wait until you are my wife!"

Drue turned her face away. He misread her disappointment for maidenly relief. Taking her gently into his arms he lifted her face and looked into her eyes.

"I swear I will never do anything to cause you unhappiness," he whispered.

The words *Then why did you stop?* formed on Drue's lips. Formed and were bitten back. It was better this way, unculminated and uncomplicated.

In that mindless moment of passion she would have given herself to this man, surrendering a maidenhead few knew existed. But now, in the cold light of reason, she knew it could never be. His own words destroyed any hope. If he waited for her to give up her knighthood to become his wife, he would wait forever!

Yet it was not that simple, for Drue wanted Connaught. Wanted him with every fiber of her body, with every ounce of her great strength, and she could not rest until they were one.

On the afternoon of the second day of their journey, the storm was suddenly upon them. The sun that had shone so deceptively during the morning hours suddenly disappeared and black engorged clouds blocked out the sky.

There was no shelter. Wind whipped against man and beast, forcing the icy rain through the thickest cloak. Carts bogged down in the mud and the men cursed steadily as they fought to free them.

At one such halt, Drue made her way to Connaught's side.

"Leave the cart and find me a horse. If I must die of cold it will not be lying sodden on my back!"

Connaught reached down to her. "Take my hand and ride with me."

"It is unseemly that two knights ride together." Her voice was firm, but she secretly longed to feel the warm strength of his body close against her.

"Is it not time we ended this farce?" Connaught struggled for patience.

"This is no farce! Now find me a horse before I have them saddle one of the cart nags."

To her relief, he did as she asked without further argument. In truth her strength was all but spent. She would do well to gain the saddle without assistance. Connaught watched her closely as the horse was brought around.

Spurred on by his scrutiny and determined not to shame herself before the men, Drue climbed into the saddle.

Warmth transmitted itself through her muscular legs as they curved about the animal's body. Pleased, Drue urged her mount forward and fell in beside Connaught as they bent their heads against the raging elements.

"My lord—" the herald pulled his horse to a halt before Connaught "—there is an abandoned monastery less than a league away. Enough stands to give shelter."

Connaught looked over his entourage. The men were wet and exhausted. Studiously he kept his eyes from centering on Drue. He was aware that she stayed in the saddle through sheer willpower. His desire to take her to his castle where she would be safe had only caused grief. His gaze fell on her hands, locked together on the reins. She guided the horse with her legs and from instinct. For Drue, if for no other reason, they must seek shelter.

"Go on," Connaught ordered. "We will follow."

The broken walls of the monastery were a welcome sight as their outline emerged through the gray mist. While most of the building was in ruins, several of the cells, the main chapel and what remained of the kitchens were intact and offered warmth and shelter. Within the hour the damp smell of wood and wool permeated the air.

Drue sat huddled before the fire at the rear of the chapel. She did not move when Connaught came toward her.

"The men have taken over the kitchen," he told her. "We will stay here."

Drue still did not acknowledge his words. The steam rose about her as heat met the cold of her garments.

"You would be warmer if you were not wrapped in that wet cloak." Connaught reached down and unfastened the clasp, drawing the sodden material from her.

He tossed the cloak along with his own over a wooden kneeler close to the fireplace.

"I will bring food as soon as it is ready," he told the still-silent Drue. "In the meantime, wrap yourself in this fur rug. It is less wet than anything else I could find."

Drue took it obediently, but the rug did nothing to warm her through the sodden garments she wore. Wearily she removed them and wrapped herself in the heavy fur. Within minutes she was asleep.

Connaught did not try to waken her, but placed the gruel and meat near the hearth. After banking the fire, he shed his wet clothing and wrapped himself in his bedroll.

Wind howled through chinks in the wall and slashed at what was left of the windows. Long-forgotten voices blended in the ghostly halls and echoed through the troubled night.

In her sleep, Drue heard them. She heard her mother's voice from long ago. The voice urged her to be good and brave and to learn to fend for herself. And then the voice was silenced forever. She heard the single cry of the first man she had ever killed. Once again she felt the surge of terror she had known at taking the life of another human being. The terror was gone with the echo of the cry and a resolve remained in its place—a resolve never to allow herself to know the fear of death again. And then that voice, too, was silenced.

She heard the clash of swords as she fought at Turlock's side. Life was good! She loved every moment! She heard Turlock's limping footsteps and his voice exhorting her to greater effort. She heard his great battle cry resounding in the thunder of darkness. She remembered the many nights they had huddled together for warmth and companionship. She heard his voice, broken with pain: "Each time you fight you will feel me at your side!" And then his voice was silenced as well. But the scream that grew in Drue's throat could not be silenced. It burst from her lips and split the night with sound.

Connaught was beside her. "Your wound..." He shook her awake. "Has it reopened?"

Drue stared at him, unable to reply. In her life, each thing she had ever dared to love had been taken from her. Her mother; Garith, who belonged to an empty-headed wife; Turlock, whose death continued to devastate her to the depths of her soul. Dare she love the man bending over her? Or would he become a shade of the past if she allowed herself to do so?

The firelight danced on Connaught's face, giving him the appearance of a satyr. His eyes gleamed like blue-black coals in the gloom. She reached up and traced the outline of his lips with her finger. He took the tip into his mouth, sucking it gently.

"My wound is fine." Drue found her voice. "I had a nightmare."

Connaught did not speak, but slipped into the rug next to her, pulling his own bedroll around them for added warmth. If he expected a woman's soft body, he was brought back to cold reality without hesitation.

As hard and tense as his own solid physique, Drue's flesh bulged with sinew. He ran his hand down the taut skin. She shivered and moved closer, but there was no melting together of soft flesh against firm muscle. Their bodies met, radiating the tension of war-hardened physiques that longed to become one with the other, yet could not accept the sacrifices union demanded.

"There will be no more nightmares for us, Drue," Connaught whispered. "Now sleep...."

It was during that long and sleepless night that Drue came to terms with herself. She wanted this man. Wanted him as she had wanted no other in her lifetime. She longed

to become one with him. To shield him within her body
and make their love a reality. There was no other love for
her, nor would there be. Without Connaught, Drue could
never be complete. She nestled more closely against the
iron-muscled body. Its warmth belied the hard strength
now dormant in sleep. Automatically, Connaught's arms
closed about her. Muscle melded to muscle as steel is
wrought to steel when subjected to intense heat. His hands
moved over her as though memorizing each contour, while
his lips invoked little tremors of wildfire that danced tan-
talizingly through her veins.

Drue's mind seemed above her, as though she were dead
and looking down from lofty heights. Was this, indeed, a
little death? In accepting womanhood, would she destroy
the brave and valiant knight she had always been?

She closed her eyes lest Connaught see the fear that
threatened to betray her. He had awakened and was raised
on one elbow. She could feel the heat of his body on her
breasts, his weight on her thighs. Her eyes opened and she
gazed into his face.

The wind had changed directions and the makeshift
shutters on the window blew open. The draft caught the
dying embers, whipping them to flame just as their bodies
were whipped to flame by desire.

Connaught looked down into her golden eyes. Drue was
not beautiful, not in the womanly sense of the word. Her
features were too strong, too splendid. There was no word
for such godlike beauty. To Connaught, she was lovelier
than the most touted court lady. She was perfection. She
was his beloved. She would become his wife and the
mother of his children.

If the idea of Drue acting the role of a mother was incongruous, Connaught cast it aside. It would come, he
assured himself.

She was like a goddess, he thought, too far gone in desire to allow his tongue to form the words. The weight of her against his body sent shudders of passion coursing through him.

Drue felt the tremors vibrating against her. Silently cursing her inadequacies, she wished she had listened to the stories of lovemaking told around the camp fires. But, alas, she had paid little attention and now, when her whole being was dedicated to pleasing this magnificent man, she did not know how to do so.

She felt his finger trace down her arm and decided to follow his moves. What Connaught would do, Drue would do also! His hand traced the outline of her breast. Without hesitation, Drue's fingers returned the compliment. Connaught almost cried out in pleasure but held himself in check, believing her action to be a coincidence.

Connaught pressed his mouth over first one breast, then the other, greedily drawing in her sweetness. As he released her, Drue returned the favor. This time a deep moan escaped his lips, and Drue knew she followed the right course.

Connaught's desire-dulled brain comprehended the game Drue had chosen to play. His heart pounding at the possibilities, he continued to explore Drue's vibrant body with his hands and lips, and Drue in turn followed his lead, until the loveplay became so volatile it threatened their very sanity.

All secrets were revealed as they searched out the unknown. By his own act of taking, Connaught gave, for Drue followed his every lead, and by doing so, she not only gave of herself, but took the wild pleasure he offered, returning in kind.

His hands were instruments of diabolical ecstasy and his tongue a magic wand, while to him, her very willingness to participate equally in their lovemaking was a miracle.

He was beyond reason, his lofty promises forgotten. The waiting, the wanting must cease and the loving begin. The need was too intense, too immediate, too long withheld. He felt Drue shift beneath him and he moved into position. He must be gentle, he reminded himself. For all her strength, Drue was a woman, and belike a virgin.

Suddenly, Drue's hands pressed his shoulders, toppling him. The hard tips of her breasts tangled in the hair on his chest as she pushed him to his back.

Connaught opened his eyes, staring in disbelief as she knelt over him, poised for a moment before encasing him in the solid sheath of herself. Her firm, suede-lined warmth engulfed the throbbing steel of his weapon. Disregarding the pain, Drue forced it to the hilt before she began moving in the throes of an ancient rhythm.

The wind caught her hair, whipping it in abandon as she began her wild ride through the valley of passion. She rode like a Valkyrie—her breasts high and proud, her head thrown back, her body gleaming with exertion. But it was Connaught's voice that sounded the battle cry as they climbed to the pinnacles of rapture's volcanic mountain, exploding into the galaxy beyond desire to touch the sun.

Chapter Fifteen

The two boys stood straight and tall as their father approached. Their eyes were wide with curiosity. They'd had many questions but no answers since they had been taken from their ancestral home and brought across the sea to the lochs of Scotland.

Connaught dismounted, but they did not rush to him. Instead, they remained in place, waiting for their father to make his wishes known.

He embraced them roughly and they relaxed somewhat, but their eyes kept creeping back to the equally splendid knight who'd ridden at their father's side.

"Who is that knight, Father?" The smaller of the two lads squirmed out of Connaught's embrace and stared openly at Drue.

"That is my...friend, Drue of Duxton. Drue will be staying with us for a time," Connaught replied. If there was a note of discomfort in his voice the boys were too young to notice. Drue smiled in satisfaction. The fact that he had introduced her as Drue of Duxton was a victory in itself. A hard-fought victory, and one she had not been certain she had won.

A withered woman bustled down the stairs into the bailey. She dispensed with formalities by showing the boys back into the building, then, stopping before Connaught, she reached up and took his face in her hands.

"Patrick," she said fondly. "You look better than you did when last I saw you. More rested, but that's as it should be." Nodding her head, she started after the boys, but Connaught stopped her.

"Mother Graham, I would have you meet Drue, our guest."

The old woman's eyes were sharp. She did not speak as she scanned the young knight.

"Is this the same Drue over whom you woke the Irish countryside with your caterwauling nightmares?"

"The same," Connaught admitted somewhat sheepishly. Then, turning to Drue, he explained, "Mother Graham was my nurse and now she has the care of my sons."

Drue bowed slightly in acknowledgment of his words. She had guessed as much by the use of Connaught's given name. Tossing the reigns to a lackey, Drue slid to the ground. To her relief, Connaught did not attempt to help her. In the days since they'd left the monastery they had spent their time hunting sporadically and trying each other in easy competition. Drue's strength had returned. Only at the end of the day's ride would she admit she was tired, but never too tired to find renewal in Connaught's arms.

The carts were laden with freshly killed game and the litter carried not human cargo, but the carcass of a stag instead. Laughing together, Drue and Connaught mounted the stairs, only to be assaulted by an object that bounced through the doors and rolled to a stop at their feet.

It took a moment for Drue to realize it was a child. Then the little face peered upward. Bright brown eyes looked into hers; the turned-up nose wrinkled, and she noticed the mass of freckles sprayed across his pudgy cheeks. He shook his mop of red-brown hair and grinned.

Drue grinned back as she reached down and set him on his short, sturdy legs.

Glancing at Connaught, she was shocked to see the scowl of disapproval on his face. "This is my third son, Kyle," he said abruptly. "Mother Graham has apparently allowed him to slip from the nursery."

The smile on the boy's face was instantly erased. A look of panic replaced it. Dark eyes shifted from one towering knight to the other. It was obvious he did not recognize either of them.

Tears formed in the boy's eyes, tears he manfully fought to suppress. As though in answer to his prayers, Mother Graham appeared at the door.

"There you are," she scolded gently. "Come to greet your father, I'll wager! Well, here he is, just as I promised."

With that, Mother Graham lifted the child and placed him in Connaught's arms. Both father and son looked uncomfortable.

"Now," Mother Graham prompted, "have you nothing to say?"

The boy tried to squirm away, and finally settled for hiding his face in Connaught's neck. Drue watched with open curiosity. She remembered little of life before her introduction to the camps of her father and was sure such behavior would never have been allowed. The thought of any child clinging to Turlock amid the men of the army brought a smile to her lips.

To her surprise, Kyle was watching her from the folds of his father's cloak. Feeling somewhat reassured, the little boy lifted his head and managed to say, "Greetings, father."

Mother Graham nodded her approval. "He is learning so quickly now. Soon he will be old enough to share a room with his brothers. It's over three years since his birth."

"I remember." Drue's words escaped without conscious thought. "I remember when we received word of the birth."

Connaught lifted the lad to his shoulder. "I remember, too," he whispered as the giant doors swung open and they entered the gloom of Morrill Castle.

The rooms were barren, but Drue found no discomfort in them. There were few hangings on the walls, and those, old and faded, of battle scenes. It was small in comparison to many castles and the comforts were few, but Drue found no fault. The rough terrain and sharp cool air suited her, as did the excellent hunting. Even the simple food was to her liking. The first weeks went by uneventfully as she accompanied Connaught on inspections of his lands.

It wasn't until after Connaught set his affairs in order that the trouble began. Drue was about to go hawking when he called her to him.

"I have been waiting to speak with you," he told her.

Drue frowned. They shared their meals, their hunts, their recreation, even their bed; surely he had ample opportunity to speak with her. Something in the tone of his voice made her skin prickle, and the hair rose on the back of her neck. She did not take the chair he offered but stood before him, legs braced for what might ensue.

"I wish you to begin to wear more suitable clothing," Connaught intoned. "I intend to tell my sons that you are a woman. It is only fitting that you dress as such."

Drue stared in disbelief. A bubble of laughter started in her throat and floated upward, bursting suddenly in the silence of the room. "You jest" she gasped. "You cannot believe what you say!"

"I assure you, I am completely serious!"

Drue could see the truth of the statement in his face, but the thought was too incongruous to contemplate. Again she dissolved into laughter.

"Drue, for God's sake, control yourself! This is no laughing matter! We are friends, we are lovers, my sons need a mother. I cannot have my wife stomping about in full armor!"

"I am not wearing full armor, and I'm *not* your wife! Your sons would think you daft should you try to make them believe I am other than Sir Drue. Your idea is mad! There is no reason for this rash act!"

She started toward the door, but in one step he stood before her, holding her in place, his lips only a whisper away. "You love me! That is reason enough!"

Drue did not try to refute his words. Instead she stared into the blue depths of his eyes. Yes, she loved him. Beyond hope of salvation, she loved this man. Her eyes swept the strong lines of his face, the tanned skin pierced by the startling blue of his eyes, the broad brow. The dark hair with the little widow's peak that gave his countenance a wicked appearance; the sensuous lips above the strong, square chin. Though she never took her eyes from his face, her mind swept his magnificent body.

Where her own strength was in wiry agility, Connaught had the deep, heavily muscled chest, the mighty biceps that could hardly be spanned by both hands. He was all she was not. She loved him, she respected him as a warrior and leader on the field of battle, but she could not give up her identity. Not for Connaught... not for the overpowering love she felt for him. What she had was too hard gained, too precious. Like her virginity, once gone it could never be reattained. The moment word was out that Sir Drue was a woman, her credibility as a knight would be destroyed.

Connaught's arms tightened about her; she could feel his breath on her lips, the warmth of his mouth. He was waiting for her to acquiesce to his wishes, for which he would reward her with a kiss.

Drue stiffened in his arms. "There is no question of my love for you, Connaught." Her voice was as hard and unyielding as her body. "It is your love for me that is lacking."

He blinked in confusion. "Before God, Drue, you know I want no other save you!"

"But on your terms. You want a wife, and a mother for your sons. You want someone who will manage your household and be at your beck and call. I am not that person and until you accept me for what I am you cannot hope to love *me!* You only love the thing you want me to be."

He released his hold and she felt suddenly bereft. For a moment she wished she were other than she was, but there was no way she could change.

To her surprise, Connaught took the offensive. "It is you who lack in love!" he all but shouted. "I am willing to make you my wife."

"And what do you offer a wife that I do not have in my own right?"

"You would share my life, all that I have would be yours! You would have my love and my protection."

"Connaught, I do not need your protection! I already share your life and I have lands and estates of my own! You offer me nothing, yet as your wife I would forfeit all I own, including my identity. Your request is ridiculous!"

Pain and rage mingled in his eyes. He was too proud to beg or bargain for a wife. His marriage with Enid had been arranged when they were children, and since her death he had been approached by the most powerful houses in Europe with offers of women to wed. Drue was being petty and impossible to treat his offer of wedlock as an insult!

He sputtered with anger, wishing he'd never seen Drue. God knew, she was no beauty. Yet the body that had so repelled him when first he realized it was indeed that of a woman, now was his chief delight. When it was matched to his own, there was no height to which they could not climb. Their sexual appetites surpassed even the most erotic fantasies Connaught had dared imagine. Drue was completely uninhibited in her lovemaking. She held nothing back and was willing to give, take and experiment. From the night of their first encounter she had followed his lead, using her imagination and ingenuity to adapt Connaught's amorous adventures to her own.

Like him, she was inexhaustible. A knight, able to fight from dawn to darkness without stopping, was equally inexhaustible in bed.

No, Connaught would never be satisfied with anyone but Drue as his partner in love, or in life. Yet he had offered her all he had and she'd thrown it in his face.

His silence damned him in her mind; he didn't understand her. Brushing his hands away, she crossed the room with long strides.

"Only when you can accept me for what I am will I believe you love me," she challenged.

His face red with anger, he muttered, "We shall see!"

Drue kept her distance during the next few days, not wanting to bring about another scene. She went to him at night, for there was little talk between them in the hours of velvety passion. If he decided not to accept her as she was, he would eventually be forced to ransom her and she would not see him again. The thought of facing him on the field of battle was incongruous. It could not happen. No war was worth living in a world without the man she loved.

Bored with the quiet life of the castle, Drue began looking for something to take up her time. She was polishing her armor one morning when she looked down on the tilting yard to see young Patrick and his brother Devin practicing the art of swordsmanship. Their movements were awkward and reminded Drue of herself and her brother, Garith, at the same age. Little Kyle stood at the side of the field, his small sword in hand, the longing in his face visible even from Drue's great distance.

With sudden resolve she put aside her task and went down to the field.

"No, no, no!" Drue's sword dropped between the astonished boys. "You are hacking at one another like old women! Has your father not shown you the finer rudiments of fighting? Look at your shield, Patrick! The only thing you are protecting is your manhood. It will do you little good if your throat is sliced open!"

Patrick looked down. His face, already red from exertion, gained another shade at her words. Devin chuckled gleefully. Drue turned to him next.

"You have no cause to laugh, young man! You use your sword as though you were slicing a loaf of bread! Are you out to kill your enemy or do you believe this implement to be a wand that will magically dispose of him with the merest touch?"

Devin hung his head. "I didn't want to hurt my brother," he apologized.

"Nor should you need to hurt him. Where are your pads? Your legs and arms should be wrapped in bunting and tied with leather thongs, to allow the blow and protect you from the hurt." Drue shook her head as she regarded them. "This will not do! You should not be allowed to fight, even in play, without proper protection and instruction."

"But I want to be a great knight like my father," Devin protested before Patrick could open his mouth.

"And so you shall be," Drue promised. "But not like this! You could do dire harm to each other this way." She turned the boys toward the castle and shoved them before her. "I will see to it you have the proper equipment and I'll teach you myself."

Patrick stopped and appraised her from head to foot. "Are you as great a knight as our father?" he asked speculatively.

Drue took a breath. "Do you remember when your father was held for ransom by the English?"

Devin shook his head, but Patrick remembered. "That was long ago," he said. "Before Kyle was born."

"Yes," Drue agreed, "long ago. But I captured him. He was my prisoner. Now, do you want my instruction or shall I go back to tending my armor?"

"Yes, please." Devin tugged at her hand.

"Yes, please, which?"

"Yes, please teach us, Sir Drue." Patrick spoke for both of them. "We would be honored."

Drue smiled, boredom forgotten as they continued across the field. A slight movement caught her attention.

"Come along, Kyle," she called. "We might as well outfit you, too. You're a great hulking lad and there's no reason you shouldn't heft a sword along with the rest."

Kyle bounced across the field like a friendly puppy and Drue wondered if she might not regret her impulsive offer.

Within two days Drue had the boys outfitted in padded armor and using lightweight, wrapped weapons. She worked with them for three hours every morning, either in the tilting yard or, if the weather was inclement, in the cavernous gloom of the great hall.

Connaught did not comment on their activities, but kept close watch on the relationship between Drue and his sons. Although he was pleased that they had become fond of one another, he was perturbed by the mode their friendship had taken. The boys admired Drue and respected her as a teacher and a knight. Still, this relationship was better than hostility. He felt they would be more apt to accept Drue as a stepmother once the truth were known and the shock overcome.

Busy with the demands of his estates, Connaught left them much to their own devices, thinking to set matters in the proper perspective as soon as he had time. It was little Kyle who brought the matter to a head.

A dispute had arisen over some property bordering Connaught's land. Connaught had been forced to take up arms against the sullen neighbor, and Drue had gladly joined him. They enjoyed fighting side by side and returned to Loch Morrill victorious.

The gloomy clouds released their burden at their arrival and the knights sloshed into the castle, shaking water from their wet cloaks.

Connaught's sons clattered down the worn stairs into the hall.

"Father!" Patrick gasped out in excitement. "We practiced in the yard before the rain. We let Kyle use my shield and he fought Devin."

Kyle catapulted into the room. "I won, Da!" he cried. "I won!"

Connaught's smile turned to a frown and then to a black scowl as his youngest son threw himself into Drue's arms.

"I beat Devin, Da!"

Drue was oblivious to the fact that Connaught's child had addressed her with a name usually reserved for a father. She flung her cloak to a lackey. "Get your sword and show me," she ordered.

Kyle hurried off, while the other boys excitedly related how their tutoring had been instrumental in Kyle's accomplishment.

When Kyle reappeared, Drue dropped to one knee. "Now, sir knight, have a go at me!"

She drew her long dagger, which was only a bit shorter than Kyle's sword. He parried and thrust with much greater skill than she had imagined him capable. "Enough!" she said finally. "What think you, Connaught? Should we take him with us on our next skirmish?"

But Connaught only growled something from his vantage point beside the massive fireplace. Thinking Connaught upset because Kyle had the lion's share of the attention, Drue told Devin to come forward. "Show me the stroke you attempted when Kyle made his touch," she ordered.

Devin thought a moment before going into action. A few moves later Drue stopped him. "There is your mistake. Raise your sword in this position when you see your enemy coming at you, so!"

Devin went over the move several times before Drue was satisfied. It was then Connaught finally broke his silence.

"Thank Drue for helping you and be off to your rooms. We have all had a tiring day."

The boys grudgingly obeyed, each making his bow, but little Kyle could not contain his exuberance and he hugged Drue, armor and all.

"Goodnight, Da," he said softly.

Connaught cringed. So it had not been a mistake on the boy's part. The child actually saw Drue as a father figure! It was unthinkable! It must be changed!

The next morning Connaught called Mother Graham to him. "I want a gown. Something plain, but elegant."

Mother Graham nodded happily. The man needed a woman. She was aware that Drue and Connaught shared the same room, and dared not think what might be happening behind the closed, locked doors. This man had been in her charge since birth. She had been his wet nurse and had nurtured him throughout his life. She could not bring herself to believe what her eyes and ears told her.

"We have many gowns in the coffers of the castle. Perhaps one of them?" she suggested.

"No! It must be large!"

"How large?"

He spanned the air with his hands. "So! And long enough to fit me."

If he noticed the look of shocked dismay on Mother Graham's face, Connaught did not comment on it.

The fashion of the day consisted of a rather shapeless underdress covered with a surcoat trimmed in fur. It was simple to adapt one size to another because of the many yards of material used in the flowing undergarment. Only the length posed a problem, but several days later, Mother Graham reluctantly produced an oversized gown.

Connaught held it up against his own body to judge the length while the old nurse looked on in abject horror.

Stunned by the prospective dishonor that was about to overpower her nursling, the old woman went to the kitchen hearth and dipped a bowl of gruel from the pot on the hob.

"You are quiet tonight, Mother," Innes, the steward, noted. "Are your young charges unwell?"

"The children are fine, it be their father I worry about," she said, shaking her head.

"Go on," the man urged. "I know of no problem with my lord."

Mother Graham let Innes think he was dragging the information from her. "Sir Drue is usurping my lord's place in the hearts of his sons." Not to mention his own heart, she thought, and eternal soul. "The young man is bored. As a prisoner Sir Drue should have been ransomed long ago!"

Innes started visibly. "I had not realized Sir Drue was a prisoner. The two men seemed . . ." He was about to say "so close," but thought better of it in deference to the old woman's sensibilities. "To be good friends!"

"Aye, that they are," Mother Graham agreed. "My lord thinks of Drue as a brother. Still, I cannot believe this prolonged captivity is good for either of them. Sir Drue should be back with his own people in England. It is only a matter of time before the lad attempts escape. Perhaps that would be best for all concerned."

She shook her head sadly, watching the steward's reaction from the corner of her eye. "I would stake my life there will be a vast reward for the person brave and canny enough to help Sir Drue return to his own land. He be wealthy in his own right, if what I hear is true."

"If ye be wrong and Sir Drue does not choose to go it could mean a man's life." Innes fell easily into the vernacular of the simple folk.

"Poor lad has no notion such is possible, thinking himself guarded day and night. Of course, it is a long, difficult trek to the borders. None of us could undertake the journey."

The steward seemed lost in thought, then said, "I know a man who might be willing to take the chance. He is newly

come to this area. A crafty Scot, he is. I will feel him out
when next I see him.''

Satisfied, Mother Graham finished her gruel. The idea
had been presented. Pray God it would not be too late!

Chapter Sixteen

The watery light of dawning filtered through the heavy hangings on the bed. Connaught slipped away from the warm naked body molded against his own. Silently, he snatched up his bedrobe and began searching out each article of clothing. Within minutes he had removed every remnant of wearing apparel, Drue's and his own. Smiling to himself, he placed the gown across the bench where Drue could not fail to see it.

He felt a moment's guilt as he ran his hand over Drue's vest, but brushed the feeling aside as he locked the garments in an empty coffer in an unused garderobe. Someday Drue would thank him, he assured himself as he dressed. Someday, if she didn't kill him first! He smiled as he hurried down the hall. It was only after he reached the lower floor of the castle that he realized he still wore his soft leather shoes, his riding boots forgotten in the room where Drue was now awakening.

"I will not wear that thing!" Drue shouted as Mother Graham set a tray of food and ale on the low table.

The old woman stared at the blanket-wrapped figure who clomped incongruously across the floor, feet encased in Connaught's forgotten boots. Mother Graham closed her eyes. "Merciful heaven, what has he done?" she gasped. So it was not for himself he wanted the dress, but for Sir Drue, and from the looks of it, the young man was not amused at the idea.

"Find me some suitable clothes, good mother," Drue pleaded. "Surely you can see I cannot wear that outrageous garment!"

As she spoke, Drue was careful to keep her body covered. Should the old woman discover her secret, Drue was relatively certain Mother Graham would not find either the idea or the garment outrageous.

"I will do what I can," Mother Graham stammered. "But I believe your things are locked away and only my lord Connaught has the key. Oh, Patrick is a naughty lad. He has surely done a bad thing this time." The old woman's eyes narrowed. "I cannot think what has possessed him. He is not himself to act so! To take out his wrath on a poor prisoner and strive to humiliate you before the whole castle! It is unheard of!" She moved toward the door, praying silently with each breath that God would help her to save her beloved nursling from sure hellfire. "How you must long to return to your own people. It's sure I'd be willing to do anything in my power to end this embarrassing interlude and see you safely home."

There! Another seed was sown! Now it was up to Sir Drue to nurture it into fruitfulness.

Drue declared a state of siege, refusing to allow Connaught to enter the room, and at the same time, refusing to come out. Wrapped in the quilt, she pouted in front of the fire.

In truth, Drue did not "long" to return to her own people. Had Connaught not been so bullheaded, she would have been content to spend the rest of her life with him, but on her terms! Once again she got to her feet and kicked the hated garment across the floor. Why had he done this to her? She missed working with the boys and knew they had been told Sir Drue was indisposed and could not leave his room.

It could not remain thus! Connaught forced her hand! She must leave Morrill Castle, leave the lads and their knightly pursuits. Oddly enough, of the children, it was the thought of leaving little Kyle that pained her the most. Perhaps now that Connaught had seen the child's potential as a natural warrior, he would be more considerate. It was obvious to Drue that Connaught hardly knew his youngest son, and the child knew so little of his father he could not pick his own sire when faced with a choice.

The thought struck her that it might be possible to take Kyle with her. Surely they would not be pursued the less whether she was alone or with Connaught's unwanted son.

She cancelled the thought as preposterous. A sop to her own premonition of lifelong loneliness. If she could not have the father, the son was a poor substitution, and a dangerous one to boot. Her only hope was to enlist sympathy and help from Mother Graham, and that sympathy would surely not extend to stealing Kyle.

She tore the linens from the bed and wrapped them tightly about her body, fashioning a pseudo vest that served to cover and secure her bodily contours, finishing only seconds before Mother Graham knocked on the door.

"I brought you some water for washing." The old woman bustled across the floor with her burden.

Drue watched the old nurse so closely the woman became nervous.

"You would not attack an old woman?" Mother Graham sputtered. "Surely that is beneath your vows of knighthood."

"And is it knighthood that has allowed Connaught to lock me up until I submit to his perverted humor and dress in this disgusting manner?" She poked at the gown.

Mother Graham shook her head. "I told you I be sorry for the lad's disposition. I cannot think what has come over him."

"It seems you are the only friend I have here," Drue said softly. "The only one who understands how I long to return to my own land, my own people. My father would pay dearly for my release."

"You mean ransom?" Mother Graham could not look Drue in the eye. She was betraying her lord and the penalty for that was death, but what Connaught was trying to force this young man to do was worse, and the penalty damnation. There was no choice.

"Call it what you like," Drue snapped across the room. "I would be away. Know you someone who might be sympathetic to my cause?"

Mother Graham prayed for forgiveness. "I could send the steward, Innes, to you. I feel certain I can convince him your release is for the best."

"I feel certain you can," Drue agreed.

It took very little time for the plans to be formulated. Mother Graham and Innes were anxious to have Drue away, but no more anxious than was Drue herself.

It would take so little to make her stay. The right word from Connaught and there was no power on earth that could make her leave his side. But he was not fain to speak that word. He came nightly and knocked on the door, requesting admittance. From the day he had shut her in and taken her clothes her answer had always been no, but tonight she answered pleasantly.

"Very well then, enter!"

Connaught opened the door cautiously, expecting an ambush. To his surprise, Drue stood far across the room next to the hearth. His heart filled with joy as he realized she was wearing the gown.

"Well," she prompted, "are you not going to tell me how lovely I look? Can you not truthfully say I am a vision to surpass all visions?

In truth, she looked uncomfortable and out of place in woman's trappings. Connaught could not bring himself to tell an outright lie, especially when she was aware of the incongruity of her appearance.

"You always look beautiful to me." That was the truth, no more, no less.

Drue swallowed a lump that rose, unbidden, to her throat. Part of her wanted to go to him and beg him to allow her to remain as she had been when they met. To plead with him to let her live the only life she knew, to live it with him, always, so that she would never be forced to leave him.

He came to her, slipping his arms around the solid firmness that was the trunk of her body.

She relaxed against him, her mind whirling as his hands moved over her. How vulnerable a woman was, she mused. Their very mode of dress gave a man easy access to their most cherished secrets. But she had no secrets from Connaught, and if she must leave him in order to survive, she would leave him with the memory of a night such as he had never dreamed.

In his initial shock at Drue's appetite for passion, Connaught had not given thought to the fact that while he explored the wonders of her body, she was learning each point of maddening eroticism that drove Connaught wild with desire. Drue had done it without thought. She had done it to please the man she loved, her whole being thrown into lovemaking with as deep a dedication as she had put into learning the art of war so many years before.

His kisses deepened but she pushed away. "I have wine," she offered.

"I want no wine but you." He reached for her again, but she strode across the room, the sound of her heavy boots echoing against the stone floor.

"Do you feel the attire on your feet is suitable?" he asked.

"Far more suitable than that on my back!" But she managed to soften the words with a smile, and Connaught allowed himself to feel assured that she did but tease.

Drue poured two goblets of rich, red wine, handing one of the cups to Connaught as she urged him to sit down at the table. There was a platter of bread, meat and cheese from which she served him.

"I had no idea you were such a charming serving wench." He grinned approvingly.

Drue pulled her grimace into some semblance of a smile. "I learned much as a page and squire, my lord. I feel sure you will find me able to fulfill your wishes and suit all your needs."

He ran his hand down her body, drawing her against him. "I have no doubt that I shall."

It was a strange game they played. Doubly dangerous, for one of them must be the loser and the other had no notion of the odds. Drue plied Connaught with wine, but his need was not for drink, but for the body that shimmered in the firelight, beckoning, enticing, tempting through the folds of the gown.

Drue's very awkwardness drove Connaught to the brink of destruction. He had been without her for the better part of a week and could think of nothing more than holding her, caressing her, becoming one with her.

Drue sensed his desperation and knew she had no hope of putting her plan into action until his appetite was assuaged. Her greatest fear was that she would be unable to carry through her escape once Connaught made love to her again. How could she live without knowing the magic of his lips, the wonder of his body, the miracle of his love? A silent sob escaped her as she turned to him, her body silhouetted by the fire. She held out her arms, palms upward, as though in supplication.

As he took her hands she allowed him to ease her onto the heavy fur before the hearth.

"This first." She lifted her foot, indicating the heavy boot.

Connaught smiled and stood astride her leg while she pushed against his body until the first boot came away. As his hand moved down her leg Drue felt a little tingle of excitement. There was something different in the feeling invoked as his hand slipped up beneath the skirt. Something secretive and promising; something Drue had never felt before. Connaught's hand moved across her naked flesh, slowly savoring every sinew. For once, Drue felt inadequate. There was no way she could match this. She lay back and allowed herself to drift on the warm breeze of his touch.

She felt soft and open, and she felt afraid. Her fear spoke.

"I have another leg, and another boot," she reminded him, amazed that her voice could be so steady.

Again he stepped across her. This time her bare foot moved in little circles along his back, squirming up beneath his doublet in an effort to find the flesh beneath. He did not move under her ministrations. Only when she placed her foot against his buttock did he take up his task in earnest. Then the other leg was free and subject to the same attention given the first. Drue sighed as she felt the skirt creep up about her waist.

Connaught stood to free himself of his own clothing, and Drue, moving with maddening slowness, held him at leg's length, rendering him helpless to do more than gaze at the shimmering promise before him. His body throbbed and quickened under the wild prodding of her feet. She wrestled with him, never allowing him the advantage of more than a glimpse of gleaming flesh.

Her movements became more sensuous, more urgent, but his became insane. He clutched her legs, desperately twisting to be away from her ministrations. This was not the Drue he had known. Some maddening enchantress had taken over the muscular body. In the dim firelight her skin took on a smooth, creamy glow. It looked soft and inviting. It tempted and insinuated promises heretofore unknown. And it would not allow him to achieve his desire. Her feet and legs trapped him, even as they played their wicked game of temptation.

Connaught's whole being became centered on Drue's body. He felt as though he must surely explode if she did not release him. He was bathed with sweat.

Drue's foot slipped from the sweat-slicked stomach, and instantly he found his goal, piercing her with the sweet shaft of desire that sent her into a dizzying vortex of sensation.

She could not deny it. Their lovemaking was good, even though she must endure it tangled in the web of cloth. In the end it was that web that made her decision for her.

As they lay together after the first onslaught of passion was assuaged, he slipped the accursed dress over her head. Her body rippled and gleamed in the firelight. Like suede, it demanded to be stroked and, like suede, it was warm and pliant beneath his hands.

She in turn followed every line of his body, memorizing each scar, each bulging sinew, for she must, from this night on, only remember. Love would be denied her, as would children. There would be no more small arms wrapping themselves about her body in delighted affection. This night would end it all. There would be no tomorrow.

As her body rode to the pinnacles of love, Drue heard her voice shouting wildly, brokenly, and then there was nothing. She was falling into the void from which she had escaped when Connaught had willed life back into her body. How she wished he had not, for the pain of leaving him was a thousand times greater now. How she wished he would have a change of heart and she would not be forced to go.

Connaught released his hold and she moved away, both of them spent with the exertion of their passion. Drue got to her feet and poured another goblet of wine, carefully adding the potion Mother Graham had supplied before offering it to him. Connaught drank thirstily.

Drue glanced into the bowl of the goblet and laughed. "You have drunk it all. I must pour again for myself." He laughed with her as she refilled his glass and returned it to him.

Within minutes she could feel his head lolling heavily against her shoulder. It was but a few minutes before he was asleep. She made to move away, but her movements awakened him. His arms clamped about her and his eyes moved over her naked body.

"You are cold." He murmured the damning words: "Put on the dress." And then he was deeply asleep.

It was as though there were two different entities vying for possession of her body, Drue mused. There was Drue,

who had come to know the art of love and used only the
direct approach, giving as well as taking pleasure in her
partner's passion. And, now, there was a character who
teased coyly. A character who had neither Drue's respect
nor acceptance. An enemy who, if given free rein, would
destroy Drue and that for which she stood. Even her great
love for Connaught could not force her to relinquish the
inborn instinct for survival. Her decision would stand. She
must leave him, for his good as well as her own.

The potion had done its job. When Connaught's
breathing became even, Drue slipped away. She watched
him, feasting her eyes on his magnificent body as she
slipped into his clothing. He must be kept from following
her should the old woman have been too sparing with her
herbs, allowing him to recover before Drue was well away.

Innes, the steward, had promised to secure a guide who
would procure horses and show her the safest road to the
border. It would all be to no avail should Connaught recover quickly enough to overtake her. It must not happen! Drue smiled as the last of her plan formed in her
mind.

She took up the dress and moved toward Connaught's
inert figure.

Innes stood outside the postern gate holding the reins of
Drue's horse.

"Your guide will meet you on the other side of the village. He knows the roads well and will see you through to
your destination."

"Very well," Drue agreed. "I will send the reward back
with him."

"No, please, my lord, do not. If you could send a messenger of your own I would feel easier. It may be that I will
not have a place should my lord Connaught discover what

has transpired this night. I would feel easier if I knew the monies would be available should they be needed for my family."

Drue nodded. The man's words said more than he intended. Apparently he did not know or trust the guide he had procured. Drue would take this into account and watch him closely.

"Go with God," Innes whispered as Drue led her horse down the dirt path.

As she rounded the corner of the outside wall she heard a sound behind her. Sword drawn, she turned, almost skewering Kyle, who ducked beneath the blade and attached himself to her leg.

"I am ready!" he gasped breathlessly.

"Ready?" Drue repeated.

"To go hunting! You promised, remember?" His voice broke on the edge of disappointment.

"I did not forget, Kyle, but this is not the usual hunt." For I will be the hunted, she added silently.

"But you promised. And I waited and watched for you to get better and leave your room all these long days."

Perhaps it was indeed the answer to her prayers. Perhaps she was meant to take this lad. But if Connaught forgave her for escaping, he would never forgive her for taking his son, though he cared little for the boy.

Time was fleeting. Drue must be away. Now she was saddled with a guide who was not to be trusted and a wayward, headstrong child. She must make her decision quickly.

Dropping to one knee, she held Kyle at arm's length. "I am not going hunting, Kyle. I must return to my own country. Your father may be angry and hurt. It is best you stay with him."

She could see the tears glistening like moist stars in the darkness. The lips moved silently as the child looked from the knight kneeling before him to the dark, looming walls of the castle.

"Take me with you, Da." His voice choked with the effort it cost him. "I will be your page. I can do it! Please, Da, I want to stay with you."

Drue closed her eyes. Connaught would raise a hue and cry that would be heard throughout the Christian world. But win or lose in this gamble with fate, she would accept the challenge. The gods had answered her prayers and she would not deny the opportunity. In one quick motion she put Kyle on her horse.

"So be it!" she murmured to the night as they started toward the village.

The man waited, as promised, by the village gates. He was small and reminded Drue of a rodent. There was something familiar about him, but in the darkness she could not make it out.

"I contracted to take only one person," he growled.

"There are two." It was a flat statement.

"Then the cost will be double."

There was no time to argue. The first glimmer of dawn appeared above the rolling hills.

"Agreed." Drue swung to the back of her horse. Kyle rode behind her in the great saddle as they galloped through the ghostly mists of the Scottish countryside.

Drue smiled to herself as she thought of Connaught discovering that not only had his prisoner but his son, as well, had escaped. Had her grudging guide known of the probable consequences, it was likely he would have demanded triple pay, and in advance.

The naked branches of the trees reached toward them with gnarled hands. Drue felt Kyle shift uneasily. Remembering Connaught's recurring nightmares, Drue turned to him.

"Are you frightened of the night?" she asked.

"I am never frightened as long as I am with you, Da," he replied, love closely akin to worship glowing in his eyes.

Drue's heart constricted in her chest. "Good," was all she could manage, as thoughts of Connaught threatened to overwhelm her.

Who now would fight off the demons that threatened Kyle's father? Why had the man insisted on announcing to the world that a woman shared his bed and held away the nightmares that plagued every knight beyond the age of puberty? What was he doing now? Had he awakened, and would he be more angry to find Drue missing or at the absence of his unloved son? Or would his fury be centered on the trick she had played on him, the last move in this game of sexual dominance that had destroyed their chance of happiness?

Connaught stirred as Mother Graham's muffled gasp disturbed his drugged sleep. The old woman clapped her hands over her mouth. She did not want her lord to awaken so soon, but had been unable to keep from entering the room and checking on his welfare. The sun was high in the sky and the room bathed in light, making the dress-clad figure lying before the hearth look all the more ridiculous.

The old woman shook her head. Surely Sir Drue had not needed to take revenge in such form. Yet it would give Connaught pause before he left the room to search for his own clothing. Perhaps the young man had been right at that. A small smile on her face, the old woman tiptoed from the room.

Chapter Seventeen

Connaught shouted for Drue until the thick walls of the castle trembled.

When she did not appear he threw open the bedroom door. The shocked look on the face of the serving girl caused him to consider his mode of dress. Rage replaced any inherent modesty Connaught might otherwise have possessed. He clutched the offensive garment and rent it from top to bottom. The scream of tortured material cut through the busy castle and all eyes turned upward as Connaught strode naked onto the gallery overlooking the great hall.

"Where is Drue?" he demanded of the astonished servants.

There was a buzz of voices and a titter from one of the serving wenches, but no one volunteered the information.

It was Mother Graham who dared face his wrath and crept up the stairs, cringing at the extent his anger must reach when he learned of the plot against him. And know he would, for her plans had gone awry. Not only was Drue gone, but the child, Kyle, was also missing. It had not occurred to the old woman that the love between the heretofore unwanted child and the young knight might be so strong as to make separation unbearable.

Mother Graham knew all too well that Connaught held little affection for his youngest son. The child had been born at a difficult time, with the father a prisoner of the English. It had been months before news of the birth had reached him, and when Connaught returned he was a changed man, avoiding not only his wife but his sons, as well. To the new babe, he paid little mind, hardly acknowledging the infant's existence.

Drue's encouragement had been the first the lad had known. It was no wonder the boy had grown to worship the young man who taught him the rudiments of weaponry and included him, along with his brothers, in lessons of knightly skill.

But surely there was no reason for Sir Drue to snatch the boy from his rightful place. Did the knight intend to hold the child for ransom, turning the tables on the father?

Connaught must be told before Sir Drue crossed the border.

The bone-aching chill turned to rain as the horses raced toward England. Tam silently thanked the heavens for the miserable weather. It had given him an excuse for keeping his face covered. He had recognized Drue immediately, though the presence of the boy had thrown him off guard. He had not heard that Sir Drue had a son, but such must be the case. The child called the knight "Da" and obviously adored him. Tam MacBurgh knew instinctively that he must not allow Sir Drue to recognize him as the man who had thwarted the attempted escape from Stirling. He thanked providence he had allowed his beard to grow during the past few months, thus altering his appearance.

Night was upon them when Drue ordered a halt.

"We should ride on." Tam sank lower into the folds of his plaid.

"The boy is tired." Drue dismounted and lifted the weary child from the saddle. "We are not followed. We will rest for a few hours."

They ate the meat and cheese Mother Graham had supplied and let the horses graze on the tough brown grass. Tam kept his distance, watching for any sign of recognition. He had fallen on hard times and was much in need of the promised reward, doubled now with the advent of the child. All would be lost if the knight suspected his identity. To his relief, Sir Drue seemed entirely engrossed with the welfare of the child.

Kyle was soaked through and Drue was grateful for the thick woolen clothing they wore. Even when wet, it retained its ability to warm. Still, she took the risk of lighting a fire. Their guide sat across from them, deep in the shadows. She stared at him across the flames. Kyle moved closer and she reached over and drew him into the folds of her cloak.

"Are you thinking of my lord Connaught, Da?" Kyle asked.

"I was thinking of my own father, Kyle, and how surprised and happy he will be to see us."

"You think he will like to see me?"

"Of course he will." Drue ruffled the boy's hair. "We will make a tour of my holdings and then I will return to my father in the field. He will have need of me." More need with Turlock gone, she added silently.

The boy's eyes shone with excitement.

"Is your father a great champion?"

"My father is one of the highest lords of the realm. My friend and teacher, Turlock, was the King's champion."

"Will I meet your friend Turlock?"

"No." Drue felt the familiar tightness in her throat. "He is dead."

"Did he die in battle?" the child persisted.

"He died to save me," Drue answered.

The child sank against Drue's warmth. "Will you tell me of his battles?" he asked.

Drue smiled, remembering how she and Garith had enjoyed listening to Turlock's tales. She had never tired of them. The thought niggled at her mind that they should be on their way, but the temptation was too great. The night was cold and wet; surely no one would be mad enough to ride out in blind pursuit. She settled herself against a log and began telling Kyle one of the stories of Turlock, the King's champion.

"I swear to you, your lordship, I know nothing more." Innes groveled on the floor. "Sir Drue wanted to be away and offered a good reward. When the man came around asking to serve as a guide, it seemed like an act of God!"

"Act of God!" Connaught snorted. "You'll be praying to God for an act before I have done with you."

Mother Graham crept toward them. She had confessed her part in the escape, and the care of Connaught's remaining sons had been taken from her.

Now she spoke again. Having Patrick and Devin taken from her and being sent back to Ireland were punishment enough. Surely there was nothing more Connaught could do to her, save death, and that would be a welcome respite from the drudgery that would henceforth be her lot.

"My lord, it was not Innes's idea." She dropped stiffly to her knees. "It was mine. I could not bear to see what was happening to you. You were forcing that poor young man to be something he was not. It was only after you ordered him to wear the dress that he asked to talk to Innes. It was as much your fault as it is that of anyone here."

"You interfere in matters of which you know nothing!" Connaught said, but even to ease the poor woman's mind he could not bring himself to betray Drue's secret. "I do not wish to hear your excuses, woman. I want to know where they went and how quickly they will reach their destination." He ran his fingers through his thick hair in agitation. "There are a dozen roads they could have taken to the border. Have you no clue as to which one they chose?" He turned again on Innes and the man cringed.

"Tam mentioned having friends near Kendal. He might have put for—"

Innes got no further, for Connaught's iron fist closed about his throat and he was jerked to his feet.

"Tam who? What was his full name? Tell me, man, before I choke it from you!"

"He said his name was Tam MacBurgh, my lord." Innes wheezed the words, falling heavily to the floor as Connaught released him.

"God in heaven! Does Drue know?"

"I have no way of knowing," Innes stammered. "They met near the village. I stayed behind."

"Then you did not see if Kyle was, indeed, with them."

Again Mother Graham could not contain her silence. "The child loved Sir Drue. He watched and waited every day this long week for the knight to take him hunting. When Kyle heard noises in the early morn, he would leap from his bed to see if Sir Drue was coming for him. If he had thought Sir Drue was leaving he would have gone to him."

"Was it not your job to watch Kyle?" Connaught asked.

"I never thought Sir Drue would take the child."

"But Drue *has* taken the child, and if what you tell me is true, they are being led across Scotland by the man responsible for the death of Drue's friend, Turlock."

"Perhaps Tam MacBurgh would be willing to see that Sir Drue is recaptured once again," Mother Graham suggested.

"Perhaps he would," Connaught agreed, "if the man has not already murdered them in their sleep."

Mother Graham caught her breath at the impact of Connaught's words. "There is no reward for dead bodies," she reminded him.

Against her better judgment and in spite of her guide's obvious agitation, Drue traveled more slowly in deference to Kyle. Although the child never complained, it was obvious he tired toward the end of the day. In truth, Kyle longed for the evening hours when he could snuggle near Drue and listen to stories of knights and battles. Sometimes Drue told him of battles she had fought. One of these recitations prompted his question. "Is my father the greatest knight you ever fought against?"

"He is," Drue answered without hesitation.

"Tell me of the first battle you had with him," the boy urged.

Drue laughed. "For centuries the Scots have been creeping across the border into England and raiding the villages. It has been thus longer than any living man can remember, and will no doubt continue to be so long after we are both dead." She paused, thinking back across the years. "It was during a border raid that I first came in contact with your father."

Drue smiled. She loved to relive even the battles she had shared with Connaught. So engrossed was she in her story, she did not notice the attention being paid them by their guide. Nor did she realize the man had pricked up his ears when Kyle had mentioned his father.

The little man drew nearer, listening attentively as Drue finished her tale.

"Would you fight my father again?" Kyle asked.

"I would not wish to fight Connaught again," Drue said honestly, "for I believe when next we meet it must be a battle to the death."

"But you love my father, just as you loved your friend Turlock. You would not want to harm him," the child protested.

"That is true, but he wants me to change and I cannot do so." Drue shook her head. "And now, he will never forgive me for taking you. Regardless of whether he pays much mind to you, Kyle, you are still his son and I have stolen you away."

Kyle paused thoughtfully. "Once I am a knight I will return and make peace with him. He will be proud of me then, for I will be a great champion, like you and Turlock."

"And your father," Drue added quietly.

"And my father," the boy repeated, unaware of the silent figure slipping into the shadows.

The boy was not Sir Drue's son after all. Instead Kyle was son to Connaught. There was no doubt in Tam MacBurgh's mind that the boy's father was hot on their trail and the meeting between the knights would not be a friendly one. If Sir Drue was killed there would be no reward, but if the boy was returned unscathed, surely a reward would be warranted. A smile passed across Tam's lips. There was more than one way to skin a cat and he knew them all.

After that, Tam's ventures in hunting took him farther from the campsite.

"It takes you longer to snare a rabbit than it would take me to kill a wild boar," Drue complained.

The little man only smiled. His beard had disguised him adequately and he no longer bothered to hide his countenance. He knew he would not be recognized.

"Most assuredly," he agreed, "but a cry would be raised from the lord who owns the land and hence, title to the boar. No, it is better if you allow me to supply food."

They were but a day's ride from the border when Tam's far-reaching search bore fruit. Scarcely an hour to the north, Tam saw signs of hard-riding horsemen. Certain it was Connaught, he returned to Drue and suggested they make camp.

"If it pleases you, sire, we would be able to cover the remainder of the distance on the morrow," he offered. "The boy would have a good and warm place to sleep at Kendal Castle tomorrow night. I have made arrangements for your welcome."

"I am not tired!" Kyle protested, but Drue overruled him and they camped at the edge of a copse of trees.

While Tam went in search of food, Drue and Kyle performed their evening ritual of practicing with weapons. The child was adept with the small sword she had fashioned for him and Drue was amazed at his prowess. Her pride knew no bounds as she encouraged him with the same phrases Turlock had used. Like Drue, Kyle wanted nothing more than to learn the rudiments of arms. She remembered the yearning she had felt at his age, and their closeness was augmented with each practice session.

So great was their concentration, neither of them noticed how long a time it had been since Tam had gone from camp. Only with the sound of horses pounding toward them did they become aware of the danger.

Instantly, Drue was on her feet. She knew the moment of reckoning had come. In her heart she prayed that Connaught would forgive her the joke of leaving him dressed in woman's clothes and understand that she, no more than he, could stand to wear them. But in her mind she knew it would not be so. She had insulted his manhood, not only by offering her love and her body without giving her spirit to his keeping, but also by allowing Kyle to accompany her.

"Go to the trees," she ordered. "Do not come forth until this is finished, one way or the other!"

Kyle went white. His legs froze to the ground, but his spirit rose up to meet the challenge. "I will stay and fight at your side."

Tears like acid burned behind Drue's eyes as she heard Turlock's voice echo the words.

"The first lesson of a good page is to obey orders. No matter how well you bear arms, if you cannot obey you will never be a knight!" She pushed him toward the wood. "Now go!"

Kyle flung himself against her armored body. "I love you, Da! No matter what happens, I love you!" And then he was gone.

Drue watched the child disappear. She knew the true meaning of his words. In his own heart Kyle did not think his father could be beaten. The lad could very well be correct. But fight they must, and both would be the loser.

She stood in the blaze of firelight, straight and tall, ready to meet the challenge. Connaught rode with four other knights and several men-at-arms. A hue and cry had been raised, indeed. The knights remained on their horses as their leader dismounted.

"Where is Kyle?" Connaught's voice was unrelenting. He still smarted from embarrassment. Part of him wanted to take his child and let Drue go her way. But that part was silenced by the taunts of his friends and the secret smiles of his subordinates. Drue was, first and foremost, his prisoner, and prisoner she would remain. Once again he demanded, "Where is Kyle!"

"He is unharmed," Drue replied in a cold, hard voice. It held no hope of mercy, no hope of parley. As she had feared, this would be a fight to the death, for she would not be taken alive. Would it be as earthshaking to be pierced by Connaught's sword of steel as it was to be pierced by the sword of his body? That was like a little death, sometimes, when the universe stopped and all that existed was their love. It had filled the world and blotted out the stars, just as it filled her now and rendered her unable to lift her sword against the man she loved. They stood staring into each other's eyes, each lost in their own thoughts, yet in perfect communion with the other, for the thoughts were the same, though unspoken.

Also unspoken was the determination that neither would give up the commitment to which they had pledged themselves. Drue would not give up her identity as a knight and Connaught would not have her unless she did.

"How did you find us?" Drew knew the answer. Tam MacBurgh's absence spoke more loudly than a hundred shouting voices.

"Your guide felt my cause more just, and more profitable." Anger overtook the outward calm. "I thought you to have more sense, Drue, than to trust Tam MacBurgh after he had betrayed you once before."

The name struck Drue like a blow. In truth, she had thought the little man to be familiar, but had cast the notion aside when he did nothing to identify himself, calling himself Thomas of Lonbough. Now she repeated his true name. "Tam MacBurgh! The man who betrayed me and caused Turlock's death?"

"The same." Connaught growled the words, knowing what her next question would be.

"Where is he?" Drue's voice was murderously cold.

"He is dead! I have saved you the trouble of avenging yourself on anyone other than me."

His icy voice gave no hint of the rage that had overtaken his fear when the little man had come demanding to be paid for his information. It was only when Tam MacBurgh had refused to answer questions regarding Drue's welfare that Connaught had lost his hard-held temper and had throttled the guide, until he hung limp and silent in the knight's mighty hands.

Connaught was not proud of his action, but love and fear had dominated all else. His relief at seeing Drue alive had been so great he had been hard-pressed to keep from taking her in his arms, yet it was obvious nothing had changed.

They stood, the camp fire between them just as their beliefs stood between them, each knowing they would fight and that it would be to the death . . . of a human being or a dream.

Drue caught her breath as the firelight played on Connaught's face. How often had she seen those features, softened by the fire of love? Why must they continue to cause the other such great pain?

"Take Kyle and allow me to continue to the border. I swear I will never fight again except to defend what is mine." Drue heard herself offer.

"I will take you both," Connaught rasped harshly. He was aware of the murmurs of the men behind him and their certain outcry should he make such a compromise as she suggested.

Drue longed to accept his offer. She wanted to return with him, but she must set the terms.

"Will you take me as a warrior and a knight?"

Connaught stepped closer. "I offer you my name and my love, Drue. Stop this foolishness and return to Morrill Castle with me."

"Your name, your love, your terms and your damnable dress!" Drue spat the words across the fire.

His face flushed as memory of his humiliation flooded him. "The dress is ruined, but never fear, I will see that you have another."

"Then it will be to bury me in!" And her sword leaped upward to be taken by his parry. The battle commenced.

Chapter Eighteen

They fought with their great two-handed swords. The crash of metal resounded throughout the forest, drowning out the raucous cheers of the other knights and the quiet sobs of the child.

Connaught had been surprised by Drue's attack. In truth, he had hoped she would see the error of her ways, return with him and live out her life as his wife, as was meet and right. Instead she attacked, and by her very words, he knew she meant to kill him if he did not disarm her first. Disarming Drue was not so easy a thing to do. Drue was one of the finest and most knowledgeable knights alive. It was too bad she was only a woman.

Connaught's foot slipped and Drue's sword whistled past his head as he jerked away. For a moment his left arm was rendered useless as the sword brushed his shoulder. His eyes narrowed. No woman had a right to fight thus! But Drue forced him back, step by step taking advantage of his momentary disability.

He rallied, clenched his teeth against the pain as he blocked her attack.

Drue could see the pain in his eyes. She pressed her advantage without thought. She dared not think, for she fought all she loved. If it came to dealing the fatal blow, would she be able to do so? If she could not, he would force her to return and be subject to his will, living as his wife, or else as a prisoner, unseen and soon forgotten. No! It was better he kill her here on the field of battle than that a little part of her be murdered each day until there was nothing left save hatred.

Drue did not fear death, not the death of her body. But she was afraid of the death of her soul. She had the soul of a knight. It was that soul that could not die. Neither love nor the blade of death could destroy it.

The familiar ache crept through her. Connaught did not spare her with his blows. Each one took its toll now. Each one was recorded in jarring pain that traveled the extremities. Her fingers tingled as steel met steel.

"If I am victorious I will take you back with me regardless of your wishes." Connaught's words were punctuated by his blows.

"You will take a corpse!"

Connaught caught her sword with his own and looked into her face. "Do you intend to fall on your sword?"

Drue's eyes softened for a second as she saw the concern in his. "No." Her words were hardly more than a breathless gasp, so great was the effort of the fight. "It is your sword that will free me."

"From my love?"

"From your stubbornness!"

She broke free and they circled, as Connaught pondered her words. He remembered the fear he had felt when he learned that her guide was Tam MacBurgh. In truth, Drue had given new meaning to the word *fear* in Connaught's mind. And yet she faced him fearlessly, waiting to accept whatever the fates had in store for them, undaunted and unbeatable. His heart swelled with admiration . . . and love.

Again the camp fire was between them. Their swords flicked above the flame, testing, waiting, watching for the advantage.

"For God's sake, Drue, give way! I love you."

Had she not seen his lips move, Drue would not have known the words were more than an extension of her imagination. She answered in kind, her voice merging with the hiss of the flames against the bared blades.

"And did you love Enid? Did you long for her? Did you glory in her body? Did you respect her opinions and enjoy listening to her prattle?" She stepped to the edge of the embers and her sword slashed down, only to be caught on his. "Did you?" A spray of sparks emphasized her words. "Did you?"

Connaught moved away quickly. His words came without thought. "No! No, to all your questions!"

"Then how in the name of all that's holy can you ask me to take her place?"

He stopped, stunned by her words. In truth, there was no other like Drue, nor would there ever be! It was her courage, her spirit, her strength, the ultimate challenge of her love that so held him. There was no one he could compare her to and no place she could be made to fill. She was an enigma unto herself and he loved her!

Stepping back, Connaught lowered his sword. "Before God, I cannot ask it!"

Drue's heart leaped in her chest. With disbelief, she heard his next words.

"I accept your terms, Sir Drue."

"All of them?" she pressed.

"All those most important to you." He sighed as she lowered her sword. "I ask for only one stipend and I will not press it at this time."

"The dress?" Drue's voice was tense with caution.

"Never again," he vowed. "I swear it! In truth, I would face my enemies stark naked rather than wear one again myself."

Drue's laughter echoed over the silent arena. Connaught joined her, and his men, realizing the fight was over and a truce had been agreed upon, relaxed and shouted their approval. Drue was a favorite, though an enemy, and well liked by all.

Because of the terms they had agreed upon, Connaught could not take Drue in his arms. Instead, he placed his gauntleted hand on her shoulder. They stood at arm's length, yet their communion was as close as if their bodies were joined.

"I love you," he said.

And she replied, "I believe you, now. I believe you!"

At a signal from Drue, Kyle came from his hiding place among the trees. He stopped before the two battle-weary knights and bowed, first to his father, as was proper, and then to Drue.

"Please do not be angry with Sir Drue, Father." His voice quavered slightly, though his back remained straight and his eyes met his father's steadily. "He did not know I followed him until it was too late to send me back."

Connaught nodded stiffly. "Come along," he said. "We return to Loch Morrill."

"You will not punish him." Drue's voice was firm, and Connaught had the feeling she would fight again to establish the fact.

"He will have punishment enough." Connaught watched her bristle and quickly added, "Mother Graham has been dismissed. The older boys have no need of a nurse, but I have decided to give Kyle into your care. He is your responsibility now. That should keep you both satisfied."

Drue's smile was his reward, but his mind had already surged ahead to rewards that were forthcoming and far greater. He would claim them before broaching the subject to which he had referred when he acquiesced to her demands. Yes, he would make love to Drue again before telling her he still planned to marry her.

They returned to Loch Morrill to find the castle in a state of uproar. English couriers awaited audience, while messengers from the Bruce roamed the echoing halls like beasts of prey.

Lionel of Perth had ridden on ahead, and now met them in the courtyard, his face a mask of excitement.

"Something is afoot, my lord," he told Connaught, "but none will speak except directly to you or Sir Drue."

Drue's expression showed nothing. She knew the English were in the castle, having seen the badges on the arms of their lackeys. She knew, too, that regardless of the ransom they might have sent, she would not leave Connaught. Her place was beside him, now and forever.

Connaught tossed his reins to a stableboy. "I will see them immediately." His words were forced. He did not want to face the possibility of conflict with Drue's family. "Tell the messengers that Sir Drue and I will see them together in the order of their arrival."

Turning to the men-at-arms who had accompanied them, he gave orders that Kyle be taken to join his brothers before he entered the great hall with Drue at his side.

It took a few minutes before their eyes became accustomed to the shadowy hall, as the light of the sun was behind them. Towering above the others, knights and laymen alike, they moved toward the low dais at the far end of the room.

"They shine like hope," Henry of Romsley whispered to the Scot at his side.

"They *are* hope!" the man replied. "Only if we join forces will we see victory."

Both men knew the importance of the next moments. Sir Drue had many holdings and controlled many armed men, besides being a well-respected field general. Henry of Romsley, who had known Drue and Garith since they were squires together, realized how great a contribution Drue would be called upon to make. Henry had been commissioned to offer a huge ransom should the need arise, but for the sake of both countries, it was hoped it would not be necessary.

Lionel stopped at the foot of the dais. "I believe Sir Henry arrived first."

Drue stepped forward and clasped the knight's arm in greeting. "Well come, Henry! Have you news of my father and my brother, Garith?"

"Much news, Drue, and you shall know it all in time. But first I have a commission I must effect."

"Go on," Drue urged. In truth, she did not want to hear his offer, for the man would never understand when she refused ransom to stay with Connaught.

"The Spanish and French have joined forces and will invade our shores in less than a fortnight."

Drue glanced at Connaught, but the startled look on his face told her he knew no more than she. She nodded, waiting for the man to continue.

"The King desires that you return to England to ready your men for battle."

"Where is my father?" Drue demanded. "My men are under his command and always ready for battle, as am I!"

"Your father is waiting for you to return to fight at his side," Henry told her. "I have the ransom."

Before Drue could speak, Connaught's words cut through the hall.

"Thank you, Sir Henry." His voice was firm and offered no opening for discussion. "As we have heard your message, it is only fair we now hear what the messenger from the King of Scotland has to say."

Graham MacHugh was an older man, well versed in carrying messages and seeing that the recipient was made to acquiesce to the demands. It occurred to him there was a closeness between these two knights that would deny separation. It was thus he chose his words, bending the order given by the Bruce to meet the current needs.

"My lords—" he bowed without giving a loss to his dignity "—my message from the Bruce is much the same, with the exception that His Majesty would be honored if Sir Drue would consent to join forces with the Earl of Connaught. Since the two of you have fought so well against each other, he feels there is no reason you would not be equally successful in fighting on the same side."

The two knights glanced at each other and MacHugh knew he had read them right.

Henry of Romsley also saw the look. It portended no good for his cause. "I must object!" he stammered. "Sir Drue's forces are pledged to the King of England."

"And think you I wish to send my men to bleed and die for the English King?" Connaught was on his feet. "France and Spain have often threatened to join forces against England. How do I know my lands are endangered?"

"The Bruce would not have sent me had there not been danger," Graham MacHugh reminded them. "He feels that if there is an early show of force on our part, the invaders will lose heart and return to their own lands, each blaming the other for defeat."

Connaught nodded. "With luck it will be no more than a skirmish and never accelerate into a full-fledged war. The last thing our enemies will expect is for our Kings to join forces!"

Voices raised from both sides as messengers, couriers and lackeys alike called out their opinions on the subject.

Drue held up her hand. "Enough!" she shouted above the noise. "I will bring my men to the border. Connaught and I will defend the coast from Northumbria to the Firth of Forth. When the enemy lands, every man will go to the massed battle."

"You must return to England, Drue!" Henry's voice rang with righteousness. "Though I feel sure Edward will agree to your suggestion, he is your King and sovereign. You must have his permission before moving your men to the border."

Drue looked quickly at Connaught. "Think you we could go to Duxton and be back in time to prepare your armies?"

Connaught was silent. Those present surmised that he was estimating the time it would take for the journey, when actually his thoughts were on another matter entirely. He wanted to wed Drue, and what better place to put the plan into action than at the place of her birth?

Garith was not in residence when they arrived at Duxton, but came a few days later.

"My progress was slowed a great deal by the excess baggage," he explained as he helped his wife from her horse.

Allyson had spent the better part of the morning readying herself to greet Drue. She had never forgotten her husband's supposed brother and still basked in the attention Drue had paid her at the time of the wedding.

After a brief greeting, Drue turned to her brother, but Allyson, having decided Drue was by far the more handsome of the men, would not allow the knight's attention to be taken from her. She alternately pouted and spoke of inane things, before flirting openly as she tried to regain Drue's eye.

Drue paid the girl no mind, but Connaught, recognizing the signs of unrequited love, was hard put to keep from laughing aloud. He wondered silently if spurning Allyson was a laughing matter, for Allyson's eyes narrowed as a wet nurse came forth carrying a child.

"Drue, Connaught—" Garith beamed "—I want you to meet my son, Andrew of Duxton!"

The men turned their attention to the child and Allyson was forgotten. Seething with anger, she turned and stomped toward the keep.

Connaught had laid his plans carefully and timed his request with the utmost care. They were alone in the solar they had shared when Drue had rescued him from his nightmare and almost destroyed them both.

"The old priest is all but blind. He would not recognize you if we wore simple robes. There would be no trouble, Drue. He would remember the entry in the church record. The Earl of Duxton had a daughter, Druanna, and now the girl comes to be wed. What could be more normal? He will perform the ceremony, make the new entry and never give thought to the fact that he has, in fact, married the Earl of Connaught to Sir Drue."

"Why do you dwell on this marriage, Connaught?" Drue's voice was quiet, but that very fact gave Connaught pause.

"I ask because I love you and I know you love me!" He watched her splendid body tense as though ready to spring into action at the slightest ill-advised move. It was warm in the room and Drue had stripped down to her hose and vest. Soon the vest, too, would fall away and Drue would be to Connaught what she was for none other... his woman, his love, his very life. But it was not enough! Until they were wed, it would never be enough!

"Our love is not in question!" Drue's words snapped like the crackling log on the fire. "What difference will it make that we are wed? You cannot announce it to the world. You cannot hold a feast or a tourney to celebrate! Before God, I do not see the difference it will make!"

She strode away and stood before the fire. While it was true Connaught had not pressured her to assume the ways of a woman since her attempted escape, his insistence on marriage troubled her. Buried deep in Drue's being was the belief that a woman wed to bear children. Those who did not accomplish this feat were failures doomed to ridicule. Drue did not fail! She excelled at all she did, but in this one thing she knew she must admit defeat. Connaught's next words brought her up short.

"It is before God I would make you my wife, so that you would be by my side forever, in this life and throughout eternity."

"You had a wife," Drue pointed out, reckless now, for his words touched her deeply. Hot tears prickled behind her eyes. She fought to hold them back. "Does Enid not wait for you in the hereafter?"

"It is with you I would share eternity."

"And I with you, but not as your wife!"

Connaught reached out to take her into his arms, but Drue pulled away.

"No! Do not touch me! And do not ask again, for I cannot give you sons. And—" she faced him squarely, her face a stiff mask "—I would not bear children even if it were possible."

Connaught was well aware that Drue's body did not function as that of other women. He had lived with her for many months and long ago realized her lack of womanly tides. At first he had thought she might be pregnant. At the time he had hoped it to be so, believing it would solve his problem and force her to marry him, but that had not come to pass. He had learned to accept Drue as she was and to ask nothing more.

"I have sons!" he replied.

His statement was filled with a truth that rang in his voice and shone in his eyes. It was that truth that allowed Drue to take what she most desired.

"So be it, then," she said, resting her hands on his hips. "So be it! I ask but one favor."

"Anything," he promised recklessly.

"Send for Mother Graham. If we are to be married, we will need have someone stand as witness. The poor woman has suffered enough thinking you in love with another man. It is time we end her suffering."

Connaught clasped Drue against him, muscle merging into muscle. "We will swear her to secrecy!" He laughed as he thought of the old nurse's surprise when she learned the truth. "But, according to law, there must be two witnesses."

"I will think on it," Drue promised, "but not now, my love. Now we have more pressing matters to think upon."

Connaught's eyes glowed like sapphires as he loosened the lacings on her vest. In a moment, Drue the knight would disappear and Drue the woman...Drue, *his* woman...would come into being. It was a time of magic and wonder. As in sorcery, a splendid knight of the realm became a wild, passionate woman. A woman able to fulfill every need, every fantasy, every silent longing. His heart leapt with anticipation as the vest fell away and Drue stepped into his arms.

The Lady Allyson was bored. Garith's father, the Earl of Duxton, had no wife and only the rudimentary women in his household, hence Allyson had no female companionship. Garith fussed over the child, Andrew, giving the little boy all the time and attention not spent on his brother and Connaught. The men did nothing but talk of war. They found no time for dancing or frolicking. They reviewed their men during the day and planned strategy long into the night, paying Allyson little mind.

Garith was seldom at her side during the hours of daylight and just as seldom in her bed at night, for the men talked unceasingly before the huge hearth into the wee hours of the morning. Drue gave Garith's wife a few kind words. In truth, Drue felt true pity for the woman. Of all the people in the castle, Allyson was the one with whom Drue would have least wanted to trade places.

Unfortunately Drue's kindness was misconstrued by the only person who noticed it. Allyson took it as an indication that Drue was still attracted to her. From the day Allyson had first seen her husband's brother, she had admired the tall, handsome knight. There was something wildly exciting about Drue, Allyson thought as she watched the men over her needlework. Garith would never be exciting. Her husband's idea of excitement was acquiring a new herd of sheep for their thriving flock, or trading a prized cow for one of another bloodline. He did not even go to London to attend the King's court more than was absolutely necessary, and then he did not take Allyson, though she begged and pleaded to be allowed to go. Little Andrew had been but a few months old the first time Garith had gone and Drue had only recently been taken prisoner by the Scots. Garith had explained he had much business to attend to and had left her behind. After that, it had been easy for him to use the same excuse and leave her on his estates.

Now, however, Drue smiled on her, and Allyson saw a way to make Garith pay for his lack of consideration.

It was not simply a matter of making Garith jealous, she told herself. Had it been only that, she would have set her charms for Connaught, a widower and renowned womanizer. But Drue had always been a favorite, and now that his hair had grown longer, in the style set by Piers Gaveston and the King, Drue was even more handsome. Putting down her needlework, Allyson sallied forth toward her husband's unsuspecting brother, her skirts swishing seductively across the rush-covered floor.

The evening was a matter of continued embarrassment for Drue and of contained mirth for Connaught. The coy smiles, the intimate touches bestowed on Drue by Allyson became so obvious that Garith was forced to step in and reprimand his audacious wife.

Some hours later, Allyson lay alone in her bed, seething with anger. Drue had not only ignored her, but had acted as though her subtle offers were no more than a joke. And Connaught had all but laughed aloud at her efforts.

Now the men remained below and would, no doubt, talk far in to the night once again. She could not think which had angered her the most—Drue, Connaught, or her own husband, who had finally decided she was overtired and had escorted her to her rooms like a wayward child before returning to the masculine companionship awaiting him below.

She would make them pay! She would make them all pay!

As she floated on the edge of sleep she could hear Andrew's angry cries from the nursery, finally silenced by his nurse. Yes, Allyson vowed, they would all pay, and that squalling baby of whom Garith was so proud would be the instrument through which she would effect her vengeance.

Connaught dangled Garith's son on his knee. Andrew was a chubby lad, reminding Connaught of Kyle. Though he mentioned the fact to Drue, knowing her affinity toward his youngest son, it did little to whet her interest in her nephew.

The men looked up as Allyson joined them. Her face was pale and puffy from lack of sleep. The night had not been kind to Allyson.

A pang of pity touched Drue and she looked away quickly. Her gaze fell on little Andrew, and Allyson's eyes followed.

"I see you do not care much for children, dear brother." Allyson's voice sliced through the room, causing even the babe to look up in surprise.

"I know little of children," Drue agreed. "Until a lad is old enough to be a page he is of little interest."

"Ah, but you should be interested in this one," Allyson persisted, indicating the blond hair and golden eyes of the little boy who scrambled from Connaught's lap and went to his mother.

She turned the child toward Drue, holding his little face between her hands. "Does he not resemble someone you know, my lords?" She searched each of their faces in turn.

"He looks more like Garith than yourself, my lady," Connaught volunteered. The woman was up to no good; he could sense it but knew not what she planned. "A good sign, and one for which many women would give great thanks.''

The men laughed, but Allyson did not join them.

''Think you because the child bears resemblance to Garith it need be his son?'' Her voice tinkled brittlely, like icicles falling against stone. ''But, look you. Andrew resembles Sir Drue in coloring and features as well as name.''

''And so he might,'' Garith agreed, ''seeing Drue is my brother and the child's uncle.''

Connaught smiled. It seemed Drue had indeed been correct in her assumption that even her family had forgotten she had been born a wench.

''Drue is more than Andrew's uncle, my lord.'' Allyson's face contorted as she formed the words. ''Drue is the child's father!''

Garith jumped to his feet. Drue froze, stunned by the immensity of the lie. But Connaught could stand no more. For days he had watched Allyson trying to seduce Drue and had fought valiantly to contain his mirth. This was too much! Unable to be held back any longer, Connaught's laughter rang out through the room.

''When? How?'' Garith demanded.

''After the wedding, before Drue left with Turlock! We made love and Andrew is Drue's child. Drue's and mine!'' She glared at Connaught as she spoke. How could the fool laugh at this moment of dramatic revelation?

But Connaught could not stop laughing. Each word made the situation more ridiculous. He could not stop when tears rolled down his face and he writhed in pain. He could not stop even when he saw Garith draw his sword and challenge Drue.

Chapter Nineteen

The sword trembled in Garith's hand. Well he remembered how Drue had followed Allyson about the castle like a lovesick hound. Anger blotted out the common sense that told Garith he was no match for his brother, and something else as well, something niggling at the back of his mind that insisted Allyson's words could not be true. Yet the anger prevailed.

"Draw your sword!" Garith thundered. "Draw your sword or I will kill you where you stand!"

Garith's words brought Drue to her senses. Realizing he meant what he said, she brought forth her sword, resolving to use it only to ward off his wild blows.

"Allyson's words are not true, Garith—surely you must realize that! I would never betray you so!"

But Garith was past listening to reason or truth. He saw no cause for his wife to lie, when she must know her own life was forfeit. He pressed on, making Drue use every skill she knew to defend herself.

The hall filled as the sound of swords echoed from the thick walls. Garith fought with an intensity brought about by desperation. Drue knew he would wound her if she did not stop this quickly.

"Allyson lies, Garith!" Drue's concern for her brother overpowered discretion. "What she says cannot be true! Ask Connaught! He will bear out my words!"

The hall clattered with the sound of steel and the chatter of many tongues as the men shouted at the brothers, not realizing the seriousness of the matter. Connaught's continual laughter made light of the situation.

"Connaught! Connaught, damn you, tell this idiot his wife's words cannot be true! Connaught! Connaught, where are you?"

"I swear... I swear... on my honor as a knight," Connaught gasped, "Drue cannot be the father!" Again he collapsed as laughter overwhelmed him, but Garith did not think it funny.

"You could not know!" he countered. "You were not here!"

Connaught wiped the tears from his face. "I *do* know, Garith! I give you my word. The woman lies."

Garith's sword came down on Drue's.

Had Drue taken a vow of celibacy? Garith had heard nothing mentioned of that sort. Surely he would have remembered such a thing, yet Drue had never married. Drue's only ambition was to be a knight!

Again his sword whistled through the air.

The mists of memory crept around the edges of his consciousness. Dimly Garith remembered the day Drue had made that announcement. It had been here in this very castle. Garith remembered lying on a pallet in the little room hidden behind the solar fireplace, while Drue stood by the arrow slot overlooking the devastated countryside.

Swords spat fire as Drue blocked his blow.

He could see the room as plainly as though it were yesterday rather than some twenty years before. "I will be a knight, like Turlock!" Drue had said as the light reflected around the sturdy, dress-clad figure standing at the arrow slot. The figure of his sister, Druanna!

Garith's sword dropped to the ground. Too stunned to speak, he could only open and close his mouth and stare at the person before him.

As though it were a signal, Connaught sobered and hurried forward, clasping his side from the pain of laughter.

"Drue, come, help me get your brother to our apartments. We have much to talk about."

Before Garith could recover his speech, Drue and Connaught had whisked him from the room.

"I never gave it a thought!" Garith paced the room. "Why, Drue is a prime example of all a knight should be. He...she...you could have killed me at will in that skirmish below."

"Exactly!" Connaught agreed. "And that is why we ask your pledge of secrecy. Drue wishes to remain as she is!"

Garith shook his head, still unable to comprehend the sudden turn of events. "But why would Allyson make up such a lie?"

"In truth, Garith, you have paid her little mind since coming to Duxton. The woman is no doubt jealous of the time you spend with Drue and myself. Had you but eyes in your head you would have seen the Lady Allyson flirting with Drue, but neither of you seemed to notice. Unable to obtain your attention in any other way, your wife lied to gain your notice."

"Be not too hard on her, Garith," Drue offered as she stretched her legs out before the fire. "Allyson has inadvertently solved a problem for me."

Garith sat down in the chair across the table from Drue and speared a chunk of meat with his knife. "And that is?"

"Connaught and I wish to wed. We need another witness. A trustworthy, discrete witness who will never tell a soul, not even the old priest, that Sir Drue is marrying the Earl of Connaught."

Garith choked on the meat and turned to Connaught. "Is this true?"

Connaught's eyes rested on Drue for a moment before he answered. He took her words into his mind and recorded them in his heart . . . *Connaught and I wish to wed.* It was for her as it was for him. "It is true," Connaught affirmed, "but the ceremony is for our own gratification. It must never be made public. Drue will remain a knight. Only you, Drue, myself and my old nurse, Mother Graham, will know the truth."

"Our father—" Garith began.

"I have apprised him of the matter. He realizes the need for secrecy and has sworn to do all he can to help us. He is gravely concerned that Edward will discover he has knighted a woman and will destroy our house in a fit of anger."

Garith nodded as he saw the clear reasoning of her words. His mind was abuzz with memories, most of them of times when Drue had overpowered him, or beaten him in trial combat. It seemed impossible that she could be other than a knight, strong and skilled.

He turned to her, the meat poised on his knife halfway to his mouth. "Are you certain?" he questioned.

Drue's eyes went from her brother to Connaught. He answered for her. "We are!"

"You realize that Drue will never be content to sit at home and manage a castle!" The depth of Garith's instant understanding shocked both Connaught and Drue.

"I realize it," Connaught affirmed. "I love Drue as she is! I do not want her to change. I would have her no other way, but I would have her as my wife before God, even if before man she must continue to be only my companion-at-arms."

"And your friend," Drue added.

"And my friend." Connaught repeated the words as though they were a prayer.

Garith squirmed in his seat, faced with a depth of love he could not completely grasp. "I would I had a wife who was my friend and companion rather than a jealous, petty, troublemaking wench."

"Perhaps if you paid her more mind she would be your friend," Drue suggested.

"A man must be able to talk to his friends about the things that interest them both," Garith pointed out. "It can never be so with Allyson. Her interests are limited to sewing, dressing and the latest gossip."

"Few men find a wife they can talk to as an equal," Connaught agreed. "I felt the same as you when married to Enid. She brought me lands and wealth and bore my children. Yet we had little to say to each other." He sighed, and a smile played impishly about his lips. "At least you do not have to worry that Allyson will challenge you for a believed wrong."

"And beat you." Drue added the teasing note to Connaught's words.

Garith sighed. "I see I do have something for which to be thankful. It is bad enough that my brother...sister... bests me regularly. It would be doubly hard to take if my wife did likewise."

Their laughter filled the room as Connaught poured good English ale into their tankards.

"When do you wish to wed?" Garith asked.

"Mother Graham arrived this afternoon," Connaught told them.

"Very well." Garith got to his feet. "I will go to the priest and ask that he perform the ceremony for my sister, who has secretly returned to Duxton. Because of the shortness of time and the large stipend I plan to give the church, I feel sure the old man will be happy to dispense with the usual banns." He stared into Drue's golden eyes. There was no hint of coy femininity in this creature before him. She was magnificent, and her beauty defied the limits of sex.

Had God meant for either of them to have been a female, it would more likely have been himself, Garith thought wryly. He was of slighter build and had not the firm muscles of the knight before him. He shook his head. "You are still one of the best men I know, Drue." His voice caught in his throat as he clasped her shoulders. "I'm glad that Connaught has the sense to see that you cannot change."

Drue smiled at Connaught. A small, secret smile that spoke of another time, when Connaught had not been so willing to accept Drue's terms. But Garith need never know, and the look that passed between Drue and Connaught spoke eloquently in silent understanding.

It was just dusk as the heavy door to the chapel creaked open. The old priest waited before the altar. He watched in astonishment as three towering figures moved toward him.

Except that two were fair and one dark, there was little difference as far as he could tell. He rubbed his eyes in an effort to clear his bleary vision, but to no avail. He could recognize none of them in the flickering candlelight.

As they stopped before him, the old man was aware that two were dressed in white robes trimmed in gold. Neither wore any sort of headgear as was wont for a woman when in the church of God. He looked from one to the other in confusion. Except that one was dark and one light of hair, it was as though the old cleric saw double. He looked toward the third man.

"As I told you, good Father," Garith's voice was easily recognized in the silence of the chapel, "my sister Druanna has returned to be married to the Earl of Connaught. Because of the imminent threat of war it must be done immediately and in all secrecy. Will you begin?"

The old man squinted and leaned toward the towering figures, faltering over the familiar passages. The sound of his own voice gave him confidence as he repeated the ancient words.

A small womanly figure had appeared to stand beside the fair person in white. The priest directed his words in her direction. Upon receiving the proper response, the old man declared Connaught and Druanna to be man and wife before God, and all knelt for his blessing. There was no kissing, but a great deal of good-natured backslapping. The only person to be embraced was the little woman, who stood to the side, apparently as confused by the whole procedure as was the priest himself.

Garith stood beside the old man, directing his hand as he made the entry in the church record that Lady Druanna of Duxton had wed Patrick, Earl of Connaught, with her brother, Garith, and one Bridget Graham as witnesses. A heavy purse was pressed into his hands and he watched as the figures strode from the church with long masculine strides.

He turned and began extinguishing the candles as the sound of laughter floated back to him. Then the door closed, and like a dream sequence, they were gone. The priest turned to the altar and sank painfully to his knees. He had been asked to marry the daughter of the house of Duxton to a noble and powerful lord. As a priest, retained by the house of Duxton for the better part of his life, the old man knew it was his duty to comply with their wishes, but for the life of him, he could not be sure which had been the bride and which the groom. He bowed his head, and as he had done so many times in the past, put his faith in his God.

Dinner in the great hall that night was a festive affair. The cooks had been instructed to prepare a feast and had worked throughout the day in an endeavor to do so.

"But I do not understand," Allyson was saying. "Drue and Connaught must leave on the morrow. What cause is that to celebrate?"

Garith smiled silently. If Allyson had not ferreted out Drue's secret, it was most likely safely kept. He would have given his wife some inane excuse, but Drue answered the query.

"For the first time Connaught and I will fight on the same side. It is cause for celebration!"

The goblets were raised again and again as toasts were drunk to the new partnership between Connaught and Drue, those proposing the toasts never realizing they actually drank to a bride and groom. Garith had overcome his shock and fully enjoyed being part of a secret, one that had turned into a fantastic lark.

As the lackeys cleared away the dishes, and the tables were removed to make way for tumblers and jesters hastily summoned from the nearest castle, Drue turned to Connaught.

"I had Garith draw up papers today. Should aught happen to me, all my estates go to Kyle."

Connaught did not touch her, but his eyes caressed her face as surely and sensually as though he ran his lips across it. "Think you I would live if you were gone?"

"Sometimes we do not have a choice of life over death, Connaught. We are knights! We will do that which we must, but while we live, we will be together."

Drue and Connaught stood beneath the starless sky. Black ships loomed on the horizon off the coast of Northumbria. Beneath the shroud of darkness they drifted toward the shore. The silent threat of doom advanced, unwavering in its purpose.

A word from Drue sent the signal fires flaring to life. All down the coast and along the border their flames burst upon the horizon, one by one. The enemy was sighted.

The archers took their positions among the craggy cliffs, and cries rang out as the arrows found their marks. There would be no landing this night.

"We must take word to the Kings," Connaught said, as the dark shapes bobbed on the water in confusion.

"I will go to Edward," Drue replied. "You go to your uncle, the Bruce. God willing, we will meet when the battle is joined."

"Then go with God," he whispered as he touched her face with gentle fingertips.

Even the persuasiveness of two respected knights could not move two armies with the speed needed to intercept the enemy. By the time Drue returned, Connaught's men were already forming for attack.

"The Bruce?" she asked, her eyes overlooking the camp with trepidation. Their force was so small compared to the legions that poured from the sea.

"He began marching as I left. But they are two days behind me, for they move slowly, hampered by artillery and foot soldiers."

Drue nodded. "So it is with me. My father comes, but not as swiftly." She did not add that she had all but exhausted her horse and her men in an effort to return to Connaught's side. "Have they attacked?"

"So far only skirmishes, but they are forming, as are our men."

The two walked to a point overlooking the sea. It seemed impossible that the small force they employed would be able to hold back the black waves of invaders. Both sensed the immensity of the task before them.

"Your orders, my lord." Drue deferred to Connaught's rank and title.

"We are equal in command," he corrected. "What are your thoughts?"

Drue studied the situation as the seconds ticked away. There was no easy solution. "We cannot make a frontal attack and hope to survive. Our best course is to attack and fall back, hitting their lines in several places at once."

Connaught nodded. "Rather like a border raid," he said, then, seeing the look on Drue's face, remembered their first encounter. He removed his gauntlet and placed his hand on hers. "I would Turlock were here with us today."

Drue swallowed with difficulty. It was several minutes before she could speak. "He will be with us when the pipes of battle sound." Her voice was quiet but firm. "His last words were that he would always be there, fighting at my side."

The horns called the men to form ranks and, in the distance, the Scots pipers began the shrill whine that signaled the filling of their pipes.

They mounted, fully realizing the danger they must face as they led their small army to harass the enemy. At any time, the French or Spanish commanders could discover their intent and send a massed force against them. Yet there was nothing else to do. Drue and Connaught must hold the enemy as near the coast as possible until the allied force could gather in an area that would give them the advantage.

Drue wheeled her horse about and rode back, shouting orders mingled with words of encouragement to the men. Their cheers followed her again to Connaught's side. The laughter and excitement faded from her eyes as she saw the sorrow in his face.

"I would we could go into battle with a huge force behind us and victory a foregone conclusion."

She knew his fear. It was the same as her own. Not of death for herself, but of death for the one she loved more than life. Her eyes shone as though radiating the warm rays of the sun from their depths.

"With Turlock beside me in spirit and you beside me in flesh, how can I help but know victory?"

But Connaught could not dispel the new and unsettling fear that had come to him along with the love he bore this unusual woman. "Go back," he urged. "Wait for the Kings to come. I will meet you at Dumfries in two weeks' time!"

"The Bruce is your uncle, you should be the one to go!" she countered. "Why should I miss a good battle?"

"I order you to go!" His voice rose as the horses pranced nervously, sensing not only the imminent battle, but the friction between the two commanders.

"You cannot order me!" Drue returned hotly. "I hold equal rank and command equal men. We go together!"

Connaught's jaw set with determination. "We are badly outnumbered. You could be killed."

"As could you!"

The silent fear had been voiced. It hung in the air between them, as intangible as the sunlight, as sacred as a prayer, as endless as the ancient land for which they would both soon fight.

He wanted to kiss her then. To feel once more the firm, pliant lips against his; to inhale the scent of sunlight she emanated.

Drue's eyes scanned his face. She could read his thoughts, and the longing was almost more than she could bear. Yet, the fates had given them a different task to perform in order to be judged worthy of the love they bore each other. Instead of tearfully kissing her man and sending him off to battle, Drue would ride with him, fighting at his side. She would not have it any other way, and in that moment of spiritual communion, she knew that neither would Connaught.

Drue reached out and Connaught grasped her gauntleted forearm in the gesture made by comrades-at-arms through time immemorial. They drew their swords, holding them aloft as their standard-bearers lifted the emblems of their rank. Now the horns sounded in earnest and the cheers of the men echoed across the countryside. The sound of drums merged with the thunder of the army as the men moved forward to defend the land they loved.

"Onward to victory!" Connaught roared above the sound.

"You are my victory." Drue's lips formed the words. "For having known your love, I can never be defeated."

And they went forward together to meet the challenge, to reach the heights, to touch the sun....

*   *   *   *   *

Take 4 bestselling love stories FREE

Plus get a FREE surprise gift!

HARLEQUIN®
OFFICIAL SWEEPSTAKES RULES

NO PURCHASE NECESSARY

1. To enter, complete an Official Entry Form or 3"× 5" index card by hand-printing, in plain block letters, your complete name, address, phone number and age, and mailing it to: Harlequin Fashion A Whole New You Sweepstakes, P.O. Box 9056, Buffalo, NY 14269-9056.

   No responsibility is assumed for lost, late or misdirected mail. Entries must be sent separately with first class postage affixed, and be received no later than December 31, 1991 for eligibility.

2. Winners will be selected by D.L. Blair, Inc., an independent judging organization whose decisions are final, in random drawings to be held on January 30, 1992 in Blair, NE at 10:00 a.m. from among all eligible entries received.

3. The prizes to be awarded and their approximate retail values are as follows: Grand Prize — A brand-new Mercury Sable LS plus a trip for two (2) to Paris, including round-trip air transportation, six (6) nights hotel accommodation, a $1,400 meal/spending money stipend and $2,000 cash toward a new fashion wardrobe (approximate value: $28,000) or $15,000 cash; two (2) Second Prizes — A trip to Paris, including round-trip air transportation, six (6) nights hotel accommodation, a $1,400 meal/spending money stipend and $2,000 cash toward a new fashion wardrobe (approximate value: $11,000) or $5,000 cash; three (3) Third Prizes — $2,000 cash toward a new fashion wardrobe. All prizes are valued in U.S. currency. Travel award air transportation is from the commercial airport nearest winner's home. Travel is subject to space and accommodation availability, and must be completed by June 30, 1993. Sweepstakes offer is open to residents of the U.S. and Canada who are 21 years of age or older as of December 31, 1991, except residents of Puerto Rico, employees and immediate family members of Torstar Corp., its affiliates, subsidiaries, and all agencies, entities and persons connected with the use, marketing, or conduct of this sweepstakes. All federal, state, provincial, municipal and local laws apply. Offer void wherever prohibited by law. Taxes and/or duties, applicable registration and licensing fees, are the sole responsibility of the winners. Any litigation within the province of Quebec respecting the conduct and awarding of a prize may be submitted to the Régie des loteries et courses du Québec. All prizes will be awarded; winners will be notified by mail. No substitution of prizes is permitted.

4. Potential winners must sign and return any required Affidavit of Eligibility/Release of Liability within 30 days of notification. In the event of noncompliance within this time period, the prize may be awarded to an alternate winner. Any prize or prize notification returned as undeliverable may result in the awarding of that prize to an alternate winner. By acceptance of their prize, winners consent to use of their names, photographs or their likenesses for purposes of advertising, trade and promotion on behalf of Torstar Corp. without further compensation. Canadian winners must correctly answer a time-limited arithmetical question in order to be awarded a prize.

5. For a list of winners (available after 3/31/92), send a separate stamped, self-addressed envelope to: Harlequin Fashion A Whole New You Sweepstakes, P.O. Box 4694, Blair, NE 68009.

PREMIUM OFFER TERMS

To receive your gift, complete the Offer Certificate according to directions. Be certain to enclose the required number of "Fashion A Whole New You" proofs of product purchase (which are found on the last page of every specially marked "Fashion A Whole New You" Harlequin or Silhouette romance novel). Requests must be received no later than December 31, 1991. Limit: four (4) gifts per name, family, group, organization or address. Items depicted are for illustrative purposes only and may not be exactly as shown. Please allow 6 to 8 weeks for receipt of order. Offer good while quantities of gifts last. In the event an ordered gift is no longer available, you will receive a free, previously unpublished Harlequin or Silhouette book for every proof of purchase you have submitted with your request, plus a refund of the postage and handling charge you have included. Offer good in the U.S. and Canada only.   HQFW-SWPR

HARLEQUIN® OFFICIAL
SWEEPSTAKES ENTRY FORM

4-FWHHS-3

Complete and return this Entry Form immediately – the more entries you submit, the better your chances of winning!

- Entries must be received by **December 31, 1991.**
- A Random draw will take place on **January 30, 1992.**
- No purchase necessary.

Yes, I want to win a FASHION A WHOLE NEW YOU Classic and Romantic prize from Harlequin:

Name _____ Telephone _____ Age _____

Address _____

City _____ State _____ Zip _____

Return Entries to: **Harlequin FASHION A WHOLE NEW YOU,**
P.O. Box 9056, Buffalo, NY 14269-9056   © 1991 Harlequin Enterprises Limited

PREMIUM OFFER

To receive your free gift, send us the required number of proofs-of-purchase from any specially marked FASHION A WHOLE NEW YOU Harlequin or Silhouette Book with the Offer Certificate properly completed, plus a check or money order (do not send cash) to cover postage and handling payable to Harlequin FASHION A WHOLE NEW YOU Offer. We will send you the specified gift.

OFFER CERTIFICATE

Item	A. ROMANTIC COLLECTOR'S DOLL (Suggested Retail Price $60.00)	B. CLASSIC PICTURE FRAME (Suggested Retail Price $25.00)
# of proofs-of-purchase	18	12
Postage and Handling	$3.50	$2.95
Check one	☐	☐

Name _____

Address _____

City _____ State _____ Zip _____

Mail this certificate, designated number of proofs-of-purchase and check or money order for postage and handling to: **Harlequin FASHION A WHOLE NEW YOU Gift Offer,** P.O. Box 9057, Buffalo, NY 14269-9057. Requests must be received by December 31, 1991.

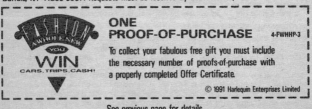

ONE
PROOF-OF-PURCHASE

4-FWHHP-3

To collect your fabulous free gift you must include the necessary number of proofs-of-purchase with a properly completed Offer Certificate.

© 1991 Harlequin Enterprises Limited

See previous page for details.